THE LAST REDOUBT

The kidnapping of a young doctor leads to some puzzling developments, which have their origin in a small island in the Adriatic. The doctor's sister, Valerie, tormented by the disappearance of her brother, decides to act independently of the Police. She and Inspector McLean eventually find themselves marooned on The Isle of Mystery, at the mercy of a gang of criminals — but an inspired strategem on the part of McLean turns the tables completely.

*Books by George Goodchild
in the Linford Mystery Library:*

THE DANGER LINE
McLEAN DISPOSES

GEORGE GOODCHILD

THE LAST REDOUBT

A McLean Mystery

Complete and Unabridged

LINFORD
Leicester

First published in Great Britain in 1952

First Linford Edition
published March 1995

British Library CIP Data

Goodchild, George
  The last redoubt.—Large print ed.—
Linford mystery library
I. Title II. Series
823.914 [F]

ISBN 0–7089–7653–0

Published by
F. A. Thorpe (Publishing) Ltd.
Anstey, Leicestershire

Set by Words & Graphics Ltd.
Anstey, Leicestershire
Printed and bound in Great Britain by
T. J. Press (Padstow) Ltd., Padstow, Cornwall

This book is printed on acid-free paper

1

IT was another of Inspector McLean's unlucky days. Everything had gone wrong since he set foot into his office that morning, and now at five o'clock in the afternoon he learned that a man he was holding on a serious charge had produced an alibi that was as perfect as an alibi could be. Sergeant Brook, who had brought the proof, shrugged his big shoulders compassionately.

"I'd have put my shirt on his guilt," he said.

"So should I, and do still," replied McLean. "But we can't hold him any longer in the face of these depositions. I'll have to see the Chief."

The subsequent interview with the Chief was not pleasant, and McLean eventually left with a proverbial flea in his ear. The detained man was given

1

his freedom, and he, too, had a few choice words to say before he went on his way.

"And now I'm going straight to my solicitor," he threatened.

"Oh no you're not," snapped McLean. "You're going to let the whole matter drop like a hot brick. That's the way out. Go, while the going's good."

He hoped that would be the end of a most thankless day, and for an hour or so he worked with Brook, polishing off a number of odds and ends. It was more than an hour later when the telephone informed him that Miss Donkin wished to see him, and the message made his former hope a reality.

"Send Miss Donkin up," he said. "All right, Brook. We'll call it a day."

Valerie Donkin sailed into the office just as Brook was leaving. She was younger than McLean and the sister of one of his best friends. It was her habit to sail into McLean's life at the most unexpected moments, and she was like a breath of fresh country air.

"That assistant of yours gets bigger and bigger," she said, when the door had closed on Brook.

"Fatter and fatter. He's out of condition. But what are you doing in London?"

"Getting away from the chores that are wrecking my young life. Do you realize we haven't seen a sign of you for nearly a year?"

"Is it as long as that? Well, sit down and tell me all the news."

He passed her a chair, and Valerie gazed at the hard polished seat.

"Same old austerity," she said. "And that rug has been here since the first time I came to see you. I wouldn't like to say how many years ago that was."

"Ten, and you were just seventeen and as pretty as a picture in those days."

"Beast!" she retorted. "But really, Mac, this is no fit office for a famous member of the C.I.D. Why don't you do something about it?"

3

"My dear child, this is a spot where work is done, not a show place. When you have finished castigating my furniture perhaps you will tell me how Ian is getting on."

"So-so. You know what Ian is. He's never up and never down. Between shoals of patients he's writing a book, at least a treatise. Heaven knows what it's all about, but he seems to think he is on the verge of making a stupendous discovery. I have to drag him away from it round about midnight, and pack him off to bed. The man's a maniac for work, but there's nothing in it — no material reward. Doctoring used to be a dignified and respectable profession, but now it's downright drudgery. He's nothing but a slave of the welfare state."

"I thought he had made up his mind to have nothing to do with the National Health scheme."

"He had, but a great number of his private patients went over to it, and so he had to come off his high horse. Oh dear, it's a horrid world."

McLean smiled as he ran his eye over her nice Spring costume, the neat shoes and gleaming nylons. Her flame-coloured hair had quite obviously been expensively coiffured, and her whole appearance suggested prosperity, if not opulence.

"You don't seem to be doing so badly," he said.

"Well, this is a special occasion. I received my annual dividends last week, and I resolved to blow the whole lot in a defiant gesture to the bankrupt world. Now you can tell me in your forthright fashion how childish I am."

"Not I. The point is does it make you feel any better?"

"Heaps better. I am now prepared to go down the drain with my colours flying. Now tell me how the body-snatching business is progressing. Have you had any good murders lately?"

"Just the usual brutal stuff. It's surprising how unenterprising the average murderer is. I wonder they don't get some tips from Crime novelists."

"That wouldn't pay," laughed Valerie. "Because the Crime novelists invariably see that the sleuth-hound gets his man."

"You're quite bright," said McLean. "But why are we talking this nonsense, when we might be doing more interesting things? Don't look at your watch. There are plenty of trains."

"Meaning just what?"

"That you are coming out to dine with me. That brother of yours is quite capable of getting a meal for himself. In any case you can blame it all on to me."

"I oughtn't to," said Valerie, with gleaming eyes.

"But you will?"

"On one condition."

"Name it."

"That you'll come to dine with Ian and me on Thursday."

"That's not too onerous. It's a bargain."

"Good! Oh, may I ring up Ian?"

"Of course. I'll get the number for you, and then you can tell him the awful truth."

He put the call through, and in a few moments Doctor Ian Donkin was on the other end of the line. Valerie took over the receiver, and after a little banter with her invisible brother she replaced the receiver.

"Caught him in the middle of his surgery hour," she said. "He's glad to hear about Thursday. Now I'm ready. Where shall we go?"

"It's up to you. Somewhere respectable but very dull, or the worst place in London — to be exact, just out of London, and not so dull."

"The latter sounds more exciting — if the food's good."

"At such places the food is always good."

In a few minutes they were in McLean's car, making southward through the dense traffic, but very soon McLean dived off into secondary

7

roads, passing through districts strange to Valerie, until finally they left the main built-up area behind them and emerged into pleasant country. It was now getting dark, and the brighter stars were already visible in the clear sky, with the slip of a new moon away in the west.

"Never see the new moon through glass," ruminated Valerie. "Oh Lord, I've done it."

"Turn over your money," said McLean. "That's the infallible antidote."

"I haven't got any money. But where is our mysterious objective?"

"We're almost there. An old country house turned into a restaurant, with a full licence. Most of the original furniture too. Run by a Frenchman named Gustave. He's the most ingratiating scoundrel I've ever met."

"In what way?"

"Lots of ways. But provided he doesn't go beyond a certain point we leave him alone, for such a man can be useful at times."

"Meaning you have got him in your pocket?"

"Not exactly. But he knows just how far to go if he is to continue running his excellent business, and when we want a little information about certain persons Gustave is sometimes able to supply it."

"Then he knows you are a policeman?"

"Oh yes, but it goes no farther. He's not such a fool as to advertise the fact. But don't bother your head about it. It's all very complicated."

When finally they parked the car outside the magnificent old mansion and went inside Valerie was agreeably surprised at what she saw. Everything was in excellent taste, from the expensive draped curtains at the wide windows to the Persian rugs on the parquetted floor, and the fine linen table-cloths and serviettes. The head waiter, who conducted them to a vacant table not far from the raised platform where a string orchestra performed, might have stepped straight from the Ritz or the

Carlton. Majestically he beckoned a waiter to their service.

"Golly!" whispered Valerie. "You certainly know your way about."

McLean laughed at her astonished expression, and the waiter thrust menus into their hands. When they had both made a selection of the multifarious food items, the wine waiter came along and McLean, feeling that he deserved a respite, ordered champagne.

Valerie, glancing round at the assemblage, could see nothing to justify some of McLean's early remarks. The women were all very well turned out, and were mainly on the young side. She thought there was a little ostentation in places, but everyone seemed to be behaving perfectly. This went for the orchestra also, which was now playing selections from *Tosca* with considerable success.

"This is lovely," she said. "If the food is as good as the appointments it ought to be divine."

"You'll find the food all right. None

of these people would come here if it wasn't."

When the food began to arrive Valerie had to admit she had no cause for complaint of any sort, and the champagne was as good as it looked.

"Mud in your eye!" said McLean, and raised his glass.

"There's mud in yours," Valerie retorted. "I can't see any sin hanging around."

"You won't. They're all on their best behaviour. And why not? Even the most incorrigible crook likes to enjoy a few hours of virtuous life, away from the cares that pursue him for the rest of the day. Take, for example, that young man on your right, with the girl of the inflated bosom. Two years ago he was mixed up in the biggest financial swindle of modern times — and he got away with it. There's an older man, behind him, looking rather decrepit for this place. Yet I happen to know that he organizes the theft of motor cars on a huge scale.

11

He's for the burning later on, but not yet. And here comes Gustave himself, as cheerful and immaculate as ever."

The diminutive Frenchman hove into Valerie's view, bowing and smiling to his more familiar patrons. When he reached McLean's table he stopped and asked him if everything was to his satisfaction, and was assured that it was.

"Excellent," he said. "It is a pleasure to see you again, sir — and you, madame."

Valerie sighed and shook her head as Gustave went on his tour of inspection.

"I believe you are playing a game on me, Mac," she said. "You promised me scorpions and all you produce is white mice, not to mention the most beautiful food I've ever tasted. Oh dear, I'm going to make a hog of myself."

McLean laughed, for he, too, was enjoying the whole thing, but what he had said about the place was perfectly true. Every few minutes he saw a face which was vaguely familiar, and after a few moments his excellent memory placed the face in Scotland Yard's very extensive list of persons known to be engaged in activities slightly, or to a greater extent, outside the law. Then suddenly some late arrivals were escorted by the head waiter to a large table which had been reserved, and the party of four sat down. They were two men and two women, and all of them were in full evening dress. McLean chuckled as he replenished the champagne glasses.

"Ever seen a murderer?" he asked.

"Not in the flesh."

"Then you have a treat in store. The large man who has just arrived with his friends is such a person. He murdered his young wife some sixteen years ago."

Valerie shot a swift glance at the man in question.

"Oh, Mac," she protested. "He looks rather like a simple clergyman, up from the country."

"He talked like one too, when his

counsel was bold enough to put him in the witness-box. It was that fact which was largely responsible for his missing the gallows. He got imprisonment for life instead, and after fifteen years in jail, where his conduct was exemplary, he was set free upon society again. Makes one think, doesn't it?"

"No more," begged Valerie. "You're spoiling my meal."

"I'm sorry. Let's forget all about it. I really didn't bring you here to inflict man's inhumanity to man upon you. Tell me all about yourself. What are you doing, apart from domestic chores?"

"I've taken up painting again, and getting a tremendous kick out of it. I paint everything, including myself. Ian thinks I'm quite mad, but then Ian never had feeling for Art. I tried to get him to pose for me, but he looked quite murderous at the bare suggestion. Anyway, he'd be the worst of models, because he can't sit still for a moment. Now you're the sort of man who would be God's gift to young aspiring artists — "

"Oh no you don't," said McLean. "I can't even face a camera, let alone a ferocious young woman, taking in every defect which Nature lavished on me. Get thee to a nunnery."

Valerie laughed infectiously. The soft music, the softer lighting, and the bubble champagne were bringing out the best of her charming generous nature, and McLean let her do most of the talking because he liked the ring of her healthy young voice, and the changing expressions which passed over her admirable features. The last drop of champagne vanished just when coffee and liqueur were due. By this time the floor show started, and after a couple of songs which Valerie called 'tear jerkers' the 'star' of the evening was introduced by Gustave, with many superlatives. According to Gustave she had appeared in every European capital, in America, India, and the Far East, in all of which countries she had been received with acclamation. He was sure that his patrons would agree that her world-wide reputation was deserved.

"Ladies and gentlemen, it is my pleasure to present the glorious, one and only, Stella Polaris," he concluded.

The black curtains at the back of the stage were parted, and the lady herself stepped into the limelight, to a roll of the kettledrum, and the clapping of hands. She was the most perfect blonde that McLean had ever seen, with a mass of golden hair that was coiled up in an enormous bunch at the back of her head. Her dress was Grecian to match the hair style, and her tiny feet were bare, and the toe-nails gilded. The clapping ceased and the orchestra started to play music which McLean recognized as Ravel. Stella began to dance and posture most admirably, and one was led to believe the turn was no more than that, but Stella had more strings to her bow. Cunningly the music changed its tempo and style, and the dance changed with it, hotting up into cacophonic jazz, and Stella suddenly slipped her outer classical garment and deftly kicked it across the stage. In turn other flimsy garments came adrift, while the music became wilder and wilder, until finally the frantic dancer was left with nothing but a bikini.

"Not much else she can shed," muttered Valerie.

But at that moment the bikini fluttered off like a butterfly, and Stella, realizing her predicament with well simulated horror, let down her mass of golden hair, which fell like a curtain to her knees, and with a coy expression vanished behind the black curtain, to another long roll of the drum, and roars of applause from a delighted audience.

"Well!" muttered McLean. "The one and only Stella Polaris. I didn't expect that. I hope you're not shocked."

"Not as shocked as you are. I thought there was a catch in it."

"I didn't. She danced so well at first that I expected she was serious. But of course that would never go down here. What a lot of wasted talent there is."

They stayed for two more turns, which were not quite respectable, and then Valerie, with a little sigh, said it was time she got on her way.

McLean took her to the car and then drove her to a railway station, where he discovered there was a train due in a few minutes which would take her within a mile of her home. There she thanked him prettily for the very pleasant evening, and reminded him of the promise to dine with her and her brother on the following Thursday.

"Any time after seven," she said. "Ian will then have got his surgery over."

"I'll be there."

When the train finally arrived her slim warm hand lingered in his for a moment.

"Thanks for everything, Mac," she said. "You're a darling."

McLean drove back to his rather lonely flat.

2

DOCTOR IAN DONKIN'S house and surgery was situated in that still unspoiled piece of country south of Esher. He could hear the hum of traffic on the busy by-pass, but his immediate outlook was as rustic as anything could be. The practice was small and scattered, but sufficient for the needs of a bachelor. Valerie, who lived with him, and almost mothered him, held him in great respect, for she never doubted his ability to rise to the top of his profession had he wanted to. But Donkin had no such ambitions. He liked being a G.P. He liked living away from big cities, and having sufficient time to engage in research work the results of which were published in learned journals, or given orally before professional audiences. There was no money in this, but Donkin had an utter disregard for money. His own patrimony had been used in the equipping of a small laboratory in the house, in which most of his spare time was spent.

Had his heart not been given to Medicine he might have been a first-class athlete, for he was built on splendid lines, and had played 'rugger' for Scotland in his younger days. His best friend was probably McLean, whom he had first met at the University, and this friendship was not diminished by the lack of correspondence, for McLean was a man rather after his own heart, too deeply engaged in his work to indulge in the rather futile occupation of letter-writing.

"When is it that Mac is coming?" he asked Valerie.

"Tonight," replied Valerie. "Why do you think I'm roasting that fowl?"

"But you said Thursday."

"Today is Thursday. It's six o'clock, and the waiting-room is already half-full of patients. You'd better get weaving."

"You're right. Did you get that bottle of Johnnie Walker?"

"I did, and it goes on the housekeeping bill. Ian, you can't see your patients in that filthy old coat."

"You go and look after your fowl, and leave my clothing to me. If Mac comes before I'm finished, there's a half-bottle of sherry in the lab."

"So that's where it went!" gasped Valerie. "I was looking for that to put in the trifle."

"A waste of good liquor. And remember not to keep Mac yarning too long after dinner. He owes me my revenge at chess. The last time he came here he gave me the whale of a licking."

"And what do I do while you two sit like mummies staring at chessmen?"

"You can paint us. Then we shall have perfect silence."

Valerie threw a table-mat at him, which he deftly caught and placed on the dining-table. Then with an amused chuckle he passed through a door to his surgery.

By seven o'clock Valerie had everything organized. The dining-table was laid, with a floral decoration, and the chicken was going on nicely. It took her but a few minutes to put the final touches to her own appearance, and then Ian came back from the surgery.

"You're punctual," she said. "Got rid of them all?"

"Yes. I think I'll go and tidy myself."

"I should think so too. You're probably impregnated with germs. I'll see to the lounge fire."

It was about a quarter of an hour later that the door-bell rang, and Donkin, on his way downstairs, answered it himself, rather than disturb his sister in her culinary duties. He opened the door to find a large saloon car outside, and a tall dark man on the doorstep.

"Good evening!" he said. "Do you happen to be Doctor Donkin?"

"I am."

"My name is Baldock. I live not

22

far from here — at Dunham's Cross, and am a new-comer to the district. I fear my brother is dying. He suddenly collapsed about a quarter of an hour ago. The telephone at my house has not yet been reinstalled, and so I couldn't ring anyone. Then I remembered having seen your plate on two occasions when I have used the road outside. So I lost no time in getting here. Can you come and look at my brother?"

"It isn't very convenient," demurred Donkin. "I am expecting a visitor at any moment."

The visitor wrung his hands pathetically.

"But this is a matter of life and death," he said. "If I go chasing round for a doctor my brother may die. It's a stroke of some kind, and he cannot speak. Please, please do come. I could take you in my car, and my chauffeur will drive you back afterwards."

Donkin looked at the big car, beside which a uniformed chauffeur was now standing. He found it difficult to refuse such an appeal.

"I'll come," he said. "If you will give me a minute or two to collect a coat and a few things."

"Thank you, Doctor. I'm most grateful to you. I'll sit in the car until you are ready."

As Donkin closed the door Valerie entered the hall from the kitchen.

"Who was it?" she asked.

"A Mr. Baldock whose brother has had a stroke, out at Dunham's Cross. He is also without a telephone. It's a nuisance but I shall have to go."

"Is he one of your patients?"

"No. He's a new-comer to the district."

"Then why didn't you send him to another doctor?"

"The matter appears to be too urgent to waste time. If Mac arrives before I am back you can entertain him. He will understand."

"This would have to happen," complained Valerie. "Just when I've got the fowl done to a turn. Ah well, that's what comes of being cook and

24

bottle-washer to a doctor. What you need is a little more flint in your heart."

Donkin laughed, and snatched a light coat and a hat, also his bag from the surgery.

"I'm off," he called to Valerie. "I'll be back as soon as I possibly can."

"You'd better," replied Valerie. "Don't be surprised if Mac and I finish up the whole bird, not to mention that bottle of Scotch."

A few moments later Donkin was sitting in the back of the car with Baldock, and the chauffeur, who was already at the wheel, set the vehicle moving into the gathering darkness.

"Has your brother ever had a similar attack?" asked Donkin, as they sped through the narrow lanes which led to Dunham's Cross.

"No. I don't understand it at all. We were just about to sit down to a meal, when he gave a curious little cry, clapped a hand to his heart and fell heavily. I managed to carry him upstairs and tried to get him to take a sip of brandy, but his jaw was set hard. Then I realized I had to get a doctor somehow."

"What age is your brother?"

"Thirty-eight."

"And he's always had good health?"

"Yes. Very good indeed."

"So you're a stranger in this district?"

"Yes. My brother and I came from Malaya a few months ago. The place became a bit too hot for us. We had a small rubber plantation in a very remote spot, and on two occasions we were very nearly murdered by bandits. Finally we decided to sell out. It meant a great loss in terms of capital, but we were very glad to get back to a peaceful country. We managed to find a house — a bit too big for us it's true, but one can't be choosey these days."

The car was now moving very fast, and in the narrow dark lanes Donkin had some difficulty in recognizing his whereabouts.

"Have we passed Dunham's Cross?" he asked.

"Yes — the last turning to the left. The house isn't very far now."

But after ten minutes of silence the car was still making great speed. Donkin looked at his wrist-watch, and found that it was nearly half-past seven.

"I hope it isn't much farther," he said.

"Less than half a mile. The first house on the left in fact."

Donking grunted as he realized that Baldock had under-estimated the distance, but then the car began to slow down, and very soon it turned through double gates, and up a winding drive which finally ended in a wide open space outside a large, white, Georgian house.

"Here we are," said Baldock. "Barnes, you had better wait in the car. The doctor will need to be driven back shortly."

The chauffeur touched his peaked cap, and Baldock and Donkin hurried to the front door, which the former opened. Inside the large hall was an elderly man, who looked like a servant.

"Any change?" asked Baldock anxiously.

"No, sir," said the old man. "He hasn't come to."

Baldock escorted Donkin up the broad staircase to a bedroom along the corridor. The blind had been pulled and the lights were on. It was quite a small room, and very sparsely furnished, and lying in the bed was a middle-aged man, of dark complexion. He was flat on his back, and was still partially clothed. The coat and waistcoat were on a chair beside the bed, but he wore his shirt, which was now open at the neck.

"I thought it was best to give him some air," said Baldock. "He — he doesn't seem to be breathing."

This was perfectly true, but Donkin made no comment, as he opened his bag and took out a stethoscope. While Donkin made various tests Baldock grew more and more anxious, until

Donkin gave him a quick glance which clearly indicated that he preferred to be alone with his patient.

"I'll come back in a few minutes," said Baldock. "I'm feeling a little faint."

Donkin sighed his relief as the door closed on Baldock. The man on the bed was undoubtedly dead, but the cause of his death was yet veiled in mystery. Donkin opened the shirt fully at the front and rolled up the thin vest. The body down to the waist was well developed, and there was no sign of any injury there, or on the scalp which he examined. He did not look like a 'hearty' man, but that did not rule out the possibility of some unexpected heart trouble. Only a post-mortem could settle that question.

He replaced the bed-clothes, and walked across to the wash-basin to wash his hands. There his attention was drawn to a small crimson stain on one of the taps. It looked remarkably like blood, and the fact caused him to cogitate. How had blood got on to the tap except from the last human hand to touch it? Then, just under the bed, he noticed a pair of shoes and some socks. He pulled the socks from the shoes, and noticed that one of them was saturated with blood, and in one of the shoes there was more blood.

Astonished by this he went to the bed and pulled the bed-clothes right down. The dead man was wearing grey trousers and a belt, and his feet were bare. Above the left ankle there was a bandage obviously tied by a novice. Donkin unfastened it and laid bare what appeared to be a bullet wound which extended right through the fleshy part of the limb. In a few moments he had the nether garments off, but there were no more injuries. He was replacing the bed-clothes when Baldock crept into the room.

"Well?" he asked.

"He's dead," said Donkin. "He was dead when I arrived."

"My God! Was it — his heart?"

30

"I don't know. How did he come to get that wound in his leg?"

"Oh, that was yesterday. He was playing about with a small rook rifle and shot himself."

"You didn't tell me that."

"I didn't think it could possibly have any connection with his collapse."

"Well, that's all I can do."

"You mean you can't write a certificate?"

"Certainly not, in the circumstances. I shall have to report the matter, and then there will be a post-mortem. What was your brother's full name?"

"Henry Arthur Baldock."

Donken pencilled the name in his note-book, and then picked up his bag.

"I must get back," he said. "I'm sorry I was too late."

The despairing expression on Baldock's face changed.

"Not yet, Doctor," he said grimly.

"What do you mean?"

"I mean that circumstances make

your departure a little difficult. I'm grateful to you for coming here, but I scarcely expected this dramatic ending. For reasons which I don't propose to go into I shall be obliged to delay your return."

Donkin's response to this amazing speech was to march straight to the door and open it. Outside was a man wearing a dinner-jacket, and an improvised mask across the nose and mouth. In his right hand he clutched an automatic.

"What the blazes!" ejaculated Donkin.

The man with the automatic made no response, preferring to leave that to Baldock.

"You see the position, my dear Doctor," said Baldock. "All I ask is that you remain here for a certain time — a matter of hours."

"I'll do nothing of the kind. I'm a doctor and I have certain responsibilities and duties. One of those duties is to report this case immediately. Will you order that crazy fool to stand aside?"

Before Baldock could reply a second armed man joined the first and, like him, he was masked.

"Why not be reasonable, Doctor?" asked Baldock. "I do not expect you to lose over this unfortunate business. Accept the situation and in a few hours you will be free and in possession of ample payment for inconveniences caused."

"And if not?" snapped Donkin.

Baldock's dark eyes flashed ominously.

"I'm afraid there's no 'if' about it," he said.

Donkin hesitated for a moment and then the ignominy of the situation drove him to desperation.

"There's nothing more to say," he grunted. "I'm leaving — now!"

He walked straight through the open door, whereupon both gunmen crowded on him and pushed their pistols against him. Infuriated, he lashed out with his left fist and dealt the nearer of the two men a shattering blow. The fellow went down like a ninepin and his pistol clattered to the floor. In a flash Donkin's arm went back again, and then there came a loud report and a sensation like a red-hot iron in his left shoulder. Dropping the bag he let loose with his right fist, and felt it land on an almost invisible face. Then everything seemed to revolve about him, and his big form crumpled and came down on the hard floor with a crash. After that — darkness.

★ ★ ★

It was barely more than five minutes after Donkin had left in Baldock's car that McLean arrived at the house. Valerie let him in, with a sigh of mingled relief and disappointment.

"Anything wrong?" asked McLean. "Don't tell me you have forgotten that I was coming."

"Far from it. The fact is Ian had an unexpected call, and couldn't resist it."

"A rich private patient probably?"

34

"No. A complete stranger. Ian had only just finished his surgery when the fellow turned up in a panic. His brother had had a stroke or something, and the house is minus a telephone. Anyway, Ian promised he wouldn't be long and I was to apologize for him. That done, the next thing is a drink."

McLean passed into the comfortable lounge, where a big fire was burning. He knew that room very well, and liked its appointments, all of which were due to Valerie. Periodically she changed things round, but the effect was always pleasant and artistic.

"It's got to be whisky or sherry," she said. "I suppose sherry is the right stuff before meals?"

"Sherry will do very nicely. Heavens! What have you done to your hair?"

"That hair-do I had in town was a wash-out. It all fell to pieces the next day, so I had a go at it myself. Don't you like it?"

"Very much. It reveals more of your admirable neck. Ladies with lovely necks ought to make a point of showing them. Don't look so bellicose, I mean it."

"Not you," scoffed Valerie. "You've never paid a girl a compliment in your life. At the moment this neck of mine needs lubricating inside. Chin chin!"

McLean stretched himself out in the comfortable chair by the fire, and Valerie, as was her wont, took the large pouffe with her hands clasped round her knees. It was her favourite form of physical relaxation, and McLean recalled her in that position years and years ago.

"How's the painting going?" he asked.

"Not too badly."

"When am I going to be allowed to see the results of your labours?"

Valerie laughed and took another drink from her glass.

"I always imagined you to be a very observant person," she said. "Don't you notice anything different here?"

"You've changed the furniture around,

and some of the pictures since I was last here."

"Say on."

"The piano used to be on that side, and is now moved to the south wall."

"That's right. You're very slow about it all."

"Oh, wait a minute. There's a picture I haven't seen before — over the piano. It looks rather interesting."

His gaze quickly switched to Valerie's reddening cheeks.

"Guilty," she said. "A little duckling among the swans. Ian swears I've hung it upside down, but I ought to know."

McLean got up and went to the picture. It was more than a trifle impressionistic, but there was unmistakable talent in it, and McLean, who loved pictures almost as much as he loved music, was considerably impressed.

"Excellent," he said. "I think I know that bit of country. Isn't it close to Friday Street?"

"You're cleverer than I thought.

Come and have another sherry."

"I will. But, seriously, you've missed your vocation. That really is a praiseworthy effort. Show me some more."

"There's nothing worth looking at. When I'm in the mood I dash things off in a fearful hurry, and the result is usually horrific."

But McLean egged her on, and finally she left him and came back with a number of canvases, which she passed to McLean with some reluctance. None of them was quite as striking as the one on the wall, but in all of them were signs of her immature talent.

"When Ian's practice fails I shall probably take a pitch on that wide pavement near St. Martin in the Fields and do immortal work with some bits of crayon, with a large hat close by to collect the pennies," she said. "Now I must go and look at my roast fowl and the things that go with it. If Ian isn't back on time I'll murder him."

She was absent for quite a long

time, during which McLean sat and smoked reflectively. When she returned she looked very rueful.

"Everything done to a turn," she said. "It really is naughty of Ian to be so long. I told him that dinner would be served at eight punctually."

"It's only a few minutes past the hour. How far did he have to go?"

"Only a mile or two. He went in Mr. Baldock's car, and the idea was that Baldock's chauffeur would drive him back."

"Presumably the patient needed some attention."

"Well, if he's not back in a quarter of an hour I'm going to make a start."

But when the quarter of an hour was up Ian was still absent, and Valerie then decided not to wait for him.

"He won't mind," she said. "Food means very little to Ian. It's really wasted on him. He'd just as soon eat out of tins, and, believe it or not, he doesn't know mutton from beef. Come on — I'm hungry."

They went into the dining-room, and in a few minutes Valerie had the meal served. Thereafter they gave themselves up to the excellent repast, and it was close upon nine o'clock when they went back to the lounge, where Valerie served coffee.

"I wish I knew what was happening," she said. "It must be very serious to keep Ian all this time. Milk?"

"Just a dash. I shouldn't worry if I were you," said McLean.

"But the evening is completely spoiled — for Ian, I mean. He had looked forward to it so much."

"Well, the night is yet young."

"Such a nuisance that man not being on the 'phone. I could at least have rung up to find out how long Ian would be."

"But if he knew he was going to be delayed indefinitely he could have got a message to you by some nearby telephone."

"Yes, I suppose so."

As time passed Valerie became more

and more anxious, and McLean, too, began to feel that something might be amiss. There was always the possibility of an accident to the car, in some remote spot where the incident might not be discovered for hours.

"You don't know the house to which Ian was going?" he asked.

"No. The man — Baldock — said it wasn't far from Dunham's Cross. That's about two and a half miles from here. It was rather foolish of me not to have got the exact address, but of course I didn't anticipate that Ian would be there for more than a cursory examination of the sick man."

"I suppose a directory is no use?"

"No. Baldock is a new-comer to the district. There's absolutely nothing we can do but wait."

Wait they did, while the hands stole round the clock on the mantelpiece. Normally it would have been pleasant enough sitting there with Valerie's quick tongue ranging over wide topics, but now all her infectious gaiety had left her, and it was McLean who did the talking, until even he realized that something should be done in the matter.

"You know the road to Dunham's Cross?" he asked.

"Yes."

"Then come in the car with me, and we'll cruise round that area. We can leave a note for Ian in case he returns while we are away. We can also telephone here from a public box."

Valerie was quite agreeable to this, and she quickly wrote a message and left it pinned to the wooden mantelpiece. A few minutes later she and McLean were making towards Dunham's Cross. The lanes were completely deserted, and they reached the crossing in a very short time. Here McLean stopped and consulted the road map. He put a series of arrows along the various roads and lanes in the area, and then handed the map to Valerie.

"I propose following the route

indicated by the arrows," he said. "It should finally bring us back to this spot. Check me in case I go wrong, and at the same time look out for a telephone-box."

This procedure was followed, Valerie checking each turning. Soon they came to a telephone-box and McLean stopped the car while Valerie put a call through to her house. She returned in a minute or two.

"No luck," she said. "I could hear our bell ringing. He's not back."

"Then let's continue."

It took about half an hour to complete the tour, and finally they came back to Dunham's Cross having achieved nothing. McLean drove back to the house, which they found exactly as they had left it.

"Something's wrong," said Valerie. "It's nearly midnight, and nothing can explain Ian's absence but some sinister plot. That man — Baldock — was a fake. That's why he brought his own car. He didn't want to have to tell Ian the address he was going to. Mac, must you go back?"

"What a question! I have not the slightest idea of going home while things are at this pass. The best thing I can do is get in touch with the Surrey Joint Constabulary, and get them to patrol that area. But can you give me any details of the car which called here?"

"Yes, I saw it through the window, as it was leaving. It was an American saloon — very large and modern. The colour was either dark blue or black. I think it might have been, a Chrysler, but am not sure."

"And the owner — Mr. Baldock?"

"I never saw him at all."

McLean then used the telephone, and was busy on it for some time, but finally he came back to Valerie, who had poured him out a huge whisky.

"Well?" she asked.

"They're sending out two wireless-equipped cars, and have promised to report any progress to me here. But it's only natural to presume that Baldock is a spurious name. You look tired, my dear. Wouldn't you like to lie down for a bit? It may be hours before I hear anything."

"No. I'm not a bit tired. Just worried. The idea of Ian getting into any trouble is fantastic, and yet there's no other explanation. Do you think a whisky-and-soda would do me any harm?"

"On the contrary, I am convinced it would do you a lot of good just now. Have a cigarette, too, and don't get too gloomy over this queer business. It may not be as serious as it looks."

Another hour passed, and then Valerie decided she would adopt McLean's earlier suggestion, and try to snatch a little sleep.

"You'll call me if there's any news?" she asked.

"I promise."

When she had gone to her room McLean stretched himself out on the settee, leaving the door open in order that he would hear the telephone-bell if, and when, it rang. He was far more disturbed about Donkin than he felt like revealing to Valerie, but could find no satisfactory solution to this mystery. That Donkin could leave his devoted sister in such grave doubts about his welfare could only be due to the fact that he was not free to communicate with her. That fact suggested that he had been the victim of foul play. The theory of a car accident would no longer hold water.

After a long while he dozed, to awake at intervals and remember where he was. Then, finally, when the light of day was stealing into the room, the telephone-bell rang. He imagined it was the police patrol, and hurried to the instrument. To his surprise, and relief, he heard Donkin's unmistakable voice.

"Oh, it's you, Mac. Thank God!"

"Where are you, Ian?"

"Near Effingham, I think. Can you possibly pick me up?"

"Yes, of course. Are you all right?"

"Far from it. Tell you all about it when I see you. Listen. If you take the road from Effingham that leads over that high land to the Silent Pool you are sure to find me. I guess I'm about a mile from Effingham. I'll wait in the telephone-box. Too done in to go any farther."

"I'll be with you as quick as possible."

McLean hung up the receiver and saw Valerie standing on the stairs — fully dressed.

"Ian?" she asked excitedly.

"Yes. He's away near Effingham. I'm going for him at once."

"Is he — all right?"

"I think he's injured. Now you go back and sleep. I'll have him here very soon."

"No. I want to come. I can't sleep."

"I think it would be much better if you stayed here, and prepared some food. I propose to drive dangerously for a change. He's bound to be famished."

"Perhaps you're right," she conceded.

"Shall I get you some brandy — in case — "

"I always keep a flask in the car, and a first-aid outfit. Now I must leave. See you later."

Snatching his hat and coat, McLean hurried out of the house into the breaking dawn. There was the promise of a beautiful day and the air was clear and cold. In a few minutes he was out of the twisting lanes and on the main road. Here he put his foot down hard, and the powerful car began to mop up the miles. He knew every inch of that road, and it was absolutely deserted. Within a quarter of an hour he was in Effingham, and from there he turned through the beautiful wooded upland country. The sun had now risen and was shedding its amber light through the dense timber. Suddenly the roadside telephone-box hove into sight. He was surprised to see no one near it, but pulled up the car just short of it. A glance inside the box revealed Donkin sitting on the floor, with his eyes closed. He opened the door and leaned over the sitting man.

"Ian!"

The closed eyes opened, and a smile lit up the rugged features.

"Never more glad to see you, Mac," said Donkin. "Lend me a hand, will you? I'm all right. Just a hole in my shoulder. I was having a snooze."

McLean helped him to his feet, and then noticed the blood on his coat and shirt, near the left shoulder.

"Shall I attend to that now?" he asked.

"No. It'll keep till I get home. Luckily the bullet went clean through. Lordy, I'm so tired."

McLean got him into the car, transformed the rug into a pillow, and got him into a comfortable position.

"I won't bother you with questions now," he said. "Hungry?"

"Famished."

"Valerie is attending to that. Well, here we go."

3

VALERIE subsequently received her brother, if not with open arms, at least with a warmness that left no doubt as to her affection for him. She saw the blood on his clothing, and wanted to know all the facts there and then, but McLean wagged a remonstrative finger at her.

"All in good time," he said. "First and foremost his wound needs attention. You see about that breakfast, while I help him to the surgery, and take a look at his wound. Or would you rather I called a doctor, Ian?"

"No need for that," replied Donkin. "I assure you I'm all right, Valerie. What I need is a wash-down and a bandage. I'll direct Mac in the operations. But you can help by bringing a bowl and a jug of warm water."

In the surgery Donkin was stripped to the waist, and his wound attended to. There had been a great deal of bleeding, and as a result Donkin felt weak and tired, but fortunately the small bullet had touched no bone of any kind. After the wound had been bathed and sterilized McLean carried out the rather awkward business of bandaging to Donkin's complete satisfaction.

"Feels miles better," he said. "I'll sit here and have a smoke while you go to my room and collect a complete set of fresh clothing. You'll find a favourite grey suit of mine in the wardrobe and the other things in the chest of drawers."

In about a quarter of an hour he was fully dressed, and quite ready for the very early breakfast which Valerie had prepared. To the surprise of both Valerie and McLean he made an extremely good meal.

"I needed that," he said. "Now for my story."

"Oh, one moment," said Valerie. "I

forgot to tell you, Mac, that the police telephoned soon after you left here. They regretted they had nothing to report, so I told them it was all right and that we had heard from Ian."

McLean nodded his head, and Donkin then related what had happened to him after his arrival at the house where the sick man lay.

"When I collapsed," he concluded, "they took me to a cupboard on the landing, which contained a number of brooms and brushes, and locked the door on me. I bled merrily up there, and nobody did the slightest thing about my wound. Hours passed, and then Baldock and another man, who was still masked, came and bandaged my eyes, and I was led downstairs, and shoved into a car. The car started and for about half an hour it kept up a steady pace. Then it stopped and I was taken out of it, and led, with a pistol pushed into my back, for some distance. Baldock then told me to count a hundred before I pulled off the bandage, and threatened to shoot if I disobeyed. Well, I didn't count the hundred nor anything like it, but when I tore off the bandage I was quite alone and in pitch darkness. But some distance away I could see a glow which I assumed came from the headlights of a car, and then I heard the engine fire, and the glow moved away."

He stopped for a moment, and took a drink from his still unfinished coffee.

"I stumbled across broken land to where I had seen the glow, and fell down several times, but finally I found myself in a very rough road, lined with thick trees. I had no idea at all where I was, and it was so dark that twice I wandered into a ditch. Then, after a long time, there was a lightening of the gloom, and I realized that the dawn was coming up. A little later I recognized the country I was in, and soon I found a signpost which told me that Effingham was two miles ahead. I staggered on, seeing no habitation of any kind until I came upon that

53

telephone-box. Fortunately I had the necessary change demanded by the telephone operator, and I put that call through. That's all there is to it, except that the blighters have still got my bag."

"Well!" gasped Valerie. "Of all the cheek! But, Ian, you can find that house again, can't you?"

"I'm not sure. You have to remember it was dark, and I was in the back seat with Baldock, who kept me engaged in talking for some time. It was only when I thought the journey was taking a long time that I took some notice of our surroundings. But I saw no landmark of any kind, and now I feel certain that the chauffeur deliberately went by unfrequented back lanes, and avoided all the main roads. But, of course, I saw the house, after we entered the drive. I should know that again. What do you think of it all, Mac?"

"It all seems to make sense," replied McLean. "I think a doctor was really needed — that they had good reason for wanting to save the life of the alleged brother, but foresaw the possibility of his death, and made their plans accordingly. They wanted no post-mortems, no inquiry into the matter whatsoever — at least not while they were on the premises. It is pretty certain that if we succeed in locating the house they will have gone, and perhaps the dead body too. Obviously the matter should be followed up."

"Yes, without further delay," said Donkin. "I'm ready when you are."

McLean looked a trifle doubtful, but Donkin's mind was made up, and he backed his decision by pointing out that without him any identification of the house was impossible.

"Sitting in the car won't do me any harm," he said. "I'd like very much to see that gang in custody. Valerie, you need some sleep. Go and get it, and leave all the chores to that daily woman. Mac and I are going on the war-path."

Valerie, with her chief fears removed,

made no objection, and McLean and Donkin got into the car.

"I remember the first part of the journey," said Donkin. "We turned right at the gate, and then right again, and then left. That's the usual direct way to Dunham's Cross, but I think we left that on our right. Oh yes, I remember one very steep hill, somewhere round about the Dunham area. You carry on for a bit while I look at the map."

McLean made the turnings mentioned by Donkin, and proceeded along a lane for some distance. Then again there were cross-roads. Here he stopped.

"Dunham's Cross is up on the left," said Donkin. "If we go straight on and take the first left turning there appears to be a very steep hill. That may well be the hill I remember."

McLean set the car moving again, and then suddenly came to a deep dip in the narrow lane, where the road surface was very muddy. He stopped the car and examined the mud ahead of his own car. Across this were clearly imprinted the tread of large-section tyres — obviously made quite recently.

"Goodyear tyres," he said. "Looks rather like the car which carried you. All the other tracks are older."

On taking the next turn to the left the lane began to ascend steeply. Donkin peered at the trees which grew on the high banks, and then pointed to a very old blasted elm.

"We're right," he said. "I remember the headlights of the car lighting up that old skeleton. The hill should have a right-hand hair-pin bend near the summit."

A little later the car rounded the bend, and shortly afterwards the brow of the hill passed and the lane was flat for some distance. Donkin, staring at everything outside the car shook his head.

"I'm done," he said. "Can't remember anything from now on, until we entered the drive, but there were lots of turns before that."

McLean kept the car going until again there were cross-lanes. There was a house on the right, and another farther up on the left, but Donkin was convinced that the place they sought was farther on.

"I'll try the ground," said McLean. "These roads are largely dirt."

His examination of the ground was successful, for the left turning yielded the diamond pattern of the Goodyear tyres in several places. McLean got back into the car and the quest was resumed. The lane they were now in ran for a considerable distance without a side turning of any kind, and the surface improved until it was decent tarmac.

"Not much chance of any tyre marks on this stuff," said McLean. "Hullo, there's a left turning. What do we do now?"

"Keep straight on," said Donkin, "but slowly, because I've a feeling we're somewhere near the place we want."

McLean slackened the speed, and very soon they came to a number of large houses, lying well back in wooded grounds, but at each one Donkin shook his head, and finally they came to a little colony of smaller habitations.

"We'd better go back and take that left-hand turning," said McLean.

"It looks like it."

The car was reversed and soon they made the turning. The road surface was good, and for a long way there was no sign of a house, then suddenly the car passed two closed white gates.

"Steady!" said Donkin. "That looks remarkably like the place, but the gates were open when I saw it. Back the car a bit."

The car moved backwards until they were abreast of the white gates. On one of them the name 'Leylands' had been painted, but the lettering was so worn as to be almost illegible. Donkin left the car and passed through the gate. He walked up the curving drive, until he was lost to view. Then he reappeared very quickly, and beckoned to McLean who, in the meantime, had opened the gates wide. McLean drove the car through the gates, and on reaching Donkin he saw the large, squat, Georgian house. Donkin climbed on to the running-board, and the car finally stopped outside the imposing entrance.

"This is it," said Donkin. "No sign of any smoke from the chimneys."

"What did you expect?" asked McLean. "They would never run the risk of staying on once you were free to tell your story. Still, we'll try the bell."

He pushed the large bell-button and heard the electric bell ringing lustily inside the house, but there was no response, and the door was firmly closed. McLean then passed round the side of the building and came upon a large garage. The doors were open, but there was nothing inside, except a bench and some useful tools. Moving on they came upon two other doors, both of which appeared to be bolted on the inside. One of these was the main door to the domestic quarters, and beside it was a large window. McLean peered through it, but saw nobody.

"We shall have to do a bit of housebreaking," he said, and picked up a loose half-brick from the drain. With this he smashed the lower window just under the latch and then pushed his arm through, and released the latch.

"I'll go and open the back door," he said. "Shan't keep you a minute."

He climbed through the open window, and was soon at the open back door. Donkin accompanied him along two passages until they reached the hall.

"This is the place all right," said Donkin. "I went straight up the staircase to a bedroom."

McLean nodded and then opened a door on the right of the hall. It gave entry to a large lounge, in which were the ashes of a fire in the large grate, and some dirty glasses on a side table.

The floor was littered with bits of paper and string.

"Signs of a hasty departure," mused McLean. "Well, let's see if they've removed the corpse."

Donkin led the way to the room in which the body had lain. It was still there, in the bed, but every article of clothing had vanished, and when McLean pulled back the bed-clothes the corpse was completely naked.

"Taking no chances with clothing or laundry marks," he said.

"I'm surprised they left the body."

"Wouldn't you? Driving around with a dead body is a dangerous occupation. Poor devil! I wonder just what happened to him? Should be a nice job for the County Pathologist. How many men did you actually see here?"

"Only three at one time. Baldock and the two gunmen who were armed. There was the chauffeur, but he might easily have been one of the two masked men."

An examination of the other rooms

revealed nothing of importance, except Donkin's professional bag, which was lying on a bench in the hall.

"That's something rescued from the burning," he muttered.

Leading out from the kitchen was a small room which housed the big boiler. Here there was evidence that a lot of rubbish had been recently consigned to it. McLean opened the stove and found it dead, but choked with burnt paper and cardboard. The only things of interest found there was a blackened address tag. The very stiff tag was burnt round the edges, but the writing on it was still visible. It was 'Greta Borche, Hotel Danielli, Venice'.

"Borche," said McLean. "Might be German, Scandinavian, or merely invented. May help, and may not. Now I must get on to the County Police and make a report, also get the body removed."

"But how? There's no telephone — "

"There is — in the study. I thought

you didn't notice it."

When McLean went to the telephone he found that it was in service, and he spoke for a few minutes with County Headquarters.

"The ambulance is leaving at once," he said. "We shall have to hang on here until it arrives."

"So the story about the telephone not being installed was just a lie?"

"Just one of the many lies already apparent in this case. But how are you feeling?"

"Quite all right. There's a nagging in my shoulder, but it's not really painful."

While they waited McLean probed into every corner in the hope of discovering further information about the strange persons who had inhabited the house, and behind a vase in the dining-room he found an engraved visiting card, bearing the name of Major Coleman, whose address was 'Leylands'. On the back was written: 'All correspondence to Major Coleman at Lake Hotel, Matlock — please.'

"That's interesting," said McLean. "Major Coleman is obviously the owner, and must have let his house furnished during his absence. He should be able to tell us something about his temporary tenants."

A few minutes later McLean was talking to the Major, who appeared to be a very old and ailing man. He explained that he had let the house furnished to Mr. and Mrs. Baldock for three months, through an advertisement in a London newspaper. They had called upon him, and he had liked the look of them. Baldock had paid him one month's rent in advance — in cash. McLean asked if there had been a formal agreement, and the Major said there had not. In the circumstances he didn't think that was necessary. But there had been an inventory. McLean asked about Mrs. Baldock, and the Major described her as a pretty and charming woman of about thirty years of age. He wanted to know what was wrong, and when McLean told him there were noises at the other end that suggested the Major was having a fit. Then he asked if he should come home at once, but McLean said that was not imperative — at the moment. But had Baldock given him any address at which the Baldocks had stayed prior to their coming to Leylands? The Major said it was some hotel — he couldn't remember which. Finally McLean ended the conversation.

"People behave most strangely," he complained. "He lets these people into his house, without knowing anything about them, impressed by the fact that Baldock paid him a month's rent on the nail. I suppose he didn't employ a respectable agent because he wanted to save the commission. They could easily have made off with a vanload of his excellent furniture."

It wasn't long before the ambulance arrived, and with it was a police surgeon who had a look at the dead man before he was taken away. Then he had a chat with Donkin, who told him of his unusual experience.

"How long do you think he had been dead when you examined him?" asked the police surgeon.

"A very short time — probably less than half an hour."

"Hm! He looks a healthy enough specimen; but then some of them do, until you open 'em up. What's your position in this case, Inspector?"

"Up to now it has been strictly private, but I'm rather hoping that phase is over."

"You'd like the case?"

"I think I should. It promises to be interesting."

A little later McLean drove Donkin back home, where Valerie was waiting to know of any developments. McLean told her briefly what had transpired, and intimated that his immediate return to London was essential.

"You've been telling me to get some sleep," said Valerie. "You look as if you

67

could do with some yourself."

"What I need more than sleep is a bath," replied McLean. "But that will have to wait. I have to call at County Police headquarters, and report this matter in full."

"And then quietly fade away?"

"I don't know, but I hope not."

That evening, while in his own office, McLean, who had previously had a long interview with his Chief, was informed that the case was his, and that the result of the post-mortem should be in his hands the following morning.

"You can drop everything, Brook," he said to his burly assistant. "We're in on the Leyland's case."

"Fine!" said Brook. "I can do with a sniff of country air. Where do we start, sir?"

"I'll tell you in the morning. It may be with a lady named Greta Borche, but that largely depends upon what answer I get from my telephone inquiries at Venice. Better get all the sleep you can, while you can."

On the following morning McLean received the report on the post-mortem. McLean read it and shrugged his shoulders.

"Disappointment number one," he said. "No evidence from which to deduce cause of death. The injury to the lower leg inflicted a day before death. Undoubtedly caused by bullet of small calibre. Both medical experts in full agreement."

"And Greta Borche?"

"No information yet. If there's no reply in an hour I'll get through to Venice again."

But within the hour the information which McLean hoped for came. It was from the Italian police and it informed him that Greta Borche had stayed at the Hotel Danielli from 4 March until 12 March. She was reputed to be a film actress, using the professional name of Greta Groll. With her was her manager — Hendryk Stein. Their nationalities were given as German.

They had left no address behind them to which letters might be forwarded.

"They left Venice on March the twelfth," mused McLean. "And it is now April the twentieth. Baldock took possession of Leylands just over three weeks ago. Yes, it looks as if the woman went more or less straight to Leylands. Her manager may have been Baldock, or he may not. Well, it's a good start. Here's a little job for you — go to the offices of one or two leading film magazines, and see what information you can get about Greta Groll. Any photographs of her would be most valuable, also of her manager."

This sort of work was very much up Brook's street, and he started on his quest with the greatest enthusiasm. While he was absent McLean got on the telephone to Donkin. He wanted all the details that Donkin could possibly give of the articles of clothing which he had seen in the room where the dead man had lain.

"I can help you there," replied Donkin. "The coat and waistcoat were part of a blue pin-striped suit — comparatively new they seemed to me. The shirt was a soft one, with collar attached. It was a creamy colour. The shoes were brown."

"Good! I've a pretty good recollection of the physical details. My urgent need is to get the fellow identified. I suppose you heard the result of the post-mortem?"

"No. What was it?"

"Cause of death unknown."

"I'm not surprised. Have you got the case?"

"Yes. I shall probably see you in a day or two. Take care of yourself."

"I will. Trouble is I can't drive my car at the moment, so Valerie will have to push me around. Well, the best of luck."

With all the available particulars of the dead man nicely tabulated McLean lost no time in using the B.B.C. and several of the London newspapers. He heard the broadcast later in the day, and felt that he had done all that was immediately possible.

An hour later Sergeant Brook returned from his quest with a pleased smile on his broad face, and a large envelope in his hand.

"Not as easy as I imagined," he said. "I've visited dozens of places, and been sent on all kinds of wild goose chases, but just when I was giving up I had a bit of luck, and here's the result. Probably the only photograph of Greta Groll in London. Quite an eyeful, too."

He thereupon drew from the big envelope a large picture of a glamorous woman, which had obviously been cut from a magazine. The caption was in Italian, and stated that the subject was Greta Groll, who had just completed her film based upon a story by Flaubert.

"She's certainly attractive," agreed McLean. "Did you find out anything at all about her?"

"Practically nothing. The man who found me the picture said he had never heard of her until he saw the picture. He's on the staff of a film journal, and it's his job to watch out for new and attractive foreign stars. He remembered the name because of the other Greta, whom everybody knows."

"Well, we've got to find her. If she's in London she'll probably be in one of the larger hotels — something comparable with Danielli's. We'll start working on that at once."

Scotland Yard's excellent system for combing hotels was swiftly put into operation, and within half an hour Greta Borche was located at the Phoenix.

"What now, sir?" asked Brook.

But McLean was not yet ready to commit himself to action, for the position at the moment was delicate. Any direct approach to the woman might prove hazardous. While he was making up his mind about the next step the telephone bell rang, and he was informed that there was a response to the B.B.C. broadcast. A woman named Mrs. Welcome had called in person, and was now in the waiting-room.

"Welcome, Mrs. Welcome," he said. "Go down and get her, Brook, and we'll hear what she has to say."

Brook left the office and returned in a minute or two with a middle-aged woman, who looked excited and intelligent. McLean waved her into a chair.

"Now, Mrs. Welcome," he said, "I understand you have come in response to our broadcast appeal earlier this evening?"

"Yes. The description of the man mentioned is like that of one of my paying-guests who left two days ago. I keep a private hotel in Langden Gardens. It's called the Waverley."

"I know the place," said McLean. "What was the name of this guest?"

"Mr. Joseph Banner."

"How long was he with you?"

"Ten days. He came on April the

eighteenth, and left two days ago."

"What makes you think the dead man might be him, apart from the articles of clothing?"

"The little mole which was mentioned on the right side of his nose. But not only that. It was the curious way in which he left. He didn't give me any notice, but he telephoned late in the evening and told me that he had gone into the country to see his sister, and that he found her very seriously ill, and proposed staying with her until she was better. He said he would send her chauffeur with the car to collect his baggage, and that the chauffeur had instructions to pay anything that was owing."

"Did the chauffeur turn up?"

"Yes — about an hour later. I showed him to Mr. Banner's room, and waited while he packed everything into two suit-cases. Then he paid me and left."

"Didn't you think you were a little indiscreet in handing Mr. Banner's belongings to a complete stranger?"

"Not at the time. He told me about Mr. Banner's sister being seriously ill, and mentioned the fact that he had telephoned Mr. Banner early that morning to tell him of Miss Banner's sudden illness."

"Was that true?"

"Yes. There was a telephone call that morning, and I sent the maid up to tell Mr. Banner."

"When you received the telephone message later did you recognize Banner's voice?"

"No. I can't say I did, but I thought it was him by the easy way he talked. It was only afterwards that I wondered if I ought to have taken steps to find out if everything was all right."

"What sort of a man was this chauffeur?"

"Fairly tall, and young. He was clean-shaven and wore a blue uniform."

"Did you see the car he used?"

"Yes. But it was dark, and I couldn't describe it."

"Are you willing to come at once and attempt to identify the body?"

"Will — will it take long?"

"About forty minutes each way."

The woman hesitated for a moment and then said she would go. McLean at once put a telephone call through to the County Police, and then he and Brook and the important witness went to the mortuary where the body lay. When, in due course, Mrs. Welcome saw the body she nodded her head speechlessly, and then managed to gasp: "That's him — Mr. Banner."

McLean did not linger, but drove her back to her small hotel, and then saw the room which Banner had occupied. It was not in use, but it was as clean and tidy as a new pin, and not a single thing remained that could serve as a clue to the activities of the dead man.

"How did he occupy his time while he was here?" asked McLean. "Was he engaged in any business?"

"I don't know. He never spoke about

himself. All I provided was room and breakfast."

"Was he out most of the day?"

"Yes."

"Any callers?"

"None to my knowledge."

"Did he run a car?"

"Oh no, but he used taxis a great deal. He was always ringing up 'Luxicabs' to send a taxi round."

"Where are Luxicabs?"

"In Canton Street, not far from here."

McLean thanked her and decided to look up Luxicabs. It was a very small firm, running only one or two vehicles in addition to a row of pumps, and at that moment both the regular drivers were on the premises. McLean made his business known, and the proprietor called a pie-faced bald-headed old fellow into the office.

"Jim, you bin picking up fares from the Waverley, haven't you?" he asked.

"That's right," growled Jim.

"Have you ever been engaged by a

Mr. Banner?" asked McLean.

"Sure! Several times. Mostly in the mornings. He used to telephone round about ten o'clock."

"Where did you take him?" asked McLean.

"Once I took him to South Kensington Museum, and once to the Tower of London. Twice, no three times, I took him to the Foreign Office."

"Are you sure?" asked McLean.

"Course I am. He asked for it and I dropped him there. I saw him go inside before I left. He didn't want me to wait for him."

"When was the last time you took him there?"

"Oh, it was about three days ago."

"Did you drive him anywhere after that?"

"No; that was the last time he used my taxi."

McLean was intrigued by this emphatic statement, and after thanking Jim for his information he went back to the car with Brook.

"Foreign Office?" asked Brook.

"Yes, but it's not the most promising of places to make inquiries about any single person reputed to have called there. I can smell delay."

4

McLEAN was right, and for a long time he was shuttled from department to department, all very politely but fruitlessly, until at last he was passed into the office of an immaculately dressed and suave gentleman who said he had given Joseph Banner an interview.

"A very tenacious person," he said. "I had already refused him an interview a few days previously, since he had refused to state the nature of his business to my secretary."

"And did he do that on that latter occasion?" asked McLean.

"No. He said that what he had to say was for the ears of the Minister himself, or at least his chief secretary. I told him that the Minister was abroad, and that there was no possibility of his gaining an interview higher up without an appointment. I suggested that he should write, and state broadly the nature of his business."

"What did he say to that?"

"He was most impertinent. He said he was in possession of information which was of vital interest to the country, and that he was sick of being pushed around as if he were begging some favour. He asked me when the Minister would be back, and I told him that I was not in a position to give him that information — that it would, in fact, be most irregular. At that he flew into a rage and called me a — well never mind what?"

"And you have no idea what was really in his mind?"

"None at all. I was left with the impression that he was not completely *compos mentis*, and was glad to be rid of him."

"It's a pity," said McLean. "I think he did have something important to reveal. But it's too late now, for his dead body was found two days ago in sinister circumstances."

The official raised his eyebrows.

"How perfectly ghastly," he said. "But if we gave interviews to every Tom, Dick, or Harry who dropped in casually, a fine mess we should find ourselves in. I'm sorry, Inspector, not to be of greater service."

McLean was sorry too, as he made his way out of the big building, for with Banner's secret now safe the persons responsible had every reason to congratulate themselves.

"There are certainly some good brains behind this case," he admitted to Brook. "Banner was undoubtedly kidnapped before he divulged what he knew, and it was smart of the kidnappers to send that car to his lodgings and collect everything that belonged to him. We were fortunate indeed to be able to get the body identified. That leaves us with one remaining string."

"Greta Borche?"

"Yes. I think it might be a good idea

for you to drop me at the Phœnix. Possibly I may get a glimpse of the lady in the flesh, without making my interest obvious. You can then drive the car back. If I want you I'll telephone."

Brook did this, and McLean passed through the ornate vestibule into the luxurious public lounge. He found a seat, and looked round at the well-dressed throng. A waiter caught his eye and came to his table. McLean ordered a drink, and lighted a cigarette. Casually his glance went from table to table, but none of the women present bore any resemblance to the woman of the magazine cutting. His drink came and he sipped it in leisurely fashion. Away to his right was a door marked 'Residents Only' and it seemed to him more likely that the woman he sought would use that room in preference to the public one. By standing up he could see through the partition which was partially glazed. The adjoining lounge was smaller than the public one, and was even more luxurious. A number of people were sitting about in little groups, and these he scanned as well as he was able. At a writing-table a woman was sitting, writing a letter, but her back was towards him, and he could not catch a glimpse of her face. But she was clearly young and blonde, and his interest in her remained. But he could not continue standing up, and so he sat down and resolved to wait until she came out.

But after a quarter of an hour he stood up again and saw that she was still writing furiously. He decided to put an end to his doubts, and leaving his seat he went to the communicating door and passed through it. Beyond the letterwriter was a long table carrying magazines and journals. He made that his objective, and on reaching it he made a pretence of hunting for some non-existent publication. On turning he came face to face with the woman, only to discover that she bore no resemblance at all to the glamorous

Greta, even after allowing for a wide margin of flattery on the part of the studio photographer.

Back he went to the public lounge, and after scanning several new arrivals he sauntered into the vestibule, where he was attracted by some strip lighting which advertised the American Bar, the location of which was indicated by an arrow pointed down a flight of stairs. He had no need for a second drink, but descended the stairs and entered a long bar, furnished with dazzling mirrors and much chromium plating, and there facing him in the mirror, but with her back to him in reality, was unmistakably Greta of the shining locks. McLean did some quick thinking. She was sitting alone and near her right hand, at the very edge of the table was a sparkling drink. He went forward towards a vacant table, and as he passed he managed to overturn her glass.

"Oh!" he gasped.

McLean was all apologies, in a voice

that was tinged with a slight American accent.

"Oh, it doesn't matter," she replied, in perfect English.

"But your dress!"

"It missed my dress."

"Are you sure?"

"Quite sure."

"That's a relief. Guess I'm not used to cat-walking. Hey, waiter!"

The waiter hurried along and quickly mopped up the mess.

"You must permit me to make good that drink," begged McLean.

"Oh no."

"I won't feel good unless you do."

"Well, if you insist," she said with a smile. "It was champagne cocktail."

"Very good, madam. And you, sir?" asked the waiter.

"I'll have the same."

McLean seated himself at the adjacent table, and the waiter quickly brought the drinks. McLean handed him a pound note, and what little change was offered in return he waved aside.

Greta gave him a smile as she raised her glass.

"Here's hoping it won't happen again," drawled McLean. "I'm not usually so clumsy."

"Well, there wasn't much room to spare," she said, from which McLean concluded she was not unwilling to chat.

"D'you know something," he said, after a pause. "I can't get it out of my mind that I've met you before."

"I don't think so," she said.

"Well, it's queer. I'm not usually wrong about faces. Could it have been in Paris?"

"I haven't been in Paris for years."

"But — Oh, wait a moment. It wasn't Paris. It was Venice, about a month ago. I went to see a friend — a film producer, who was staying at Danielli's, and you — you passed me in the vestibule. Now tell me I'm wrong."

"You may be right. I was in Venice about a month ago. But are you in the film business?"

"Well — partly. My name's Hudson — Erle Hudson, and I and some friends are forming a company to produce films, chiefly with Italian backgrounds. I'm scouting around for talent — bi-lingual if possible."

"Most interesting," she said. "Because I happen to be in the film business."

"Wal, can you beat it! Are you an actress?"

"Yes. I don't suppose you know my name, because most of my films have been produced abroad. I'm Greta Borche, but I use the name of Greta Groll — "

"Greta Groll! But I do know the name. When I was in Rome I read about a film you were making — can't remember the name."

"It was *Il Bacio*."

"That's it. Wal, what do you know?"

McLean, already steeped in prevarication, consoled his conscience by the thought that the business at hand justified such deception, irregular as it undoubtedly was. It was no time to turn back to the ways of righteousness, so he transferred his drink to the other table and sat facing Greta.

"Can we talk business?" he asked.

She laughed and drank what was left of the champagne. McLean called the waiter and the drinks were repeated.

"I am under contract not to talk business," said Greta. "You see, I have a manager, who does all the business. He knows all the answers."

"You can at least tell me if you are under contract for the next three or four months."

"I am not. I promised myself a rest."

"That's how people die — resting too much."

"Tell me about this company of yours. Has it got plenty of money?"

"You needn't worry about money. Where can I find this manager of yours?"

"You can't. He's out of town for two days. When he comes back he'll be at the Albemarle. His name is Stein. Says he can't afford to stay here."

"Two days," mused McLean. "That means Thursday."

"Yes. He's due back Thursday morning."

"Can we all get together for a talk on Thursday evening?"

"Where?"

"Here if you like. Say eight o'clock. Can you fix it?"

"Yes, I think so. Where can I get in touch with you, in case there's any hitch?"

McLean had to think quickly, and he gave the name of a hotel where he was on intimate terms with the management. Greta delved into her handbag and produced a diary in which she wrote the details.

"All right, Mr. Hudson," she said. "Unless you hear anything to the contrary we shall be waiting for you. But I should warn you that Stein talks money — real money."

McLean laughed, and at that they parted. McLean took a taxi straight to the hotel whose address he had given, and made everything right there with the management regarding any letters or messages for the spurious Mr. Hudson.

From his own flat he telephoned Sergeant Brook, who had been waiting at the office as instructed. He seemed a little disappointed to hear that his services were no longer required for that day.

"Don't moan," said McLean. "This is a game that calls for patience. I've gone as far as I can go until Thursday evening. But I've a job for you tomorrow morning, before you come to the office. Go to the Phœnix and find out when Greta checked in there, and do the same for Hendryk Stein who is staying at the Albemarle. Don't divulge to anyone the real object of your call. Just look through the register. Is that clear?"

"Perfectly clear, sir."

"Good! You are now free to enjoy the

evening in your own innocent fashion. Keep sober."

"Can't afford to be anything else," said Brook. "Well, see you in the morning."

5

THE following morning McLean found a number of letters having reference to the radio announcement. Most of the writers were certain they knew the dead man from the description given, but since that important matter had been cleared up the letters were speedily dealt with. At shortly after ten o'clock Brook turned up with the results of his inquiries.

"Both Stein and Greta checked in at their hotels on April the nineteenth," he said. "Their nationalities are given as German, and their addresses as Venice."

"So they arrived in London together," mused McLean, "and on the very night when Doctor Donkin was called to the house where the dead man lay. A little significant, I think."

"You think they came straight from Leylands House?"

"I do. But if their passports show that they did not arrive in England until that day then we are right off the track, and at a dead-end."

"Can't we check the passports right away?"

"No. Stein is not available until tomorrow, and it would be folly to arouse the least suspicion in Greta's mind. But tomorrow evening we will settle this matter. In the meantime you can drive me down to the inquest on Joseph Banner, which takes place this afternoon. The result is, of course, a foregone conclusion."

"An open verdict?"

"Yes."

McLean's prognostication proved correct. By previous arrangement he was not called upon to give evidence, since the inquest was bound to be reported in full, and he did not wish to be publicly associated with the case at that juncture. When it was all over he and Brook had tea with the Donkins, who were eager to know what progress McLean had made, if any.

"I haven't got very far," said McLean modestly. "The case bristles with difficulties."

Valerie gave him a sly, unbelieving glance, and Brook, eating his way through a pile of delicious home-made scones, kept his gaze unduly riveted on what he was doing.

"At least you identified the corpse," said Valerie.

"Not I. It was his landlady who did that. Valerie, you didn't actually see the man who called here that night — Baldock?"

"No. Ian took him off my hands by going to the door first. If I had been there I would have told him there was nothing doing, as we were expecting you. Of course Ian shouldn't have gone with him."

"That's the sort of doctor she thinks I am," said Donkin. "Well, I wish you luck, Mac."

"Thanks. I feel I shall need it. How's that shoulder behaving?"

"It's going on all right, but is still very stiff, and painful if I use the arm much. Should be all right in a few days. Valerie is still driving me around."

"Don't I know it," said Valerie. "He's the worst passenger in the world. Actually he still drives the car although I hold the steering-wheel."

McLean laughed at Donkin's guilty expression, and a few minutes later he and Brook were on their way back to London in a flood of spring sunshine.

On the following evening McLean was ready for the next real step in his investigation. No communication of any kind had been received at the hotel which he had given as his address, and presumably the 'business' meeting with Greta and her manager was on. Brook drove him to the car-park quite close to the Phœnix Hotel, where McLean alighted.

"I'd like you to wait, Brook," said McLean. "I don't know what is to be the upshot of this meeting. If this Mr. Stein appears to be a stranger to our case I may have to attempt to lead him up the garden path a bit. But keep your eye on the main entrance, and if perchance I should emerge in anyone's company, follow up with the car."

Brook nodded, and McLean made his way into the hotel. He had a good look round the public lounge before entering it, but saw no sign of Greta. So he crossed the lounge and peered through the glass partition into the private room. A number of guests were there, but not Greta. The clock gave the time as five minutes past eight. Not much margin to allow a woman vain of her looks to titivate. Instead of entering the private lounge he found a seat behind a spreading palm, from which he could see the main entrance door. A few minutes passed and then Greta appeared with a male companion. The moment McLean saw the man he recalled Ian Donkin's description of Baldock — tall and dark, and clean-shaven, with a very slight limp. There it was — limp and all, although the limp was only just detectable. Immediately McLean made himself completely invisible, and waited until the couple had vanished into the interior room. Then he left the hotel and joined Brook.

"Nothing doing, sir?" asked Brook, with raised eyebrows.

"On the contrary, much is doing or about to be done. I am convinced that Mr. Stein is none other than Mr. Baldock. I am going to take him, but not here. We'll drive to the Albemarle, and wait for him there."

"And the woman?"

"She'll keep. I'll telephone her and regret I wasn't able to keep the appointment."

On reaching the Albemarle McLean ascertained that Stein's baggage was still in his room. He thereupon telephoned the Phœnix, and left a telephone message for Greta. Then he and Brook waited for Hendryk Stein, and they had to wait a long time, for it was close upon ten o'clock when McLean, from the waiting car, saw Stein arrive in a taxi and enter the hotel. He and Brook left the car and followed Stein through the vestibule to the lift. They reached it just as the liftman was closing the door, and stood close to the unsuspecting man.

"Third floor!" said Stein.

"Third!" repeated McLean.

When they emerged from the lift Stein went to a door almost immediately opposite, and as he opened it McLean and Brook reached him.

"Mr. Stein?" asked McLean.

"Yes."

"We are police officers and I should like to ask you a few questions," said McLean.

"Certainly."

"Inside, please," said McLean.

The somewhat reluctant man nodded, and McLean and Brook filed into a large single room, which in addition to the bed and the conventional furnishings contained a large writing-table, on which was a portable typewriter.

"Well, here we are, gentlemen," said Stein, affecting an air of complaisance. "What are the questions? Am I guilty of some misdemeanour?"

"I hope not," said McLean. "You are of German nationality, I believe?"

"Yes. My father was German, my mother British."

"I should like to see your passport."

Stein went to the chest of drawers, and then handed his passport to McLean.

"I see you arrived at London Airport on March the fifteenth?" said McLean.

"Yes."

"Alone?"

"No. I had a companion — a lady named Greta Borche, who is a film actress. I look after her affairs."

"When did you arrive at this hotel?"

"Three days ago."

"From where?"

"Must I answer these very personal questions? If my passport is not in order I am very sorry. But it is no fault of mine. So far it has not been questioned."

"This inquiry has nothing to do with your passport, but with your movements after you reached this country. I want details of your movements from March the fifteenth to the date when you entered this hotel."

"I regret that I am not prepared to give you that information. I regard this as an unwarranted intrusion into my private affairs. Do you propose to charge me with some crime?"

"That may come. Have you ever used the name Baldock?"

"Certainly not. Why should I?"

"Allow me to ask the questions," said McLean crisply.

"Very well, but all this is most disturbing."

"Have you ever met a man named Joseph Banner?"

"I cannot remember having done so. But I have met thousands of persons during my career. It is possible I have forgotten him."

"You wouldn't forget Mr. Banner so quickly. Do you know a man named Doctor Donkin?"

"No."

"You insist upon that?"

"That is my answer. I am at a loss to understand the meaning of all this. Why cannot I be told of what I am suspected?"

"You will be told in due course," said McLean. "I propose now to take you to police headquarters."

"You — you mean I am under arrest?" gasped Stein, now thoroughly shaken.

"We will call it detention. Perhaps after a little reflection you will satisfy us as to your movements after landing in this country. Then — possibly — you might establish your innocence."

"This is outrageous!" protested Stein. "You cannot arrest me without a warrant. Where is your warrant?"

McLean gave Brook a sign, and

Brook quickly produced a pair of handcuffs.

"No," gulped Stein. "Not those. It's all a mistake, but I will give you no trouble."

"That would be wise," said McLean. "All right, Brook. You can put them away."

Stein asked if he might take a light overcoat, as it was now rather cold outside. This was permitted, but it was Brook who got the coat from the wardrobe, and felt in the pockets before handing it to the very troubled man.

McLean took over the door-key, and locked up the room once they had left it. They walked across to the lift gate, and McLean pushed the button. The lift came up empty, except for the liftman, and the party stepped inside. On reaching the ground floor McLean and Brook walked on either side of the prisoner, through the small lounge, where several persons were sitting, drinking. Stein now strove to appear completely composed, and smiled at a man and a woman who gave him a nod, and a minute or two later they were all in the car, making towards Scotland Yard.

After Stein had been given into custody McLean and Brook went back to the Albemarle, opened up Stein's room, and started a search of his belongings. But not a single document or letter of any kind came to view. Except for the passport there was nothing which shed any light upon his recent movements, or his business associates.

"When a man takes such care to cover up his activities one is naturally justified in assuming that he doesn't act that way without good reason," said McLean.

"A typewriter too, and not even a carbon copy of a letter," said Brook. "It's just as if he knew we were coming for him, yet that's impossible."

"You're sure you didn't mention his name when you came here to look up the register?"

"I'm not quite so dumb, sir."

McLean went to the small typewriter, and examined the black ribbon. It was a comparatively new reel, and only a small portion of it had been used, with the result that the impressions of the type upon it were quite legible.

"One thing he overlooked," he mused. "I'll remove this and you can make a copy of what is imprinted on it."

The ribbon was wound back on the reel and Brook took possession of it. Satisfied that there was nothing more of interest in the room, McLean now decided to call it a day, with the exception of making one telephone call, which he believed would afford a certain amount of pleasure to the recipient. This took place later at his flat, where Brook had dropped him, prior to taking back the car.

The telephone call was to Ian Donkin, whose tired voice was heard on the line after some delay, for it was now nearly midnight.

"Oh, it's you, Mac," he said. "You ought to know better than to drag an overworked doctor from his bed. What's on your mind at this hour?"

"Quite a lot. I believe I have got your Mr. Baldock."

"What!"

"Yes. The description is perfect. Of course he denies everything. Now I want your help."

"Identification?"

"Yes. I'll hold a parade tomorrow. Can you make it?"

"Of course. But I'd like to do my morning round first."

"That will suit me. Will you be ready at two o'clock if I send Brook along with a car?"

"Excellent! I shall look forward to it with the greatest pleasure. If it's really Baldock I'll know him in an instant. Good work, Mac. Very good work."

McLean went to bed with the feeling that things had gone very well for him, and he hoped that the detained man, on realizing that he was involved in a very serious matter, would make some statement which would clear up the mystery of Banner's death.

But the morning produced news which completely shattered all his hopes. He was in his bath at seven-thirty when the telephone bell rang. Slipping on a dressing-gown he went to the instrument and heard Valerie's voice on the line. A voice that was choked with deep emotion.

"Ian's gone," she said. "He vanished from his room in the night. I never heard a sound. Just now I took a cup of tea to his room, and found the bed empty, and a smell of chloroform."

"Steady!" he said. "I'll be with you as quick as I can. This is shocking. We won't waste any time now. Good-bye!"

Two minutes later McLean was speaking to headquarters, and having finished he got on to Sergeant Brook.

"There's a car calling for you, Brook," he said. "Snatch some breakfast quickly, and then pick me up here. Something totally unexpected has happened. Tell you about it when I see you."

McLean dressed with great speed, made himself a pot of tea, and boiled an egg. How short-lived was his triumph, and how desperate and enterprising the people he was up against! He remembered the man and the woman who had nodded at Stein as he had passed through the hotel lounge. They must have realized what was happening, and had lost no time in reporting the situation to some person, or persons, behind the scenes. The chief danger to Stein at the moment was Donkin, and action had been taken in that direction.

He had just finished his sparse meal when Brook arrived in the police car. McLean did not ask him in but went straight to the car, and gave the driver instructions. Then he sat beside Brook in the back seat.

"Something amiss, sir?" asked Brook.

"Very much amiss. I telephoned Doctor Donkin last night and arranged for you to bring him to headquarters to identify Stein. During the night Donkin was kidnapped."

"My hat!" ejaculated Brook.

"Snatched from his own bed and taken away without his sister hearing a sound. They chloroformed him first."

Brook's incredulity took the form of muttered imprecations, for he felt this set-back as keenly as McLean. That it had happened when everything appeared to be nicely in the bag was doubly humiliating.

"Low-down swine!" he muttered. "Well, they're not going to get away with this."

"Let us take our medicine without grimaces," said McLean. "I warned you that we were up against a clever gang. We may yet experience another shock."

Brook gazed at him sharply. He had heard McLean tell the driver to stop at the Phœnix, and even Brook could put two and two together.

"You think the woman may have gone?" he asked.

"I shall be surprised if she hasn't."

When they reached the big hotel it was Brook who went inside to make the inquiry. He returned almost at once to inform McLean that Greta Borche had paid her bill and left the hotel late the previous evening, following a telephone message.

McLean nodded without comment and the car moved on again through the London traffic and out on to the broad by-pass. Here the driver was permitted to use the full power of the big engine, and in a very short time it came to a halt outside Donkin's house. Valerie came to the door before McLean could ring the bell.

"Thank God!" she said. "This is terrible, isn't it?"

"It's unexpected. I must admit I was caught off balance. But that doesn't excuse me. I should have realized that Ian was in danger."

"But why?"

"Didn't you know I telephoned him last night."

"No. I went to bed early."

"I telephoned him to tell him that I had detained a man whom I feel sure is Mr. Baldock, and I asked him to come to London today to identify him."

"I see. Ian was kidnapped to prevent that happening?"

"Without doubt. Can I see his room?"

"Yes, of course."

She went with McLean up the stairs to the room which Donkin had occupied. The bed-clothes were pulled back, but there was no sign of any struggle. Near the pillow McLean could detect the odour of chloroform. But nowhere could he see Donkin's discarded clothing.

"Did they take his clothing?" he asked.

"Yes."

"And you heard absolutely nothing?"

"Not a sound. But I must confess I'm a heavy sleeper. After I telephoned you I found a hole in a pane of glass in the french window of the surgery, so that the latch could be slipped. There must have been several men involved, because Ian is tremendously heavy — over thirteen stone."

"They knew that," said McLean. "These people leave nothing to chance. The moment they knew Stein — as he calls himself — was arrested they took steps to prevent his being identified as the man who came here previously. Without that identification I have no case against Stein, and I can't hold him indefinitely."

"The brutes don't lack brains."

"No — nor audacity."

"Mac, tell me the truth. Is Ian in any real danger?"

"Frankly, I don't know. They may be content to hold him until Stein is free and they can get him out of the country."

"But mightn't — mighn't they kill

him, to make doubly sure there is no slip-up?"

"That's possible, but improbable. You see, so far this is not a murder case. We have no proof at all that Banner was murdered. My feeling is that they would fight shy of murder unless their own safety was very closely threatened. At the moment I regret that isn't the position."

"But it may come."

McLean took her hand and pressed it.

"Don't dwell upon the worst possibilities," he urged. "I still have another string to my bow. Not a very strong one I admit, but it might be sufficiently strong to make Ian's abduction useless."

"What do you mean?" she asked eagerly.

"There is another person who might identify Stein as being the man who rented that house under the name of Baldock. He is the owner of the house, a Major Coleman, who is now taking a cure at Matlock."

"But would that enable you to get a conviction?"

"It might. I admit it would not prove that Stein was the man responsible for Ian's first detention and injury. But the circumstantial evidence would be very strong. I'll put a call through now to Coleman, and then have a look at the surgery and the ground outside."

The call was put through and McLean asked to be rung back. The subsequent examination of the surgery failed to produce any clue. The facts were as stated by Valerie. A sharp diamond had been used on one of the panes of glass, and a piece of glass removed by the use of a piece of putty, which still adhered to the centre of it. McLean examined the putty for finger-prints but found none. All that remained on it were very fine hairs from a woollen glove.

"Efficient to the last degree," he complained.

Then the telephone bell rang, and

McLean hurried to it. He asked after Major Coleman, and was informed that the Major was no longer at the hotel. He had found cause for complaint, and after a stormy interview with the management, he and his chauffeur had left by car. They had left early that morning without leaving any address to which letters might be forwarded. Before he left the telephone McLean got the registration number of the Major's car.

"We can try to locate him," he said to Brook. "But it may take days. In the meantime Mr. Stein's very enterprising friends seem to have things much their own way. Did you bring that typewriter ribbon with you?"

"Yes, sir, but I haven't had time to look at it."

"We'll look at it now."

Brook produced the ribbon from an envelope, and McLean twisted the spool round in his fingers, until the whole length of it lay exposed on the table.

"Curious looking stuff," he said. "I'll read while you write it down."

Brook produced his note-book and McLean began to read off the impressions on the black ribbon. It was simply a long succession of letters and figures, without any break at all.

"Cipher," said Brook.

"Obviously. But we may be able to get it deciphered quickly at the office. Oh, here's something that isn't in cipher. It's an address — from the envelope I imagine:

Colonel Enzo Lombroso,
  Tadmarsh Manor,
    Near Tiddingford, Norfolk.

"That might be useful," said Brook. "It's the first blunder we've found in this case."

"No counting chickens," warned McLean. "Norfolk is a long way from here. But it would be nice to find out why Mr. Stein types a letter to Colonel Lombroso in cipher, and nicer still to find out just what he has to say to the gallant Colonel."

"Will there be time to do that?"

"There may be. We'll get the whole department busy on it. Get me through to Braden, and I'll talk to him."

Brook used the telephone, and a few minutes later McLean was talking to the chief of the deciphering department. He read out the symbols from Brook's note-book, and after they had been read back to him he hung up the receiver and prepared to leave.

"It may be a wild goose chase," he said to Valerie. "But I can't afford to miss any chances. Cheer up and hope for the best. For the moment, anyway, I feel sure that Ian is in no danger. I'll give you a ring this evening."

"Thanks, Mac," she said.

The car completed the return journey as speedily as it had the outward one, and McLean from his office set the machinery working in an attempt to locate Major Coleman's car. He then went to Braden's department to find him and his staff of experts busy on the cipher message.

"More difficult than it looks," said Braden. "I believe the actual message is in a foreign language, and an obscure one at that. At the moment we have got nowhere, and I can't make any promises. But you know what these things are. Something suddenly clicks and the whole thing becomes clear."

"Well, I hope something clicks soon," said McLean. "I've got a longish journey to make, and time is precious. The best thing I can do is telephone you from my destination, in four or five hours' time."

"I'll do my best," promised Braden.

McLean collected two automatics, and then rejoined Brook, who in the meantime had been looking at road maps.

"Not a mention of Tiddingford," he said. "But I got on to the G.P.O. and they tell me it's a very small village, not a great distance from Sandringham. Are we waiting for that decoding job?"

"No. It's giving Braden some anxious moments. I'll telephone him later on. Here's a gun for you — just in case."

Brook took the weapon with a grin, and slipped out the magazine, to make sure it was loaded. It looked as if McLean was expecting trouble, and Brook had no deep objection to that sort of excitement. A few minutes later they were in the car and settling down to a lengthy journey.

A very short stop was made two hours later for some refreshments, and then the car sped on again across the flat and somewhat deserted country towards the Wash. It was late in the evening that they caught a glimpse of the sea away to the north-east, which signified that they were not a great distance from their destination, and very soon they came to a road junction where a signpost gave the name Tiddingford, and the distance seven miles. But the lane which they now entered was very different from the one on which they had travelled for so long. It was narrow and full of holes, and on either side high banks effectively shut out all views. Along this gully the car moved very slowly, for there were acute bends every hundred yards and barely room for another car to pass. But finally they came out into what was little more than a hamlet, comprising a number of cottages, a couple of shops and a public house. One of the shops served also as the post office, but this was now closed.

"If I am going to telephone Braden I'd better do it from the pub," said McLean.

"Keeping a pub in these parts can't be an economical proposition," said Brook. "I wonder what the local beer is like?"

"You can sample it," agreed McLean. "But I don't want to waste any time here."

They entered the little pub, and found but one customer in the saloon bar, and he a very old weather-worn farm labourer. McLean asked to use the telephone for a call to London, and was shown into a box with a slot meter. He dialled the exchange, and asked for his number. After a few minutes delay he was told how much to put into the slot. Braden was quickly on the line, and his news was unsatisfactory. So far the cipher had beaten him and his staff, and he despaired of solving the problem that night.

"Call yourself a cipher expert," said McLean. "Well, keep trying."

When he returned to the bar Brook had finished his pint of beer, and vowed it excellent.

"Any luck?" he asked.

"Not yet," said McLean. "Oh, Landlord, do you know a place not far from here called Tadmarsh Manor?"

The landlord shook his head and explained that he hadn't been long in the district. He referred the matter to the ancient farm labourer, who stroked his scrubby beard with great solemnity, and finally nodded his head.

"Three to vour moile from 'ere I dare say," he droned. "You goes over the bridge, and turns roight. Then after two moile or zo ye'll see a water-tower. You turns up by the tower, and ye'll come to Tadmarsh. Used to be a fine place when I were a lad, but not now. There were an aerodrome there in the last war, and the 'ouse were bombed proper it were. You can't miss un."

McLean thanked him, and very soon he and Brook were back in the car and following the directions of the old man. The light was now failing, but they were able to make out the old water tower, and crawled on from there over a deeply-rutted road surface.

"Looks as if it hadn't been made up since the last war," said Brook. "Look, there's the sea again."

It was only a fleeting glimpse, seen between two low hills in the distance. Otherwise the country was as flat as a pancake, but with wide areas of afforestation obstructing the longer views.

"We must be quite near the place," said McLean, "and yet there isn't a sign of it. Oh, wait a moment. Here's a turning off to the left. Part of an old signpost too, but someone has taken the arm for firewood. Better stay here in the car while I go and have a look, otherwise we may run into a cul-de-sac and have trouble getting out."

He got out and walked up the narrow, ascending lane. It was now so dark under the tall trees that grew out of the banks that he had to use a pocket torch. It was as well that he had not turned the car, for the lane terminated at a tall, broken-down wall, under which was a bridle-path going in either direction. He clambered up the wall where there was a foothold, and in the gloaming he saw in the distance a large mansion, which was approached by a winding drive between trees. It was in complete darkness, and it looked derelict. Between him and the house were sundry buildings, and the land to the left swept away in a great level plain, on which nothing but weeds appeared to be growing. Then he remembered the old man's remark about an aerodrome, and realized that this was the place. On the eastern side the wall no longer existed, and he thought he could see the sea in the distance. Undoubtedly this was Tadmarsh Manor — or what was left of it. He made his way back to the car.

"It's there," he said. "But there's no way in. The entrance is farther on — about half a mile I should think. You'd better carry on. I'm going to climb over the wall and make my way to the house, as I want to look at some buildings on this end of the estate. There's no light to be seen in the house, so don't bring the car into the drive. If anyone should arrive and see the car they might take fright. Take it past the entrance, and conceal it if you can. Then you, Brook, come up the drive on foot, and I'll meet you at the top. If you see three quick flashes of a torch it'll be me. I want to make sure there is no one living in one of those outbuildings who might spoil things."

Brook nodded, and the car moved off at once. McLean then went up the lane and clambered over the wall. The buildings near him were old farm buildings, which had clearly not been used for years. Among them was a small cottage in tumbledown condition, but it was completely deserted. A hundred yards farther on, towards the house, there was what appeared to be an enormous barn, and as McLean approached it he came off the soft weedy land on to hard concrete, which turned out to be a broad runway, running straight from the barn as far as he could see in the semi-darkness.

He reached the front of the building to find there two huge sliding doors. He put his hand to one of these and found that it moved easily on its steel runners. Slipping through the gap he had created, he closed the door and flashed his torch. There, lying back a little way was a large two-engined aeroplane, of the latest design, but of a make quite new to him. Some wooden steps were placed in position under the entrance door, and when he climbed these McLean found the door unlocked. He stepped into the machine, and found it to be equipped with four large and comfortable seats. A door gave access to the cockpit, which was separated from the cabin by a mica partition. Behind the cabin was another narrow door. Before investigating what lay behind that he passed through into the cockpit and examined the instrument panel. The petrol indicator showed that the tank was full, and in a recess he found some navigation maps. It was while he was looking at these that he heard a sound outside the barn, and then the unmistakable slamming of a car door. He put back the maps and hurried through the cabin. He was about to descend the steps, in the hope of finding some place of concealment below, when someone shouted: "Get those doors open, Max!"

His one hope of concealment now lay behind the door at the back of the fuselage. He sprang at the door and pulled at the handle, for a moment he feared it was locked, but a stronger pull showed that the door was jammed. Now it was open, revealing a luggage compartment. He slipped into it as suddenly the doors began to move, and the whole place became brilliantly lighted.

The situation was critical in the extreme, for now he heard several voices, and conversation both in Italian and English, followed by some bumps which suggested the dumping of luggage. Then a voice said: "Up you go, Greta. Max, I want all the luggage aboard quickly."

McLean had to make a decision. He had either to make some sort of show with the pistol or attempt to hoodwink them. The first alternative offered little hope, since he had already counted at least four different men's voices. The second scheme, even if it failed, would not worsen his position. So he put the electric torch in his pocket and gripped the handle of the door with both hands. Almost immediately there came the sound of heavy footsteps approaching the door, and the handle was gripped on the other side. McLean hung on for dear life, and there was heavy panting as the door refused to budge.

"Stuck!" said a voice. "Here, let me have a go at it."

"Never mind!" said the voice of authority. "There's plenty of room here. Pack it behind those seats."

McLean breathed a deep sigh of relief as the pressure was relaxed, but he still clung to the handle in case someone else might try his luck on it. There came several more bumps, and then Greta's voice — asking for a rug, as she was cold. Everything was painfully clear to him now. Greta's presence helped to make it so. The gang was clearing out, and he and Brook were just a few minutes too late to prevent it. While he had been examining the outbuildings the gang had been packing up. Brook at that moment was probably coming up the drive, watching for McLean's signal. It was indeed a most unpleasant predicament, and how it would end was in grave doubt.

"Chocks away!" yelled a voice.

Instantly the engines began to fire, and McLean was conscious of a slow movement of the plane, as it taxied out of the hangar. Soon the engines sprang into full power and there were a number of bumps as it passed over rough bits of the runway. But suddenly these ceased and the motion grew smooth. He realized that the machine was airborne, and climbing at a steep angle. For a long time this continued, imparting to him a tendency to slide towards the tail. But finally the machine found a level keel, and he became more comfortable.

But soon there developed a new trouble. The luggage compartment was unventilated, and the air grew stale and almost unbreathable. He felt he must have some fresh air or be suffocated, and the only way to get it was to open the door slightly. This he thought would be safe, as almost certainly the passengers would be facing the engine. Also he hoped to be able to discover just how many passengers there were.

Very cautiously he pulled the door towards him a few inches and peered out. But the cabin was in complete darkness, the only light being in the cockpit, and that no more than a glimmer. He left the door slightly open, and sat down on the floor beside it, to be ready for any possible emergency.

But nothing happened. The drone of the powerful engines never altered as the plane sped through the night, and that consistent note was like an anodyne, and time and again he would find himself on the verge of sleep. But he fought against it successfully. As the hours passed one thing became clear. He was out of the bounds of Britain whatever the pilot's course, but he had not the slightest idea what that course was.

Soon there came a change in the conditions. He was aware that it was getting colder and colder. His feet became numbed and then his hands. Also he began to slide towards the tail again, and suddenly he experienced the sickening sensation of falling, which was finally arrested by violent bumping. It was the sort of thing which happened over mountains and it caused him to suspect he was over the Alps. Then more climbing and further bumps. But finally all this unpleasantness ceased, as the plane began to lose altitude, and the cold became less intense. He believed that a landing was soon to be made, but this was soon proved to be untrue.

He looked at his wrist-watch and read the time by the luminous hands — half-past one! Already he had been in the air over four hours. How much longer was it to continue? Where would the journey finally end? Another two hours were to pass before the first question was answered. There was a sudden falling off in engine revolutions, and the plane began to lose altitude quickly. He rose to his feet and quietly closed the door, holding firmly to the handle, while the plane banked steeply. Then, when they were on a flat keel the engine stopped and shortly afterwards he felt the landing-wheels touch lightly, then rise and touch down again for good, with the whole machine vibrating on a rough runway. Then, very slowly, it pulled up and stopped.

Now all the old anxiety was reborn. Would one of the gang take it into his head to try the door again, and start another exhausting tug-of-war? But his fears were groundless. He heard the luggage being removed, and Greta complaining that she was frozen and hungry, and then finally there came complete silence. He opened the door slightly and peered round it. Everything was wrapped in darkness.

6

ON descending from the plane and switching on his pocket torch he was suprised to find himself in an enormous cavern, the floor of which had been concreted. The sides and roof were of natural rock, which at some time had been blasted, for there was no sign of erosion by water. What should have been the open end was now closed by large doors. He went to them and found they were not fastened in any way, and moved easily on steel runners when he put his hand to them. Cautiously he ventured outside.

Above him were brilliant stars and away to the west a half moon which gave good illumination to his immediate surroundings. Before him was a wide stretch of flat hard sand, partly enclosed by outcrops of rock, and reaching as far as he could see. On it were tracks made by the landing-wheels of the plane. As he stood there, gulping in the fresh cool air, he heard a low moaning which could only have been caused by the sea breaking on a sandy beach.

His present position was undoubtedly dangerous, so he moved across to the comparatively narrow opening in the rocks, dragging his feet wearily over the rough ground. So tired was he that even the incomparable beauty of the night failed to evoke any admiration. Beyond the rocks was more flat land, and then another and higher ridge. He reached this and scrambled to the top, from which he saw an unending moonlit sea.

What was this place? Looking back he could see nothing but upheaved rock, with no sign of any human habitation. Yet habitations there must be — in view of the existence of the hangar. But the mystery of his whereabouts was secondary to his immediate needs. He felt he needed sleep more than he had ever needed it in his life, and he was still miserably cold.

Wandering to the fringe of the moaning sea, he struck away to his left, where there was a stretch of cliff, and here he found a small cave, above any possible high-tide mark, with a sandy bottom and good protection against any wind that might spring up. Here he lay down, and after scraping a hollow for his hip, he fell into a deep sleep.

★ ★ ★

When he awoke it was to gaze out at a sunlit beautiful sea of a blueness only seen in the south. He looked at his wrist-watch, but found it had stopped through his failure to wind it up. But the position of the sun was sufficient to assure him that the morning was well advanced. It was almost at the zenith, and he thought it safe to put his watch to noon. Outside the cave it was hot — so hot that he discarded his coat and left it in the cave.

The desirability to know more about his surroundings impelled him to the top of the cliff above the cave, and after some minutes of hard climbing he reached what appeared to be the best viewpoint anywhere. To his surprise there was blue water on all sides. Far away to the north-west there appeared to be land, and to the north-east there was a similar break in the watery horizon. Undoubtedly he was on an island, of about two miles long by a mile or so in width. To the west was scattered vegetation, but as a whole it was of volcanic rock, interspersed with stretches of sand.

Away to the south, and not a great distance from the hangar, there was a curious mass of buildings, most of which appeared to be ruins. But he could see a tower, and also a long white building which had the appearance of a residence. The whole formed a kind of citadel, and was on rising ground. The question was — should he go to the white villa and seek food and water, or suffer these needs until he found out more about the mysterious occupants? If he went there, pretending to be a wrecked yachtsman, there was the risk that Greta — presuming she was there — would recognize him as the alleged film director, in which case Greta would surely have the sense to see what a remarkable coincidence it was, and his chance of learning anything would be nil. On the other hand, something had to be done about his raging thirst and increasing hunger.

He descended from the pile and made in the direction of the vegetation. By skirting the rocks he was able to proceed on hard white sand but a few yards from the lazy sea. There was a languorous feeling in the air, and his clothing, reduced as it was, was still far too heavy. Finally he rounded a spur of rock and came upon a green patch, which extended up a narrow gully, opening out in one spot where there was light grey soil. Many of the stunted trees and bushes were strangers to him, but a few he recognized. Amid this wild riot of greenery he found a ruin. It had been a kind of hut, formed of the local rock and bound together with poor cement. The heavy stones had fallen apart and many creeping plants swarmed over the debris. One wall remained fairly intact and by this grew an ancient fig tree. Moreover, it bore figs in various stages of ripeness. He was soon gathering the riper ones in his hat, and when he sat down to eat his meal in comfort it was with increased respect for the tree which had provided Eve with her first inadequate garment.

The figs were delicious, and many of them were juicy enough to slake his thirst. He wandered over the ruins, looking for anything which might give him a clue to his whereabouts, but all he succeeded in doing was to arouse a number of lizards from their sun-bathing. From the state of the scrambling undergrowth it looked as if the place had not been occupied for many years. With his hat full of figs, he resumed his walk, climbing over the western slope of the little valley. The vegetation faded away and again he was amid grey rock, with only a few sparse bushes to break the monotony.

Slowly the horizon to the south was brought up. In that direction there was certainly no land in sight, nor any sea-going craft. It was an invidious position to be in, and it looked very much as if, like it or not, he would have to risk a call at the white building.

Farther on an arm of the sea broke through the rocks to form a beautiful lagoon, with shelving beaches and shallow water at the fringes, but the deeper blue towards the centre suggested a channel of considerable depth. Here he found some interesting shells and some uncommon specimens of seaweed. The lagoon extended for about a mile, at the termination of which was a jetty, with tall buildings away to the left. He meandered in this direction and then suddenly stopped and stared, for on the surface of the still water was a large oily patch. It was as clear and unmistakable as anything could be, and it signified that a motor craft had used the waterway comparatively recently.

On reflection he decided not to follow the winding course of the lagoon, since he might suddenly fall in with persons it was undesirable to meet. So he crossed the sand and climbed up over the rocks, thence going forward cautiously. For some time the lagoon was lost to sight, but at last he reached a point where he could see the end part of it in full, and there, lying under a part of the jetty which had previously been invisible, was a large motor-launch. It was the pleasantest sight he had seen since landing on this strange island.

The afternoon was well advanced, and he considered it wiser not to attempt to approach either the launch or the white building while daylight lasted. The best thing to do was to kill time and to resume his investigation under cover of darkness. Finding a sheltered spot, he lay down, and gave himself up to meditation.

But for the circumstances he would have enjoyed the change of life. Here there were no telephones to make life a curse, no masses of documents to peruse and digest, no tearing traffic in suffocating streets. Nothing but colour and quietude. He watched the blue fade out of the sky as he munched figs, and felt the very soul drawn out of him as the declining sun brought off a miracle. Away in the east a star appeared — then another. The flaming ribbons in the western sky began to darken — like the embers of a fire that was slowing dying. More stars pushed their way through the deepening pall. Night had come, softly and gently, to bring a new meaning to everything.

He roused himself to action and climbed on to a rock from which he could see the massed buildings in silhouette, with the launch floating on the quiet lagoon away to the right, and as he looked a light appeared in the darkness. It moved towards the jetty, and now he could see two men making for the place where the launch was moored. Eventually they descended some steps and there entered a small tender, which had been concealed under the wall. The mooring line was slipped and the two men went aboard, after putting the tender in tow. Then there came lights on the launch itself, and very soon he heard the low throb of a powerful engine. The launch began to move, and very soon it was lost round the first wide bend.

Thus his hope of getting away in the launch was frustrated, and he wished now that he had taken the risk of getting aboard while the opportunity offered. But it still left the white villa. He went forward, using his pocket torch to guide him.

Soon he came to a beaten track which appeared to go straight to the building, and as he drew near it he switched off the torch, and made his way as best he could in the darkness through a gate which gave access to a planned garden, surrounded by a low wall. It was a curious construction, and he suspected that the upper part had been built on to an old foundation in quite recent years — possibly an old fortress. Its long front was approached by a wide terrace, to which there was access by means of several casement windows. He refrained from ascending the steps to the terrace, and was attracted to the side of the villa by some rays of light. On moving round the corner of the block he saw that the light came from a single large window, beyond which was the main entrance. Creeping up under the window he found that the light was due to an imperfectly fitting blind of the Venetian type, and through a long vertical space he obtained a view into the room.

It was a handsome room containing some interesting items of furniture, and at a long central table four persons were sitting. One of these

McLean recognized instantly. It was Greta Borche, and she was dressed as if she were dining at the Ritz. But it was the man sitting at the head of the table who was the most impressive of the party. He appeared to be about fifty years of age, and had a face like a hawk. His skin was as dark as that of a Malay, but his short hair, beard, and trim moustache were white. The contrast was striking, and made all the more so by his very dark eyes. The other two diners were also men. One of these had his back to McLean, but the other sat facing the swarthy man. He was obviously older than the white-haired man, and was almost devoid of cranial covering. He wore glasses and was most shabbily dressed.

They were all eating and McLean could recognize the dish. It was *Spaghetti Napolitaine*, and to him, after the frugal fig repast, the sight of it was most appetizing. Over the table was an elaborate chandelier, carrying many lamps of an amber shade. This was surprising, for it pointed to the existence of a generating plant. The white-haired man rang a bell, and a servant in a short velvet coat and wide trousers entered and cleared away the plates. He returned very quickly with the next course and while he was serving it the white-haired man appeared to be laying down the law, with some emphasis. The spectacled man started to say something but was swiftly cut short by a gesture and made to look like a naughty child.

Finally McLean moved on but soon found that there was no outlet on the northern side. That side of the house looked down on a kind of ravine, opposite which were ruins of ancient buildings. In a wall joined to the house there was an arch leading to some steps, and he went down these to find himself in a courtyard, which seemed to serve no purpose whatever. Leading from this was another arch, and some more steps. Soon he found himself in a series of smaller courtyards, joined by narrow alleys, and in these alleys were old doorways leading down to what he believed had been old dungeons. He stopped at one of these and peered down the steps. From below there came the distinct humming of a dynamo. But there were other sounds too — voices and laughter, and working machinery. The whole set-up was puzzling in the extreme. He shone his torch down the steps, and it rested on an open wooden box. In the box was an article of grim significance. It was a modern machine-gun, obviously in process of being unpacked. Hearing footsteps approaching from below he switched off the torch and made away.

Yes, it was indeed puzzling. Persons who engaged in honest pursuits did not equip themselves with machine-guns. What were these people really up to? It caused him to wonder whether the death of Joseph Banner was connected with this place? Had Banner some association with it, and later considered it his duty, or his business, to reveal what he knew to some highly-placed British government official? Well, Banner was dead, and here was he, McLean, more by luck than design, taking the kind of risk which might conceivably send him to join Banner. How easy it would be too, since no one in the world had the faintest notion where he was!

He was moving away from the doorway when suddenly a man emerged from a door slightly ahead of him. McLean slipped back to the doorway, but in doing so he made a slight noise, and heard the man stop dead in his tracks. Then, to his great relief, the footsteps were heard again — going in the opposite direction. McLean took this opportunity to get away from the danger area, and went to the spot where he had last seen the launch. Dark as it was he could see that the anchorage was vacant. The obvious thing to do was wait until the launch came back, and then make an attempt to get to the mainland and obtain particulars of the island and its occupants. To attempt to do more that night would be folly.

7

SO McLean spent another night in the little cave, awaking to a beautiful dawn which bathed the island in soft light. His first thought was of the launch, and he set out for the spot from which he could see the anchorage. As before, it was vacant. Parched and hungry he made his way to the old fig tree, and there selected the few remaining ripe fruit. But these did little towards slaking his thirst, and it seemed that unless the launch returned very soon he would be compelled to pay a visit to the villa, and risk the consequences.

To kill time he resolved to make a tour of the parts of the island which he had not already seen, avoiding the inhabited portion as far as he was able. It occupied all the morning and part of the afternoon, for he indulged in a long bathe in a quiet backwater. Once more he looked for the launch, with no better result than before.

Now he pondered the next move. If he called at the villa certain questions would undoubtedly be asked, and he had to have ready answers. It was no use saying he was a seaman who had fallen overboard, for his clothing would give him away. If he pleaded that he had been a passenger on a pleasure cruise, who had had a mishap, they would naturally want to know the name of the ship and from whence it had sailed, and might easily bowl him out in a lie. Suppose he pretended to have lost his memory through long immersion in the sea? That would certainly circumvent questions, but would they not become suspicious? Then there was Greta. Would she recognize him as the dapper alleged film director, with the American accent? He thought it was possible she might not, with that thick growth of beard on his face and his drenched clothing. Also exposure to the burning sun during the past few days had fried him to the colour of a lobster.

Finally he decided to use the lost memory idea, and he made his way to the beach to carry out the first essentials. Leaving his pistol, torch, cigarette-case, lighter, and wallet on the sand, he took a bathe in his clothes, and enjoyed it up to a point. Then he waded ashore and pocketed the personal articles. His hat and coat he resolved to leave in the cave.

He was in process of doing this when he heard the unmistakable sounds of footpads outside, and he prepared to play the part of a man without a memory — if necessary. He could now hear the panting of the approaching person, who had obviously been hurrying, and then suddenly the person came to view. To his amazement it was Valerie Donkin!

She was evidently as startled as he was. He hurried to her, but at the movement she turned to run. Then he called her name, and she stopped and stared at him.

"Mac!" she gasped. "What on earth are you doing here?"

"That's my question, not yours. Do I look so villainous that you have to flee from me?"

"You look pretty repulsive with that scrubbing-brush jaw, and soaked to the skin. Oh, but am I glad to see you!"

She came forward and gripped his hands warmly.

"Never mind about my story," he said. "Tell me yours. How did you get here?"

"By motor boat!"

"Whose boat?"

"A hired one — from Trieste."

"Trieste! Are we in the Adriatic?"

"Yes. Didn't you know?"

"No. Look — we can't talk here. It is too near a source of danger. Come with me and then we can get everything clear. Where did you leave the boat?"

"In a little bay — over there. I was afraid of running aground, and it was too deep to wade ashore, so I

153

managed to get a mooring rope round a rock, and get ashore over a little headland."

She pointed to the eastern end of the island, and McLean led her away.

"Have you any fresh water aboard?" he asked.

"Oh yes — a big keg."

"You're an angel from heaven. Let's get to the boat. My throat feels like sand-paper, so don't expect me to be very bright until I've had about a gallon of water. Any food?"

"Only some cold meat and some biscuits and cheese."

"Only!" he ejaculated. "Have you ever tried to live on a diet of green figs?"

"Never."

"Well, don't. This beard in which you appear to be so interested is not intended to be permanent. It's a case of Hobson's choice. I hope that boat is well hidden."

"I think it is. I chose that sort of spot."

"Clever girl!"

At last they reached the little sandy bay, which was backed by cliffs about twenty feet high, and from the cliffs there jutted a rocky promontory, a few yards from the end of which was the motor boat, rocking gently on the calm sea. On reaching the end of the rocks they hauled on the mooring-line and slowly brought the boat to a position where it could be boarded. It was a well-equipped little vessel with a long cabin and bunks for four, and here McLean sat while Valerie produced a jug of water, a drinking glass, and some slabs of bread and pressed beef.

"Primitive, but nourishing," she said. "I suppose it's no use asking you for a cigarette?"

"That happens to be about the one useful service I can render. I had the sense to keep them dry when I immersed myself in the sea. Here!"

He passed the cigarette-case and Valerie took a cigarette and produced some strip matches from her handbag.

She smoked contently while he finished the repast, and drank glass after glass of water.

"That's better," he sighed. "Now tell me how you brought off this miracle?"

"It was three nights ago. I was worried out of my life at not hearing anything, and then the telephone bell rang. I hurried to the telephone, and immediately I lifted the receiver I heard Ian's voice. It was weak and hoarse. He said: 'I've only got a few seconds. Tell McLean the place is called Delbros, an island lying off Trieste. I believe they are going to take me there. I'm not — ' And then there was a noise followed by dead silence as if somebody had suddenly intervened. I asked the operator if she could trace the call, and she said it wasn't possible. Then I looked up an atlas, but couldn't find any island named Delbros. I drove up to Scotland Yard, and saw an inspector named Drew. He was very nice but didn't appear to be very intelligent."

"He isn't," said McLean.

"He said you weren't available, and didn't know when you would be. I then asked for Sergeant Brook, but he said Brook was also unavailable. I asked him to tell you that I had called, and that you could get in touch with me at the telephone number of a friend, which I wrote down for him. I waited at my friend's house for two hours, from which I telephoned your flat several times. Finally I telephoned Inspector Drew, but he still gave me the same reply. Then I went home.

"The next morning I tried again to get in touch with you, but all to no purpose. Then I resolved to do something on my own. I simply couldn't sit still. Fortunately my passport was still in date, so I went to my bank, and asked if I could get my foreign travel allowance quickly. I was told I could have a hundred pounds in traveller's cheques at once. I drew the money, packed a suit-case and went to London Airport. There, after some delay, I got on to a plane, and finally reached Trieste. I wasn't entirely alone there, as I knew a man in the British Consulate. He told me there was an island named Delbros, but that it was a very small and uninhabited spot. He said there was some dispute about its ownership, but in any case it was absolutely useless. Finally he got a large-scale map, and pin-pointed the place. It bore an unpronounceable Yugo-Slavian name. I asked him to lend me the map, and finally he agreed. Then I asked him if he knew where I could hire a motor-boat for a day. He took me down to the waterfront and found an Italian who said he knew the island and would take me there and back for twenty thousand lire. I agreed to meet him early this morning, and to have the money ready. But last night I received a message through my friend to the effect that the owner of the boat had been taken ill. There seemed to be no other boat available so I begged my friend to see Angelo — the owner — and beg him to let me have the boat on my own. But Angelo refused, on the grounds that it would not comply with the conditions of the insurance policy. I was stuck, and my friend seemed to be relieved, because he had never liked the idea of my making the trip. It looked as if I was done."

"And then?" asked McLean.

"Then — then I did what you will doubtless consider a silly thing."

"You stole the boat?"

"I — I borrowed the boat. It was easy to get at, and I found the tank full of petrol. I had that map, and the sea was like a mill-pond. And here I am."

McLean shrugged his shoulders. What was the use of telling Valerie that she was guilty of a punishable offence when she had come so opportunely.

"Have you got that map?" he asked.

"Yes."

She brought him the map, on which the island was clearly marked, and he reckoned the distance to be about thirty miles from Trieste, but only about twelve miles from the Yugo-Slavian coast.

"How long did it take you to get here?" he asked.

"Four hours. I passed a number of other small islands, but I've done a good deal of cruising, and I checked my course pretty thoroughly. This is Delbros all right."

"I'm not doubting it."

"Now tell me how you got here."

McLean told his story very briefly, while Valerie listened incredulously.

"So that's why I couldn't get in touch with you," she said, when he had finished. "Mac, what is the meaning of all this? Have you any idea?"

"Quite a lot, none of which may be correct. That message from Ian has so far been borne out. The question is whether the latter part is true, and Ian held a prisoner here."

"We can best settle that by going back to Trieste, and getting help there."

McLean shook his head as his mind

ranged over the problem. If, as Valerie had been told, the nationality of the island was in dispute, the Italian government would not be willing to increase the tension which already existed between themselves and their neighbours by taking any immediate action. Certainly they would require far more information than McLean was able to give. Even then it would mean delay.

"No. I must have more data," he said. "And the only way to get that is to make contact with them. I was about to do that when you arrived."

"But if you go to the building you told me about you are bound to be suspect at once."

"I'm not so sure. They can have no idea I was in that plane."

"But the woman — Greta — would recognize you."

"Would she? You had some difficulty in recognizing me just now, and you have known me for a long time. For all I know she may not be there

161

any longer. Anyway, I've got to risk that. Your arrival makes things easier. Listen! This is the programme. I want you to stay here for two hours. If I'm not back by that time go to Trieste, and see your friend at the Consulate. Tell him to get through to London and inform them that I am being held prisoner, for by that time it will be true. In the meantime keep your eyes open, and if anyone sees you lose not an instant in getting away. Is that clear?"

"Too clear. Mac, I don't like it."

"If you want to help Ian — presuming he is here — that is the best way. I'll leave such garments as I don't need with you, and make myself look rather more like a genuine shipwrecked man. Here, take them."

He took off his coat and waistcoat, and handed these to her, along with his hat. He certainly looked more like the part, standing there in his drenched trousers, with his shirt open at the neck and his hair awry. The pistol in his hip-pocket bulged somewhat, but he didn't feel like parting with that.

"Take care of my wallet. In it is my warrant. It will corroborate your story — if the worst happens. But I'll take the cigarette-case and the lighter. Now, how do I look?"

"Horrible," she replied. "Oh, Mac, I wish I were coming with you."

"That would make a fantastic story more fantastic. How should I explain you?"

"Couldn't you say I was your wife?"

"Who would believe that a glamorous girl like you would marry a scrubby-faced ruffian like me?"

"Stranger things have happened. But I know it is no use arguing because you are immune to feminine appeal."

McLean laughed and then gripped both her hands, and became deadly serious.

"You're not to hesitate," he said. "One glimpse of any stranger and you start that engine and get going."

"I promise."

McLean then hauled on the mooring-rope, and finally stepped on to the rocks. He hurried across them, turning to wave his hand. His route to the buildings led him past the sandy inlet where the aeroplane had touched down, and which served as an excellent runway. Looking up this he saw that the doors of the distant hangar were closed, and that they were painted to match the greyness of the surrounding rock, so cleverly as to deceive anyone at a distance. From here the house and the adjacent ruins were approached by a stiff climb, and finally he passed through a gate in a crumbling wall, and reached a terrace on which was the main entrance.

Before he approached he cogitated on the matter of the pistol. It bulged far too prominently to be missed by any pair of normal eyes. To enter the house, obviously armed, would certainly tell against him. The sensible thing to do was to conceal it where he could quickly retrieve it. Looking around he saw a young agave growing out of a crevice, and making sure he was unobserved, he took the pistol from his hip-pocket and thrust it deep down between the long prickly leaves.

Then he staggered to the entrance of the house, and found there an old-fashioned ornate bell-pull. He tugged at the rusty handle and heard the bell clanging lustily inside the house.

8

THE man who answered the summons stared hard at the drenched and dishevelled form of the caller. It was the fellow McLean had seen the previous evening, waiting at table, and the latter's astonishment was complete. McLean addressed him in English, and on recovering from his surprise the man answered in the same tongue, but in guttural tones.

"Where you come from?"

"From a yacht," said McLean, displaying all the signs of an exhausted man. "There was a fire last night, and I was compelled to jump overboard. I was lucky to get ashore. Who lives here?"

"Colonel Lombroso."

"Could I — could I — ?"

Here he staggered and the man caught him by the arm, and led him inside to a chair, in which McLean flopped.

"You stay here. I bring Colonel."

When he had gone McLean looked about him. He was in a wide hall, on the south side of the house, and to the right of the dining-room into which he had peered the previous evening. The floor was of stone with a wide surround of mosaic obviously of great age, and of beautiful design. There were three doors leading out from the hall, and in the back a broad staircase, beyond which there was an inner hall. The furniture was sparse but of excellent quality, and scattered about the floor were numerous oriental carpets. Above the chair in which he sat there was a lovely mirror in a gilt Florentine frame. He stood up for a moment and looked into this.

"My goodness!" he muttered, aghast at what the mirror revealed, and quickly sat down again.

On hearing a door being opened he lowered his head into his hands

167

and resumed his exhausted appearance. Through his fingers he saw the white-haired man approaching. He was very stiff and upright and his expression was hard and unsympathetic.

"A victim of the sea?" he asked, in almost perfect English, but with just a suspicion of an accent.

McLean gave a start and looked up.

"Are you — Colonel Lombroso?" he asked.

"At your service."

"I'm sorry to break in on you like this. At first I thought the island was uninhabited — if it is an island."

"It is."

"My name is Charles Ward, of Manchester. I have been staying with an Italian friend in Venice, who owned a small motor-boat, and for some days we have been cruising along the coast. This morning my friend had trouble with the Primus stove we were using. It exploded, and caught the boat on fire. We tried to douse it but it got the better of us, and we had to take to the water."

"That was bad luck. And your friend?"

"I'm afraid — " McLean shook his head sadly. "He swam with me for a mile or two, but he was a poor swimmer, and finally I had to abandon him."

"Drowned?"

McLean nodded his head miserably, and prayed inwardly to be forgiven.

"Is there a telephone here?" he asked. "Can I get in touch with the mainland?"

"I'm afraid not."

"But surely there is some means of getting there?"

"We keep a boat here, but at the moment it is making a trip. I am expecting it back tomorrow."

"Would it be asking too much to — ?"

"Not at all. I will see that you are taken across to the mainland as soon as the boat returns. In the meantime you would probably like some food?"

"You're very kind. But first of all I need a drink. I've been in the sea for hours, and wandering about in the hot sun. I looked for fresh water but found none."

"There is none. The only well on the island is here. But come with me and I will fit you up with some clothing while your own clothes are being dried."

McLean thanked him with a wan smile, and followed him up the broad staircase to a bedroom which overlooked the brilliantly blue lagoon.

"Now," said Lombroso, "I will send you some fresh water and some clothing. You appear to be just about my own size. The bathroom is behind that curtain. Give your wet clothing to Marco. He will attend to it. Soon we shall be having a meal."

McLean thanked him, and sighed when the door closed after him. So far things had gone very well, but it was yet far too early to start congratulating himself, for Lombroso was not the type of man to reveal what he was thinking, and his facile acceptance of McLean's story proved nothing. From this pleasant room, which overlooked almost everything on the island, nothing of Valerie or her boat could be seen.

He looked in the bathroom, and found there several fresh towels, soap, and what not. When he tried the hot tap the water came out almost boiling, so he let it run while he stripped himself of his few garments, and finally got into the bath. While he was there splashing about there was a rap on the door, and a thick-set swarthy man entered.

"Are you Marco?" asked McLean.

"*Si, Signore*. I leave the clothing in the bedroom, and the fresh water."

"*Grazie*. So you speak English?"

"Leetle piece — yes. I taka these things?"

"Yes, but not the shoes."

Marco gathered up the wet garments, and soon made off leaving McLean to enjoy the rest of his ablutions. There was no doubt in his mind that Marco at least was genuine Italian, but he had his doubts about Colonel Lombroso, despite his name. Having dried himself off he went into the bedroom to find there a complete outfit. A two-piece linen suit, beautifully laundered, a light blue silk shirt with collar attached, a tie, a pair of socks, and some excellent underwear. But with the carafe was an article which presented quite a delicate problem. It was a safety razor.

The pernickety Colonel naturally expected that his guest would wish to remove that stubble from his lower face. The perfect host would indeed think of that. But to McLean the kindly gesture was unwelcome. That young and flourishing dark beard of his was almost as good as a mask. He had taken it into consideration when planning this dangerous business. Without it his features were quite capable of ringing a bell in Greta's mind — should he come face to face with her — and that would put an end to the tragi-comedy.

But if he failed to take advantage of the razor what then would the Colonel think? One might, of course, plead that having started a promising crop of face fungus he meant to continue with it. He considered the matter for a few minutes and then decided on a compromise. He would shave but leave the semblance of a bristly moustache, and two small 'sideboards'.

The subsequent operation was most successful — even better than he expected, for it really did change his appearance, and he laughed aloud to consider what the critical Valerie would say about it. On donning the clothing he found the outer garments fitted him extremely well, but never in his life had he worn such sub-tropical attire.

Finally he opened the door and crept downstairs. In the hall was Marco, who regarded him with evident approval, and then conducted him to the lounge. The great moment had come, for standing near a grand piano was Greta and the thin bald-headed man, whom he had seen previously.

"Oh, I beg — " he commenced.

"It's all right," said Greta. "The Colonel has told us about your adventure, Mr. Ward. I am Greta Borche, and this gentleman is Doctor Roy. We are guests here."

McLean bowed and said he hoped he wasn't interrupting any music.

"Oh no," said Greta. "We were talking about you. It must have been a very terrible experience."

"It was. Something I am not likely to forget."

"You started from Venice, didn't you?"

"Yes."

"Lovely place," sighed Greta. "I think it's the most wonderful city in the world. I made part of a film there quite recently. The rest of it was done in Rome."

"So you are a film actress?"

"In a small way. I don't suppose you have ever heard of me in England. But you will."

"I have no doubt about that," said McLean, as his gaze wandered over her admirable form, accentuated as it was by a clinging frock which displayed a large part of her torso.

"My dear Greta," admonished Roy. "Mr. Ward may not have the slightest interest in films, as I have not."

"Oh you!" retorted Greta. "All you are interested in is dead bodies and microscopes. It would do you good to see a few films."

"I have seen a few — hence my lack of interest. They give a completely false picture of life, and induce young girls who would be better engaged scrubbing floors, to starve themselves to death while waiting to be picked up by some talent scout, whose only interest is in their shape and not their intelligence."

Greta glared at him, and then laughed.

"Is that your opinion, Mr. Ward?"

"I'm neutral in this," said McLean, and switched his gaze to the handsome electric light pendant. "You're lucky to have electric light here," he said, as if he had not been previously aware of this fact.

"The Colonel installed it a few years ago," said Roy. "It is supplied by a small generating plant. It is housed down in the old dungeons. This used to be an old fortress, built against the Saracen invasions I believe."

"But does the Colonel live here permanently?" asked McLean innocently.

"Oh no — only during the spring. It can be very hot here in the summer, and very cold in the winter. He will be leaving shortly for Rome where he has a villa."

"Well, my luck was certainly in," said McLean. "If I had found nobody here my plight would have been most desperate."

"It would indeed," said Greta. "Ah, here is Enzo!"

Lombroso entered the lounge. He had changed since McLean last saw him, and now wore a black velvet coat over a pair of grey cloth trousers.

The doctor's garb was equally unconventional. He was in fact quite shabby.

"Ah, so you are down, Mr. Ward," said Lombroso. "That suit is an admirable fit."

"It's very cool and comfortable," said McLean. "I have been admiring your home. It's unique."

"Glad you like it. I bought it for a song. In the past I did a lot of yachting round here, and this deserted island always appealed to me. It was a headache making it habitable, but it offers me a nice retreat from the troubled world. Why not a song, Greta?"

"My voice is like the piano — out of tune," complained Greta.

"I'm sorry," said Lombroso. "But piano tuners are not easy to get. Won't you try?"

Greta, despite her complaint, seemed not at all unwilling. She went to the piano, arranged her dress, played a few chords, and then broke into an enchanting song about roses, and moonlight, and love, which caused McLean to smile to himself. But her voice had a fine rich quality and she knew how to use it to advantage, and somehow McLean found himself impressed although he hated the sugary sentimentality of the verses.

"Bravo!" said Lombroso, when the song ended. "Are you musical, Mr. Ward?"

"Very," admitted McLean. "But I don't perform."

"That is a pity. Half the joy of music lies in the performing of it. Personally I can't live without a piano, although I am the poorest of performers."

"He's not," said Greta. "He plays beautifully — even on an out-of-tune instrument. Do play something, Enzo."

But Lombroso shook his head with unmistakable finality, and McLean was conscious of a kind of tenseness in the atmosphere. He was quite sure that Lombroso was far from taking him at his face value, and that went for Roy as well. Strangely enough it was

Greta, whom he had feared most, who seemed to have no suspicions at all.

"Well, if you won't play, Enzo," she said. "What about dinner? I'm starving."

"I regret that dinner will be a little late."

McLean remembered Valerie, waiting out there in the motor-boat, and considered this just the opportunity to let her know how things had gone.

"In that case do you mind if I take a little walk?" he said. "I should like to look round the island as I shall be here so short a time."

"By all means," said Lombroso. "If you would return in half an hour I think dinner will be ready."

"I'll come with you," said Greta. "I should love a breath of fresh air."

"I'd rather you didn't, Greta," said Lombroso. "I've got a little matter I want to discuss with you."

"Surely it can wait."

"It could, but I'd rather deal with it

now. I'm sure Mr. Ward will excuse you."

"Of course," said McLean, greatly relieved.

Greta sighed and shrugged her shoulders, and McLean then withdrew. When the door closed after him Lombroso gave a hard little laugh.

"What's the joke?" demanded Greta.

"The joke is on Mr. Ward, so-called. He thinks he is going to the mainland, but he is going to suffer a bitter disappointment."

"I don't understand."

"Neither do I. There is a lot I don't understand. But one thing I am certain about. That man is a spy."

"What!" ejaculated Roy.

"There was no shipwreck — no fire. His story is a lie from beginning to end. I mistrusted him and sent some of the men to look round. They found a motor-boat moored in Sandy Cove, under the rocks. There was a woman in it, and she tried to get away, but they were successful in preventing it, and brought her back here. She says she is Miss Sutcliffe, and tied up because she had trouble with the engine. But that too was a lie, because it was soon proved that the engine was in perfect condition. In the cabin were a man's garments — precisely the garments of which Mr. Ward was short."

"Did she attempt to account for them?" asked Roy.

"Yes. She said they had been left there by her brother, who last used the boat."

"You think that Ward came in that boat?"

"Yes. What else can one think? There's no knowing how long they have been here, nor how much Ward may have discovered. This situation has to be dealt with, and without delay. The girl must be compelled to talk."

Roy nodded his bald head.

"What about Ward?" he asked. "Was it wise to let him walk out as he did?"

"He can do nothing but starve to

death. Had the boat been there it would have been different. We can round him up whenever we like. There's been a slip-up somewhere. I wish I knew just where it was."

"We might be able to settle the matter of the clothing," said Roy. "It might match up with the trousers which Marco is drying. I'll get Marco in and we'll settle that point."

Lombroso gave a scowling nod, and Roy pushed a bell, which brought Marco on the scene very quickly.

"Is that clothing of Mr. Ward's dry yet?" asked Roy.

"Not quite, Doctor."

"Well bring the trousers in, and at the same time ask Max to give you the clothing that was found in the boat. Don't stare at me. Max will understand."

It was not long before Marco came back with his arms full of clothing. Lombroso's keen eyes went to the bundle, and he pulled out a pair of damp trousers, and a coat. They were dark blue, with a thin pin stripe, and they matched perfectly.

"What did I tell you," grunted Lombroso. "All right, Marco, you can take them away."

"No — wait!" panted Greta. "I've just thought of something. I've seen that suit before. I took special note of it, because I thought I should like a tailored suit of the same material."

"Can you be sure of a minor detail like that?" asked Roy.

"Clothing isn't a minor detail to a woman. Yes, now I'm positive."

Lombroso waved Marco out of the room, and then glared at Greta.

"Now you can talk," he said. "Where do you think you saw that suit before, and when?"

"In the London hotel where I was staying. It was two days before Hendryk was arrested. A man in the bar knocked over my drink by mistake, and we got talking. He said his name was Hudson, and he was American. He had come to England to start a film company, so naturally I was interested."

Lombroso curled his lip derisively.

"You and your damned films!" he snarled. "What else did you talk about besides films?"

"Nothing."

"Did you mention Hendryk?"

Greta was silent for a moment.

"Did you?" screamed Lombroso.

"Y-yes. I told him that Hendryk was my manager?"

"Why in God's name — why?"

"Because Hudson had heard of me, and wanted to talk business. I told him he would have to see Hendryk."

"And gave him Hendryk's address?"

"Yes."

Lombroso's face was now white with rage. He banged a table and dislodged a beautiful vase which fell with a crash.

"You lunatic!" he raved. "Two days later Hendryk was arrested and I'll bet you never saw this Mr. Hudson again."

"No. He didn't turn up for the

meeting we had planned."

"I should think not. My God, you've landed me into trouble, with your childish vanity. Didn't you recognize this Mr. Ward when you saw him this evening?"

"No. The man I saw was clean-shaven, and he spoke with a rich American accent. Those clothes you lent him made him look quite different."

"But you have no doubt now that he is the same man?"

"He — he might be. Yes, he might be."

Lombroso turned to Roy, who was looking no less grim than he was himself, but unlike him Roy was perfectly self-controlled.

"Undoubtedly harm has been done to our cause," he said. "But it need not be irremediable. You have the girl, and it is quite impossible for Ward to get away. I think a certain amount of persuasion — shall we call it — may cause one or both of them to tell all they know."

"But how do we know it all ends there? How came they to know about this island? What are they to each other? For whom are they acting?"

"That information should come in due course. Have you yet seen the girl?"

"No."

"Then I think you should make good that omission, without undue delay. I will come with you."

9

AT that moment Valerie was cursing herself in no uncertain manner, and blaming her lack of vigilance for the position in which she now found herself. But in this she did herself less than justice, for what had happened had taken place with a speed and cunning that could not have been improved upon.

For half an hour after McLean's departure nothing had happened. She had taken in some slack on the mooring-rope, and kept the motor-boat within a few feet of the rock, in order that she could slip the mooring in an instant if the emergency arose. In the dead calm the boat made scarcely a movement, and she sat and admired the wonderful colour scheme of sand, sea, and sky, peering from time to time into the deep water, where there was a different colour scheme, and one in which the fascinating life of the sea played a part. Far beneath her she could see shoals of brightly-coloured fishes, and strange weeds reaching up for the surface and waving tentacles of pink and yellow in hypnotic fashion.

But fascinating as these things were she did not permit them to distract her attention completely from her prime task. She hoped that McLean would not stay the full two hours, or anything like it, because it would then mean doing the latter part of the journey back to Trieste in darkness. Then suddenly, without the slightest warning, the danger was upon her. Over the top of the cliff came three men, two of whom were naked to the waist. They ran like cats along the rocky spur towards the mooring-line, the fully-clad man waving a pistol, and shouting to her.

She managed to slip the mooring in time, and then ran to the starter. The pistol went off and a bullet smashed against the engine cowling.

"Stand away from that engine!" bellowed the marksman.

Valerie gulped but carried out her purpose, and the engine fired. Then one of the two half-naked men did a wild jump from the top of the crag into the cockpit of the boat. He landed quite close to her and grabbed her by the legs, bringing her down on top of him. For a few moments she fought like a wild cat, but it was all useless, and finally she was manhandled and thrown into the cabin, with the door closed on her. Breathless and bruised she had wits enough to remember McLean's wallet, inside her handbag. Quickly she took it out, and removed from it the tell-tale warrant card, which she destroyed and pushed through a port-hole. The garments left by McLean she hid under one of the lower bunks.

By this time the other two men had got aboard, and suddenly the engine, which had been ticking over, roared into power and the boat moved rapidly along the coast, in the opposite direction from which she had come, and finally rounded a point which gave entry to the long lagoon, on the left of which was a mass of buildings. Jutting out at this point was a curving stone jetty, which formed a neat little anchorage.

Very soon the boat passed through the narrow entrance and the engine was switched off. It had enough way on to drift towards some steps, close to which was an iron ring set in the stone wall. Here it was tied up, and the cabin door was flung open. The thick-set dark man, who had fired the pistol, stood outside.

"Come on!" he said.

She stepped out into the cockpit, and was helped up the steep steps, at the bottom of which one of the half-naked men was waiting for her. The thick-set man followed her, and immediately the party moved away, leaving the third ruffian aboard. They passed along the jetty, and through an arch in the very ancient, crumbling wall.

"Where are you taking me?" she asked.

"You'll find out."

Inside the arch the place was like a labyrinth, but finally they came to a series of iron doors. One of these was half-open, and from the rusted lock projected a huge key. Through this they went, and descended about half a dozen stone steps, into a dingy chamber in which were a number of old chests, and a lot of refuse. At the far end was a narrow, barred window, through which she could see the brilliantly lit scene outside, looking across the lagoon.

"Now," said the leader. "Perhaps you will explain."

"What is there to explain?" she asked. "Surely it's for you to explain why you treat me like this?"

"Where did you come from?"

"Trieste."

"Alone?"

"Yes."

"What's your name?"

"Sutcliffe. Miss Sutcliffe," she lied.

"Didn't you know this island is private property?"

"No. But even if it is, I didn't land on it. I simply tied up my boat because I had trouble with the engine, and wanted to investigate the trouble."

"We found no trouble with it."

"Of course not. I had already made it right when you pounced on me like a lot of wild creatures. Since I've told you my name, perhaps you'll tell me yours?"

"That's neither here nor there. I have to report this matter. Give me that handbag."

He snatched her handbag before she could prevent him, but that did not disconcert her since she knew it contained nothing which would invalidate her story.

"Is this your wallet?" he asked, taking out McLean's slim leather case.

"Yes."

"Do you usually carry your money

in two different lots?"

"Yes. You will notice that I keep a certain amount of English money in the wallet. The foreign money I keep separately."

He still seemed to be far from satisfied.

"What were you doing in Trieste?" he asked.

"Taking a holiday. Why shouldn't I?"

At that moment a man came hurrying into the gloomy place, carrying something in his hands. She saw at once that it was McLean's discarded clothing. The man gabbled something in a language which was lost on her. The dark man took the clothing, and showed the items to her, with a glint in his eyes.

"Found in your boat," he said. "Do you still ask me to believe that you came alone in that boat?"

"I'm not asking you to believe anything," replied Valerie. "It happens to be true, but you needn't believe it if you don't want to."

"Then whose clothing is this?" he snapped.

"My brother's I expect. He often leaves articles of clothing in the boat."

"So you have a brother?"

"Yes."

"Where is he now?"

"In Trieste. He lives there. That's why I chose to take a holiday there."

"All right. I hope for your sake you are telling me the truth. Now I will go and report."

"And leave me in this filthy place? Is that your employer's usual standard of hospitality?"

He made no reply to this scathing remark, and went off with the others. She heard the upper door clang, and knew it was useless to go and see if she were a prisoner. Her mind immediately turned to McLean, and it required more than ordinary optimism to believe that things were all right with him, for the arrival of the three men at that particular moment could scarcely have been a coincidence. But at least she was glad of one thing — the fact that she had managed to conceal the one piece of evidence as to his real identity. But that was poor enough consolation for the plight they were in.

These strange people undoubtedly had much to hide, and if, as seemed most probable, her brother was already a close prisoner on the island, it looked as if they were desperate enough to stick at nothing which would serve their ends.

She sat on the end of an upturned crate and wondered how long it would be before the next move would be played. Already the sun was well down in the west, and the light which filtered through the small grating was changing to deeper hues of gold and purple. She crept closer to the grating, but could see nothing of the jetty or the motor-boat, nor of a living soul.

Then it occurred to her, that if McLean was still free he would go to the cove where he had left her in the boat, and find it gone. Since he had told her to leave at once if she was seen by anyone, he would obviously believe that this had happened and that now she was on her way to Trieste, to bring help.

"Poor Mac!" she muttered. "Oh what an idiot I've been!"

It was of course possible that later he might see the motor-boat in the lagoon and draw the right conclusions from that. But it would merely put him on the alert. She did not see that he could do anything about it.

A noise outside interrupted her cogitations. She heard the old iron door wheeze and clang, and then the sound of approaching footsteps. She went back to the wooden box, and the next moment two men came to view. In the half light she took in their details. One was thin and scraggy, with spectacles, and the other was well-built, and immaculate in his rather strange attire. She noticed that his short crisp hair was almost white.

"Well, Miss Sutcliffe," he said. "I'm sorry to receive you in such sordid surroundings."

"You can speedily put that right," she replied. "I presume you are the owner of the island?"

"That is so. My name is Colonel Lombroso, and this gentleman is my friend, Doctor Roy."

"Pleased to meet you," said Valerie. "Now perhaps you will be kind enough to explain the situation."

"The situation is that I am engaged in research work of an important nature, and that I do not welcome uninvited guests."

"But I did not invade your privacy. All I did was tie up my boat for a few minutes. Did that give your servants, or employees, the right to board my boat by force, and take it into custody?"

"My information is that you resisted."

"I was shot at."

"Only after you resisted, and the shot was only intended to be a warning."

"It was unpleasantly near. Anyway,

I am very anxious to get back to Trieste."

"Naturally."

"Does that mean I may?"

Two pairs of eyes were now regarding her icily, and she divined that their owners were a long way from being satisfied.

"Whether you return to Trieste or not depends upon whether you are ready to tell the truth about your business here," said Lombroso. "You see, Miss Sutcliffe, I have proof that you did not come alone."

"That is nonsense. Why should I lie to you?"

"Because, I presume, it happens to suit your purpose. What do you know of Mr. Ward?"

"Nothing at all. Who is he?"

"He is the man who owns the clothing which was found in the boat."

"That was my brother's clothing."

"In that case the man we hold must be your brother. Scarcely consistent with your story, is it?"

Valerie now found herself being driven into a corner. That they had McLean she did not doubt, and further lies seemed useless.

"Now we will have the truth, please," said Roy.

"I've nothing more to say, except to repeat for the last time that I came here alone."

Roy stretched a long arm and caught her right wrist in a grip of iron. He then pushed her arm behind her back to a position which caused excruciating pain. Lombroso did not appear to enjoy this, but he said nothing.

"Now," said Roy, "the sooner you tell the truth the quicker it will be over. What is your real name?"

"I — I've told you," she gasped.

The arm was pushed still farther up her back, and all she could do now was make inarticulate noises.

"Steady, Doc!" said Lombroso.

The agonizing pressure was eased for a moment.

"Your real name — and the man's?" snarled Roy.

Valerie shook her head, and closed her eyes as the awful pressure was applied again. A low groan broke from her lips, and once more the pressure was eased. She was beyond words now, but not beyond action. She saw Roy's slightly bent knee quite close to her very sensible, solid, brogue shoe, and in a flash the shoe went back and struck out and upwards, to land with a thud right under that knobbly knee-cap. Roy gave a scream that would have done credit to a scalded cat, grabbed his injured limb in both hands, and broke into the most violent abuse, not in plain English, but heavy German. Valerie, not understanding half that was said, nursed her almost dislocated arm, and gave back as good as she got.

"Stop!" cried Lombroso. "This is intolerable."

"Intolerable!" howled Roy. "I'll show you how intolerable it is. Leave her to me. I'll teach her a lesson."

"I think it's a bad lesson. That's enough, Roy. There are other ways of getting at the truth. When she has been here a few days without food or water I think she will be more amenable. Come on!"

There was no doubt that he was used to having the last word, and Roy, after glaring at Valerie like a madman, limped after his master, bent almost double in his agony. Valerie heard the iron door slam, and sighed as she realized how serious the position really was.

10

McLEAN, in the meantime, had suffered a disappointment no less than Valerie's. On leaving the house his first step was to retrieve his hidden pistol, and with this weapon safely in his pocket, he felt a sense of relief, for one thing had been clear at the house — his story, despite Lombroso's suavity and hospitality, was not believed. On the way to the cove he examined the weapon to make sure it had not been found and tampered with, but he found the magazine fully loaded, and the mechanism perfect. From time to time he stopped, and looked about him, but he saw no living creature anywhere.

The question now was whether he should go back at once with Valerie, and get such help as he could from the Italian police, or whether he should dispatch Valerie on that quest, and devote his time to attempting to find where Ian Donkin was hidden, presuming that he was indeed on the island. The second plan appealed to him the more because there was always the possibility that Lombroso take fright and remove his prisoner to another place. Finally he decided to adopt the second plan.

He was now very close to the top of the slight cliff which gave access to the rocky headland. The extremities of the little cove came up at him, roseate and lovely in the evening light, and a few more steps brought him to the sandy summit. He stared along the headland, and muttered his astonishment. The boat was no longer there, and the whole wide expanse of sea was completely empty. Running down to the beach he searched along the sand, but found no marks of any kind. There was only one conclusion to draw — and that was that Valerie had seen someone on the island and had lost no time in carrying out his instructions.

It simply meant that plan Number Two was in operation with the difference that Lombroso by now would have his earlier suspicions corroborated. That meant that the situation called for extra caution. To continue round the island eastward involved crossing the open flat beach which served as the aeroplane runway. There was a risk of being seen on that flat surface, but he still thought it was preferable to going back the way he had come. After a few moments reflection he decided to take the risk, and made a bolt for it.

Within five minutes he had made the crossing, and was now in a region of tumbled rock, which provided abundant cover. Picking his way cautiously he scaled some heavy slabs of rock, and then saw below him the long lagoon, coming in from the sea. Away to his left was the house and the other squat buildings, and as he proceeded he brought to view the curving stone jetty which he had seen before. To his great joy there was a motor-boat out in midstream. His heart leaped at this sight, but as he drew nearer and nearer to the boat it took on a familiar shape in the gloaming. Yes, now he was sure of it — it was Valerie's boat! This was a crushing blow, for it meant that Valerie had not gone, but was a prisoner. Then, as he stared at the craft, he saw something else. It was a man seated in the cockpit, armed with a rifle.

Here, indeed, was a situation. All was lost unless by some means he could get possession of that craft. But what chance had any man with a pistol against another with a rifle? And the first shot would undoubtedly bring a whole gang of ruffians from those sinister buildings on the foreshore. He crouched for a minute or two behind a rock, trying to make up his mind about the next move. A direct attack on the boat seemed out of the question — certainly while there was any daylight left. If the thing was possible at all it could only be done in the middle of the night when the armed sentry might be half asleep and off his guard.

Having come to a sensible conclusion about that, he began to move back over the rocks, but was stopped dead in his tracks by the sight of three men who had apparently come from the buildings behind the house. They were clearly silhouetted against the sky, and he could see that one of them carried a rifle, and the others pistols. They fanned out a little and went away to the south. Another glance towards the boat told the other half of the story. From the arch along the quay, two more men appeared, both armed. They waved to the man in the boat, and then came towards him, along the path which skirted the lagoon.

To a man who had spent long years hunting other men the situation was ironical. It meant that the man-hunt was on, and that he was the quarry and not the hunter. Now he cursed the beautiful white suit which Lombroso had lent him, for it was the worst possible attire for a man in his plight.

Peering at the men along the lagoon he saw them separate, one continuing along the waterfront and the other climbing up over the rocks towards him. Swiftly he moved away to the left, and sought cover amid the boulders there, only to realize a little later that the man was coming dead at him. He wriggled away on his stomach, and dived into a hole, with the pistol gripped in his hand. Now he could hear the fellow's boots on the rocks close to him, and expected at any moment to be discovered, for the man loitered in the neighbourhood for quite a long time. Then there came a shout from the distance, which was answered from quite close at hand. Then, again, there were footsteps, fortunately going away from him. He waited quite a long time and finally emerged from his fox-hole, with a sigh of relief.

It was now nearly dark, and he

climbed up a rock with the idea of getting his exact bearings. He was standing up when a powerful ray of light stabbed out of the distance. He tried to avoid it but it moved too swiftly and fell for a moment on his dazzling suit. As he sank to his knees a shot rang out and a bullet smashed itself to pieces about a yard from him, then another.

Like a hare he turned in his tracks, and dropped into a gully along which he went at full speed, injuring his knees and elbows in his furious attempt to get away from that spot. Brought to a halt by a blank wall of rock he went off at a tangent away from the line of the searchlight which still lingered. It was now so dark in these twisting gulleys that he was compelled to use the little pocket torch, and after a long time the track which he was following came to an end, at a spot where two unscalable rocks had fallen in the past, leaving a small opening at the base. It was a possible hiding-place provided he had left no foot-prints behind him. He flashed the torch in his rear and was satisfied on that score. Near him was a large loose piece of rock, and he trundled it near the opening, leaving just enough space for him to pass round it. Once inside he reached out and pulled the loose rock closer and closer to the hole, finally closing the gap completely.

He was only just in time, for when he sat back to get his breath he could hear distant voices. At times they came closer, sometimes they grew fainter. It meant that there was now a concentration of men combing the neighbouring area. He flashed the torch again to see what space there was for him, and was surprised to see that the hole connected with a hewn passage, which went away to his right, and slightly upwards. Slowly he crept up this passage, the ceiling height of which increased until he was able to stand upright, and then suddenly the light of the torch brought to view the wing of an aeroplane. A moment later he was looking down into the improvised hangar from one of the rocky walls. On the farther side was another wider breach in the rock wall, and this was approached by some rough steps.

What had happened seemed fairly clear. The cave had been blasted across an old subterranean passage to give outlet to the only possible landing-place for an aeroplane. The wider opening certainly led somewhere. He believed that when he was in the luggage compartment of the plane the passengers had left the cavern by that means. In that case the obvious deduction was that it led to the house, fort, or whatever one cared to call that queer mass of buildings. This was an important discovery, but it was yet far too early in the evening to make any investigations in that direction. He groped his way back to where he had been, conserving the life of the small torch as much as possible.

Time passed and he heard no sound

of any kind. He tried to sleep but could not, for there was far too much on his active mind. After what seemed an eternity he looked at his wrist-watch and found the time nearly midnight. Still he resolved to wait another hour, by which time the gang might have given up the hunt — at least for that night.

Finally he crawled along to the hangar. The aeroplane was certainly a tantalizing sight, but there was nothing he could do about it. Cautiously he descended from his perch, and reached the ground without any mishap. Then, with the pistol in one hand and the torch in the other, he proceeded to climb the steps of the main tunnel. There were only a score at the bottom, after which the tunnel went up gradually over the natural rock. But a couple of spirals brought him finally to a series of well-made stone steps, and here he stood for a moment listening intently.

Hearing no sound of any kind, he

proceeded to climb the steep steps. There were over fifty of them and they terminated at a stout oak door. He listened again and then very slowly turned the iron handle. It opened on darkness, and when no sound came to him he flashed the torch inside, and found a big chamber, with narrow slits in the walls to permit ventilation. Stacked against the walls were innumerable wooden cases, all of which appeared to be empty. On the farther side was an arched doorway, but no door. He passed through this and came to a second chamber, rather smaller than the first, and empty. Immediately opposite him was another door, and away to the right yet another. He tried the door opposite and found that it was immovable — obviously locked or bolted on the other side.

Advance in that direction being ruled out, he turned his attention to the second door. This was of wood, studded with rusted iron nails. It was equipped with two heavy bolts, both of which were forced home, and he noticed that both of them had recently been oiled. Very slowly he withdrew the first bolt. He was busy with the second when he heard the unmistakable sound of a sneeze, and it appeared to come from the other side of the door. He stopped his activities immediately, and pondered the situation. This was no time to take chances. For all he knew it might be full of men, all ready to fill him with lead at sight. And yet the fact that the door was bolted on his side suggested a helpless prisoner on the other. He resolved to put the matter to a test, and if the result was unsatisfactory to beat a hasty retreat. With his mouth close to the door-jamb he gave a long hiss. There was a brief silence and then suddenly another long hiss came back.

"Is that Ian?" he asked.

"By God it is," said Donkin's unmistakable voice. "Who is speaking?"

McLean gave a little sigh and pulled the second bolt. The next moment the thin light of the torch illuminated the dishevelled unshaven form of Ian Donkin, who almost fell into his arms in his speechless joy. McLean gazed round the small filthy cell, with its pile of straw as bed, and a tin bowl half full of water. The only ventilation was supplied by a six-inch slit in the stone wall, and the smell of the place was appalling. Ian himself was still speechless, but after a few gulps he found his voice.

"How the devil did you find me?" he asked. "And why are you dressed like that?"

"That's a long story. We had better not talk here. Far too near the hide-out of the gang. Are you all right?"

"Not too bad. My shoulder is almost well, and the brutes have fed me up to a point. What do we do now? Have you got any help on hand?"

"I'm afraid not. The situation is delicate. But come away from here. We can talk farther down the passage. I'll bolt this door again, in case anyone should come this way. Where does that other door lead?"

"I don't know."

"Never mind. Let's get going."

They went back the way McLean had come, and it was obvious from Donkin's surprise that the tunnel was new to him. Finally they reached the hangar, and here Donkin broke the silence, as he saw the plane almost filling the big space.

"Well, I'll be — !" he ejaculated. "Where the devil are we?"

"Can't you guess? It was you who gave us the clue. You managed to send a broken message to Valerie. Don't you recall that?"

Donkins passed a hand across his brow.

"It's all so damned mixed-up," he said. "I was drugged in my sleep and taken away in a car. When I woke up I was lying on a bed in some house. In the meantime they had managed to dress me in my own clothes. Some of them came to look at me, but I feigned unconsciousness. I heard some conversation in Italian, and I gathered they were taking me to some island."

"Delbros."

"That's it — a place lying off Trieste. I was feeling pretty lousy, for the fools had given me far too much chloroform, but I determined to remember that. It was evening when they came again and I knew it was no use pretending I was still under the drug. There were two of them, both masked and armed. I still felt sick and weak, but I was resolved to make a bid for liberty. While I was drinking a glass of water I suddenly let loose, and bashed the hanging electric light to bits, at the same time hitting round blindly. I found some targets too, and when a gun flashed I saw the door, and made a dive for it. I got through it and locked it on the other side. As I went down the stairs a fellow tried to stop me. I hit him as hard as I could, and then made for the front door, and down a long drive. It was very nearly dark and I came out into a deserted lane, and staggered along it. I was feeling ill, and knew I couldn't hope to get far. But suddenly I saw a public telephone box ahead of me. I skipped into it, and found to my joy that there was still cash in my pocket. I put a call through to Valerie, because I thought that dialling 999 would be useless in the circumstances. As I got through to her I peered round the door of the box and saw three men running towards me. I had only time to say a few words before they were on me. A car followed them and I was bundled into it and driven back to the house. There the swine doped me again, and that's all I know, until I found myself in that filthy chamber with a head that threatened to burst wide open. They had given me enough dope to have put an elephant under. Whether they brought me in that plane I don't know. Where am I, anyway?"

"Delbros as stated."

"Then Valerie, God bless her, put you on my track?"

"No. She couldn't get in touch with me, because, unless I am greatly mistaken I came here on the same plane as you, but from misadventure. I'll tell you the rest later, because time is precious. But one thing I must tell you, Valerie is here, and a prisoner."

"What!" cried Donkin.

"Yes. When she found she couldn't get in touch with me she took action on her own, on the strength of your message."

"Great Scott! How could she be so incredibly stupid?"

"I'm not so sure that she was stupid. But no more now, Ian. We've got to deal with the situation as it is, without a moment's delay. Let's get out of this place, but not by the main doors. Follow me."

McLean led him across the hangar and up the steep wall to the ledge which gave access to the smaller tunnel, and finally to the fresh air, under the bright stars, and the lovely half-moon, which had risen since McLean had gone underground. Donkin drew his lungs full of the cool salted air.

"Marvellous!" he said. "Jove, I've never seen such stars."

"This place is marvellous enough, but at the moment it is packed with danger, and it increases with every moment that passes. So let's to business."

"I'm listening."

"There's one chance left to us. Valerie came in a motorboat which she borrowed at Trieste. She was captured in the boat while she was waiting for me to join her. They took the boat round to the lagoon, where there is a kind of small harbour, but at the moment there is a ruffian sitting in it, armed with a rifle. I happen to know there is enough petrol aboard to get to Trieste, and also a sailing chart. Our job is to capture the boat."

"That doesn't sound too easy."

"No. But we are not as badly off as you may imagine. I happen to have this."

McLean produced the automatic

which glinted in the moonlight.

"Oh, that puts a different complexion on things," said Donkin. "Is it fully loaded?"

"Yes — eight rounds. But if we allow him to start on us with the rifle it will be fatal because the buildings are swarming with men and arms."

"Then what's the plan of campaign?"

"It involves some little risk."

"Why tell me that?"

"Don't get so frosty. I thought you had better know. Anyway, this is the plan. If you don't like it you can say so. You see, I dare not approach that boat in this white suit, because the man in it is looking for a man in a white suit, and would give the alarm immediately he saw me. The boat is swinging out on a fairly long mooring from the jetty. On the quay side, at right angles to the jetty there is an arch which gives access to the buildings. I think I can find my way to the arch, without exposing ourselves to the sentry in the boat. Presuming we make that spot, you could put him off his guard at once by flashing this torch, and then going along the quay to the place where the boat is tied up. He will probably imagine you have come from the house with a message. How's your Italian?"

"Almost nil."

"German?"

"Not so bad. I might get away with that."

"Then pretend you have a message for him. Say that Lombroso told you to tell him that the Englishman has been captured, and that he may come ashore."

"Suppose he is suspicious, and wants to know my name?"

"All the better. The great thing is to distract his attention from me. The moment you are in conversation with him I propose to enter the water quietly, and swim for all I'm worth to the boat. There's quite a low freeboard in the stern, and I think I can nail him before he gets wise to the situation."

"How far will you have to swim?"

"Not more than thirty yards, if he's where he was when I last saw him."

"But if he should see you he'll shoot at once, and probably kill you in an instant."

"That's where the pistol comes in. If he turns on me let loose the whole magazine. What do you say?"

Donkin stroked his scrubby jaw reflectively.

"You're taking a terrific risk, Mac," he said.

"Not greater than the circumstances warrant. There is positively no other way out. When daylight comes they are bound to find us, and what do you think will happen then?"

Donkin nodded.

"You're right, Mac. Give me the pistol and the torch."

"Here's the pistol, but I'll need the torch to find that arch I told you about. A word about the pistol — you have to cock it before you use it. After that, it will fire every time you press the trigger, until the magazine is empty."

"It's a Luger, isn't it?"

"Yes."

"I know the weapon. Now let's go."

They made their way cautiously over the rocks, helped by the bright moon, and very soon they drew near the mass of buildings. The house was in complete darkness, and McLean gave it as wide a berth as possible, entering the labyrinth of passages well to the left of it. Here they went forward on tip-toe, to pass through queer alleys and courtyards, mostly fallen into decay. For a little while McLean believed he was lost, but suddenly the torch revealed an arch directly ahead, through which he could detect the reflected light of the moon on water.

"There it is," he whispered. "Can't see the boat yet. Keep close to the wall."

They approached the arch in the deep shadow of the high wall, and ultimately caught a glimpse of the boat, still riding the quiet water. The man with the rifle was seated in the stern with his back towards them, and the moonlight glinted on the barrel of the weapon. They were now standing within a yard of the arch. Donkin held out his hand for the torch which McLean passed to him.

"Just one thing," said Donkin. "If all goes well, what then?"

"I want you to take the boat to Trieste. You were always good with boats, and here's your chance. I hope the chart is still aboard, but if not set a course dead north-west, when you get out of the lagoon. There's the Pole Star, so you can't go far wrong."

"What about you?"

"You can drop me on the beach at the end of the lagoon. I've got some things to do here. When you get to Trieste get in touch with Scotland Yard, tell them the situation, and say that quick action is essential. Better do that through the British Consulate. It will save time."

"That's clear enough. But for heaven's sake don't take to the water too early."

"Not until I see you on the jetty."

"Good! Well, here goes!"

He put out his hand and gripped McLean's. Then he stepped out on to the narrow quay, and commenced to whistle blithely, while he flashed the torch a couple of times towards the boat. McLean saw the man in the boat swing round. He shouted something in Italian, and Donkin replied in German, to the effect that he had a message and was coming round. McLean held his breath, as Donkin moved round to the jetty. Here was the critical moment. He wished it were over. The man in the boat had changed his position and was now watching Donkin as he neared the mooring-place.

In a second or two McLean was across the quay and over the side. He took a long breath, and swam under the water as far as he was able, straight in the direction of the boat. Finally he came up about ten yards from it, and saw the lone occupant arguing with Donkin. He seemed to have decided doubts about Donkin, and was demanding his name. McLean reached the boat in a couple of powerful strokes, and had got one arm over the gunwale when the sentry chanced to turn his head. He gave a wild shout at what he saw and brought the rifle barrel round, but before it was level with McLean's head there came three sharp reports from the pistol, followed by several louder reports from the rifle, as the wounded man pulled the trigger blindly. A moment later McLean was spread-eagled over him, wresting the rifle from his hands. Donkin lost no time hauling the boat close to the steps. Then he grabbed the boathook which McLean offered, and a moment later he was in the cockpit.

"Get the engine going," said McLean. "They'll be here in a few moments."

The engine fired at the first kick, and the boat came round and headed down the lagoon, making enough noise in the silence to waken the dead. They had gone about a hundred yards when half a dozen men came running through the arch. Rifles flashed and bullets zipped in the water, but now the boat was making fine speed, and although some of the men had started running they soon gave up as the powerful little craft drew farther and farther away.

"Are you flat out?" asked McLean.

"Yes. By Jove, that was a near thing."

"It was indeed. For a moment I thought my career was at an end. Thanks, Ian!"

"Same to you. Now I'll have a look at this chap, if you'll take the wheel."

The injured man was cursing in Italian, and rolling his eyes, as if in death, but a quick examination showed that he had a bullet in his right arm, and another in the upper part of his leg.

"Nothing much wrong with him," said Donkin. "I'll see what I can do about bandages. But what the devil do we do with him after that?"

"You can land him with me. No, that won't do. I'd rather they thought I had gone with you. He'd spoil my plans."

"Why don't you come with me? We can't do much about Valerie until we get help."

"I'm thinking of that aeroplane. They mustn't be allowed to use that. No, Ian, it wouldn't do. You'll have to keep him. I'll help you to get him into one of the bunks, before I land."

"You know best. Do you want the pistol?"

"Yes, and the rifle, also the torch. Have a look for that chart."

Looking back McLean could see many lights amid the buildings where previously all had been blackness. He could well imagine the excitement there, but for the nonce things appeared to be favouring them, for he did not doubt Donkin's ability to get the craft safely to Trieste, on a calm moonlit night, chart or no chart.

But Donkin found the chart while searching for bandages, and when the injured man was dumped in one of the bunks, Donkin ran his eye over the chart.

"Nothing difficult about that," he said. "But it looks as if we are approaching the open sea. Time for parting, old chap."

"Yes, take her in a bit — to port. Steady now, or you'll be aground."

The boat was slowed down, and McLean lowered himself into the water. When he found it was only little more than waist-deep he took over the weapons and the electric torch.

"This is it," he said. "Best of luck to you."

"Look after yourself," said Donkin hoarsely. "I'll be back soon, in a big way I hope."

McLean waded ashore, and then watched the boat, going round the sandy spit at speed, to enter the open sea. It made a wide turn and then set what McLean knew to be the direct course for Trieste. For a long time he could hear the engine note, until gradually it ceased, and the great silence descended on him. From this point he was not far from the hangar, but again he was reluctant to attempt to enter it by the main door, and he made his way to the secret entrance which he had discovered.

11

BACK in Lombroso's strange villa, Greta was sitting in the main reception room, wrapped up in a heavily embroidered dressing-gown, smoking a cigarette and playing the piano in desultory fashion. From time to time she stopped and pushed back her mass of fair hair into some semblance of order. Her choice of music was of the sad variety which harmonized with her unhappy expression.

Suddenly the door opened and Roy ambled in, clad in little more than trousers and coat. He looked round the room expectantly, and then stared over his spectacles at Greta.

"What's going on?" he asked. "There seems to be no one left in the house. Where's the Colonel?"

"I've no idea. I was wakened by a

lot of shooting. Didn't you hear it?"

"Didn't I hear it! Do you imagine I am stone deaf. I've been looking for Enzo to ask him what the devil is the matter. Where's the drink kept?"

"In that cabinet. You can get me one, too. I hate being woken up in the middle of the night. I've rung the bell but nobody answers it."

Roy went to the cabinet, and pushed a button which raised the lid and exposed a number of bottles and many glasses. He helped himself to a brandy.

"What are you drinking?" he asked.

"Gin and Italian — a long one."

"You would," growled Roy. "If you ask me you're to blame for all this. You and your Mr. Hudson who turned out to be nothing but a damned spy."

Greta took her drink and glared at him.

"You keep your opinions to yourself. I never wanted to have anything to do with this business. Why did you have to drag me into it?"

"You weren't dragged into anything.

You were mad enough to fall for Hendryk, and to inveigle him into wasting his time building dream castles in a celluloid failyland."

Greta swallowed some of her drink, still eyeing Roy with undisguised enmity.

"And what are you and the others doing in this dump?" she asked. "You've never told me, and Hendryk was loyal enough never to discuss the matter. Why did you have to drag me back here? And where is it going to end?"

"Why not ask your devoted near brother-in-law? I'm sure he'd be honoured to tell you everything. But I'll tell you something, if our plans should misfire there'll be a good deal of throat-slitting, and firing squads. So watch your step, my beauty. You're in this whether you like it or not. Stop your wailing, and be thankful."

Greta shrugged her shoulders and went to the piano again. She resumed her moody music, and Roy helped himself to another long brandy. Then suddenly there were angry voices outside and Lombroso burst into the room.

"Oh, here you are!" he snorted. "Drinking and fooling about while things go up in smoke. Stop that damned noise, Greta! D'you hear me?"

Greta slammed down the lid of the piano and swung round on the stool.

"My word," she said. "You are in a passion! What's wrong?"

"Everything is wrong. The prisoner has escaped in the motor-boat."

Roy's thin lips were pressed together for a moment.

"You mean the doctor chap?" he asked.

"I do, and that damned spy who came here with his lying story was with him. They are now on their way to Trieste, judging from their course. What do you think of that, my dear Doctor?"

"It's a bad business. But how did it happen? I understood you put a guard in the motor-boat, with a rifle."

"I did, but they got the better of him."

"Have you got him — the guard?"

"No. They took him with them, or killed him and sank him in the lagoon. I don't know. I hope he's dead."

"You mean — he might talk, if he survived?"

"He might. I can't trust anybody now — not even my own brother who is in a British prison, waiting to be identified by the escaped prisoner. So far I am sure he has held his tongue, but if he is identified in respect of that other matter who knows what he may do to avoid hanging."

"Hanging!" gasped Greta. "Hendryk is no murderer. They can't hang him — "

"Who knows what they can do in the circumstances. Doctor, pour me a brandy. I'm at my wits' end. I never bargained for anything like this."

"I advised you to get rid of him at once," said Roy. "He was always a danger to us. You should never have brought him here. That was madness."

"It was necessary for something to be done at once. I never dreamed that Hendryk would make such a mess of things. I hold you responsible for that, Greta. It was a bad day when you met Hendryk."

"Oh, shut up!" retorted Greta. "I'm sick of taking the blame for your silly mistakes. You may have put the fear of God into Hendryk but you're not going to rule my life. I had a career of my own long before I met Hendryk. For the past two years he has lived on me, and my work."

"Your work," sneered Lombroso.

"It's honest, anyway; that's more than some people can say of their own queer ways. I've had enough, and am going back to bed. At least my conscience is clear."

At this she flung off and slammed the door behind her. Lombroso stared at Roy.

"I wonder just how much she

knows," he muttered.

"So do I. A little while ago she pretended she knew nothing, and swore that Hendryk kept her in ignorance of his association with you. But I wonder."

"She can do us no harm at the moment."

"What about the girl who came here, is she safe?"

"Yes."

"Then what's the position exactly?"

"I've done all I can to avert a catastrophe. The *Stella* is lying off Split. I've left Max trying to get in touch with her by wireless. If that can be done there is just a chance that she might intercept the motor-boat, and take the occupants aboard. But time is running short."

"That's an idea," agreed Roy. "And if it fails?"

"Then we must pack up and get away on the 'plane without delay."

"Where to?"

"Platz in the first instance. Herman

can shelter us until we can make new plans."

"New plans," mused Roy. "Have you considered the difficulties? It is absolutely bristling with them."

"I know — I know. We shall never find another place like this for our purpose. To think of leaving it after all these years, and scrap the organization that has been built up so carefully. It's heart-breaking."

There was a knock on the door, and a big broad-shouldered man entered and came to Lombroso.

"Well, Max?" he asked anxiously.

"I got through," he said. "I gave Walther all the details of the boat, and made clear your instructions. He said the crew was aboard and he would sail at once. He thought he would be able to intercept the craft provided it kept a more or less straight course. He reckons he should be on that course within an hour."

Lombroso's spirits rose at once and he slapped Max on his broad back.

"Well done!" he said. "Help yourself to a drink, and then get back to the instrument. Don't leave it until you hear something from Walther."

Max grinned and nodded as he got busy with his drink.

"One thing more — in case of emergency. How's the petrol situation?"

"I refuelled the plane yesterday, and there's about a thousand gallons at the dump."

"Excellent! You've done a good job, Max. I shall stay here until a message comes through from Walther. Don't lose a moment in bringing it to me."

"I won't, Colonel."

Max quickly swallowed his drink, and Lombroso sighed as he left the room.

"So far so good!" he said. "Everything depends upon Walther. But a lot may depend upon the weather conditions. Let's have a look at it."

He and Roy went out on to the veranda, and stared up at the stars and the bright moon. There was not a breath of wind and the air was heavy with the perfume of some night-scented plant in the wild garden.

"Let's hope it stays like this," mused Lombroso. "Care for a bout of chess to kill time?"

"You're too good for me," said Roy. "But it's not a bad idea. I certainly can't sleep a wink until the situation improves."

They returned to the lounge, but left the window open, since the night was as soft and balmy as a summer evening. Lombroso produced a chessboard and pieces, and play commenced. After the first few conventional moves it would have been obvious to any observer that the pair were accomplished players. Lombroso massed his heavier pieces in a tremendous attack against the wily doctor's strong defence, leaving himself a second line of attack should the major plan fail. The major plan did fail, for Roy could not be induced to make an exchange of pieces which on the face of it appeared to be to his advantage, but which would in fact have resulted in his being 'mated' within three moves.

"Nothing doing, my dear Enzo," drawled Roy. "I have faced this precise situation before, and I am too old to make the same mistake twice."

"Lucky man to be able to make that boast. Well, what is your reply to that?"

He pushed up a Bishop to threaten Lombroso's Queen, which could not be moved without uncovering the King. Roy sniffed and then interposed a Knight, guarded by a pawn. Lombroso pondered long, for the positional play was now going against him. He decided to let loose, and very soon the board was half denuded of pieces, leaving the odds still slightly in Roy's favour. After that it was a long-drawn-out battle of wits, each move taking a long time. So intent were they that neither seemed to notice the hands of the clock moving remorselessly round the dial. Then Lombroso, whilst pondering a difficult situation, happened to see the time.

"My God!" he ejaculated. "We've been two hours at this game. Something must have gone wrong. Walther has failed us."

"Make your move," said Roy.

"No time. Call it a draw."

"It isn't a draw. It's 'mate' in four moves. You can't prevent it."

Lombroso swept all the pieces into the box.

"Call it what you like," he said. "There are bigger things at stake. I've got to see Max. If there's no word we shall have to pack up."

"I didn't know you were such a bad loser," said Roy. "You beat me five times out of six and when it's my turn — "

The door suddenly burst open and Max entered, almost at a run. Two pairs of eager eyes stared into his face.

"They've got him," he said. "I've just heard it."

"Got whom?" rasped Lombroso.

"The prisoner — Doctor Donkin."

"What about the man in white, and

Luigi, who must have been in the boat?"

"Drowned. At least that is presumed. Walther said he overhauled the boat. The doctor was at the wheel, but refused to stop. Walther used a gun, but he still wouldn't stop. There was only one thing to do — run them down. He did that, and the motor-boat capsized and sank almost immediately. The launch stood by and put out a boat. They picked up the doctor, but never saw a sight of the others. He thinks they must have been in the cabin. The boat rowed round for a long time, but finally had to give up. He says he will be here in an hour."

"Well, I think that's very satisfactory," said Lombroso. "I'm sorry about Luigi, but he was fool enough to allow them to get possession of the boat. I'll weep no tears about Mr. Ward. He got what was coming to him. All right, Max. You can now have a well-earned rest. Thank God I thought of using the *Stella*."

"Any message for Walther when he arrives?" asked Max.

"Yes. He is to bring the prisoner here. Wake up Marco and tell him that. He's had enough sleep. I'll have the girl here too, and we'll get to the bottom of this business. That's all, Max."

Roy sighed as Max departed. The good news had had the effect of banishing his rancour over the chess game.

"I think we deserve a drink," he said. "Then I'll snatch a nap pending Walther's arrival."

The drinks were long and strong, and they lingered over them.

"What did you report to the Glasshouse?" asked Roy, after a pause.

"Nothing."

"You mean they didn't know what happened?"

"No. I said the prisoner had tried to escape, and there had been some shooting."

"That was risky, wasn't it?"

"Yes, I suppose it was, but I wasn't

in the mood to be lectured. Anyway, it's all turned out well. I gambled on getting him back, and I won."

★ ★ ★

An hour or so later Lombroso, who was reclining on the couch, heard the sound of a marine engine out in the lagoon, and realized that the launch had returned. He got up, and pushed a bell twice. A few moments later Marco, looking very sleepy, entered the room.

"The launch is back," said Lombroso in Italian. "I expect Max told you to take a message to Walther?"

"*Si, Signore.*"

"There's plenty of time. I want you to wake up Doctor Roy and then go to the men's quarters and tell them to bring the girl here."

"*Si, Signore.*"

Lombroso went to a toilet and tidied himself. He hated being untidy and because of that he deplored Roy's utter disregard in that respect. When he returned to the lounge Roy was already there.

"So Walther is back?" said Roy.

"Yes. I have sent for the girl. We may as well get things straightened out."

"Is there anything to straighten out now that Adams is dead?"

"Quite a lot. I want to know how the girl found out that Donkin was here. I want to know just how much leakage there has been."

"She wouldn't talk before. Why should she talk now — short of more pressure than you seem able to bear."

"There shall be pressure if she is still stubborn."

They hadn't long to wait before Valerie was brought into the room by two men. She looked tired and dispirited, and was glad to sit in the soft chair which Lombroso offered her. It was noticeable that the arm which Roy had manipulated so savagely was causing her discomfort, and when Roy looked at her she shot him a murderous glance.

"Now, Miss Sutcliffe," said Lombroso, "I want to introduce you to a young man who has got himself into considerable trouble. He should be here at any moment now."

A few minutes passed during which nobody spoke a word, and then there came the sound of heavy footsteps, and into the room came Donkin, with a guard on either side of him, and a man with a short beard following up. Valerie gulped to see her brother's sad condition. He was wet to the skin and his arms were bound behind his back. Across his jaw was congealed blood from a wound, which was concealed by a thick growth of beard. It was as much as she could do to recognize him. The guard fell back and left Donkin facing Lombroso.

"So you thought you could escape?" said Lombroso.

"Who the hell are you?" demanded Donkin.

"I should advise you to be a little more polite," said Lombroso. "If we all keep our tempers perhaps we shall get somewhere. I am under the impression that you know the young woman sitting over there."

"I ought to know her. She's my sister."

"Indeed? So she has — I should say *had* — two brothers?"

Donkin was about to deny this when he caught Valerie's eye and from it drew definite conclusions.

"Why not?" he asked.

Lombroso switched the next question to Valerie.

"In that case you will not deny that you lied previously?" he asked.

"No," said Valerie. "I lie when it suits me. He's my brother whom you kidnapped — or caused to be kidnapped from our home."

"Leave this to me, Valerie," said Donkin. "All the facts are plain enough."

"Some are — and some are not,"

said Lombroso. "You know why you were kidnapped, I presume?"

"I think so. There was that little matter of a dead man in a house in England, to whom I was called by an ingratiating scoundrel who called himself Mr. Baldock, but was later proved to be Herr Stein, and who is now in a British prison, facing a serious charge, provided he can be identified as Mr. Baldock. I fancy that you are much concerned about Mr. Stein's future."

"That is quite correct," said Lombroso. "I have no intention of letting you go until my — friend is released."

Donkin gave a scornful little laugh.

"He will never be released — not while I am missing. The coincidence is just a little too strong. The British police are not slow to draw conclusions."

"Are they not? But if they remain adamant so may I. Apart from which I am holding you now on a serious charge — the murder of the man Luigi who was aboard that motorboat, when you and your brother captured it."

"Rot! Luigi was only slightly wounded. I attended to his slight injuries and put him in the cabin to rest. It was the man in charge of the launch who did the murdering. He ran us down deliberately, and I was the only survivor."

"Who is to say that Luigi wasn't already dead when that happened? It's no use, Doctor Donkin. I am holding you responsible. But — I might take a more lenient view if your sister would enlighten me on one point."

Valerie, who had been shocked by the gist of the conversation, from which it was impossible not to conclude that McLean was dead, looked across at him with moist eyes.

"I've nothing to say," she said brokenly.

"You can tell me how you knew your brother was here. Who told you that?"

"What does it matter who told me?"

"It matters very much to me. I have nothing against you personally, Miss Donkin — "

"How generous of you!" cut in Valerie, bitterly. "You kidnap one of my brothers, and drown the other, but you have nothing against me personally. Well, I have a great deal against you, and all your gang of thugs, and I'll tell you nothing that will be of the least service to you. That is all I have to say."

Roy, who had been listening, with the usual Sphinx-like expression on his lean face, now turned to Lombroso, with a glint in his sunken eyes.

"I think you might well leave this matter to me, Colonel," he said. "This is simply developing into a talking match. There are quicker and more certain ways of learning the truth."

Donkin struggled in his bonds, but found himself powerless to do anything. What was in Roy's mind he had no doubt, and he looked at least as murderous as Roy himself.

"You abominable swine!" he blurted. "You may feel cock-a-hoop at getting me back into your clutches, but things are not exactly what you pretend to believe, and that's why you are inwardly scared to death. I can read it in your eyes despite your cowardly threats. I'll love to see you all hanged, or worse."

"You see?" said Roy to Lombroso. "More talking. I think I should take over from here."

"Not yet, Doctor," said Lombroso.

"Doctor!" exclaimed Donkin. "Doctor of what? What madman gave you a diploma?"

Roy walked up to him and slapped him savagely across the face.

"That shall be added to the score against you, Doctor Diavolo," said Donkin.

Here Lombroso intervened sharply.

"I will deal with this matter in my own way," he said to Roy. "Take them both away, Walther. There is no reason why they should not be together. They may then come to their senses. No food or water from now onwards."

"Where shall I put them?" asked Walther.

Lombroso thought for a moment.

"Put them in the belfry of the basilica, lock the door and bring me the key. If they can escape from that they are welcome to try. You may untie him when you get there."

The prisoners were thereupon marched out of the house, and through diverse passages, until finally they reached a picturesque old church, which had suffered some damage to its lower parts. Inside the entrance door two huge keys were hanging on a hook. Walther removed them and then commenced the long climb up a spiral staircase to the upper part of the tower. At the top were two iron doors left and right. Walther unlocked the left door, and pushed the prisoners inside. The light of a torch revealed a large chamber, built out of the local stone, with one narrow window divided by a stout iron bar. In the ceiling were the beams which had once supported a set of bells, but the bells themselves had been removed, as had the ropes which had operated them. It was not completely dark, for the moon sent a shaft of light through the barred window, creating a ghostly effect. The men were about to leave when Donkin drew Walther's attention to his bonds. Walther grunted, then cut the rope and took the pieces with him. Without a word he and his party left, and Donkin and Valerie heard the door clang and the great key turned in the lock. Valerie gave a little sob as her brother took her in his arms.

"Now — now!" he said. "That isn't like you."

"I'm sorry, Ian. Oh, be careful of my arm."

"What's wrong with your arm?"

"Your Doctor Diavolo did a little work on it a short time ago. He has great faith in physical persuasion."

"Good God! Let me see it."

"No. It's all right. Nothing broken. It was not on that account that I was shedding tears. I — I was thinking of poor Mac. I suppose he helped you to escape?"

"He did — bless him! But things are not quite as bad as they look — although they are bad enough."

"What do you mean?"

"Mac wasn't on that boat."

"Ian!"

Her cry of immense relief did not surprise her brother, for he was well aware of her deep affection for his best and oldest friend.

"I put him ashore at the end of the lagoon," he explained. "He said he had some things to do here, and I knew that one of them was to put the aeroplane out of use, in case they should make an attempt to get away, in the event of their failing to bring me back. Unfortunately they succeeded."

"So he's still on the island?"

"He must be, for there is no way of getting off it. At any rate he is armed. He took away the rifle of the man we over-powered and also has his own pistol, which still had some bullets in it."

"How clever of you to mislead them about Mac."

"It was the obvious thing to do. Otherwise they would have started another man-hunt. Believing him to be dead they will be off their guard, and perhaps give Mac a chance to do something."

"Yes — yes. But what can he do?"

"He might be able to signal a passing ship."

"But I never saw another craft when I came here. We seem to be off the usual shipping routes."

"I agree. That's one of the reasons why the gang is here. It's a beautiful hide-out for people who do not wish their existence to be known."

"Ian, have you any idea what they are up to?"

"None at all. Oh, there's one thing which puzzled me. Why were you so keen not to have those swine know that it was I who told you about this place?"

"Because they believe there has been

a leakage of information on the part of some member of the gang, when in fact there has not. I argued that as long as they believe that someone else may know where we are they will keep us alive. Otherwise I'm not at all sure that our lives would be safe for an instant. In short they have a healthy respect for the gallows."

"I believe you're right," said Donkin. "Valerie, you're more intelligent than I imagined."

"Thank you, sir," said Valerie, with a wan smile. "Oh dear, I'm so tired. Even a bale of straw would be a godsend."

"Wish I could help. But my clothing is saturated, and no use as a pillow."

"You poor old thing. It's been rough on you, who got into this mess by offering to visit a sick man. And what's happening to the practice?"

"What, indeed? But I think this is an occasion when we are entitled to think about ourselves rather than of others. Yet I can't help thinking of Mac, who must imagine that I am somewhere in Trieste, sending urgent messages to London. I've let him down very badly."

"Not you. No one could have done more. But I'll still back Mac to think up something."

"No man ever had a louder trumpeter," laughed Donkin.

"Well, he needs one. He's far too modest. If he had shouted his wares a bit he might be Chief Commissioner or something like that by now."

"I don't think he wants to be Chief Commissioner. Why should he?"

"A man should have ambitions, especially when he has exceptional ability. But of course you would side with him, because you are very much like him. What you both need is a wife to nag you on."

"Thanks for those pearls of wisdom. Speaking for myself I can't imagine any woman who would tolerate my unconventional mode of life for more than six months. As for Mac — well once he very nearly had a wife."

"I know," said Valerie. "What was her name?"

"Her name was Celia. It was a long time ago — before you had the slightest interest in the male side of the species. Oh, let's sit down and try to get some sleep."

They sat down very close to each other, with their backs against the hard wall, and now the moon was deserting them, and threatening soon to leave them in complete darkness.

"Ian," said Valerie, after a short silence. "What really happened to Celia?"

"I haven't an idea. She was a beautiful woman with a voice like a nightingale, and she swept Mac clean off his feet. I saw her twice, and I came to the conclusion that Mac had met his ideal woman. Then I heard that he was going to be married, and I accepted an invitation to the wedding. Two days before it was due to take place, he telephoned me to say it was all off. I shall never forget his voice. It was as if life for him had ended. When I saw him again, after a matter of weeks, I naturally expected he would confide in me, but he didn't. He took the wind out of my sails by begging me not to ask any questions. That queer business broke him to pieces for years. Even now he cannot forget her. There are some special songs which she used to sing which Mac cannot bear to listen to. She comes back in those songs."

"That explains much," said Valerie. "What do you mean?"

"I was trying to play some songs to him some months ago. One of them was 'Songs My Mother Taught Me', by Dvorak. He asked me not to play that, and turned the pages of the volume to a different piece."

"That is one of the songs," said Donkin. "I think he's very silly about it all, but one must respect another's feelings, even if they appear to be unreasonable."

"He must have loved her very much."

"Too much. No woman is worth that much love. Thank God that particular bug never bit me."

"Beast!" said Valerie. "You don't really mean that. Oh dear, isn't this floor damned hard?"

Donkin grunted his agreement. The situation as he saw it was grim. He knew desperate men when he saw them, and in the villainous doctor he recognized the born sadist. Lombroso perhaps was not quite of that calibre, but he had no doubt that in an emergency — any threat to his personal safety — Lombroso would not hesitate to remove any living thing from his path.

True McLean was at the moment free and armed, but what could one man hope to do against a formidable gang? Once it was known that McLean was still alive and on the island he would be hunted down like a wild animal. It was not a pleasant thought to have on the verge of sleep.

12

IN the meantime McLean, blissfully ignorant of the true state of affairs, had been very busy. With the aid of some tools found in the plane itself he had done such damage to it as to put it out of action for a long time. Then, weary to the state of exhaustion, he made his way back along the tunnel, and crawled out under the stars. Sleep was now an absolute necessity, and he recalled the little cave which he had found on his first tour of the island. A quarter of an hour later he reached it, and flung himself down on the welcome sand, with the rifle within reach of his hand. In a few moments he was sound asleep.

The morning sunlight was stealing into the cave when he woke up, much refreshed short though his slumber had been. One of his natural needs had been partially satisfied, but thirst and hunger remained. It meant another search for the figs which had kept him going on the previous occasion, but he persuaded himself that it wouldn't be long before something more substantial was available. Donkin must have reached Trieste hours ago, and knowing Donkin's character he backed him to have got something moving despite the awkward hour. That London would act quickly he had no doubt, for Scotland Yard had a marked dislike for the kidnapping of its staff. There was a good deal of co-operation between Rome and London, and within twelve hours he hoped to enjoy the welcome sight of an Italian craft packed with policemen steaming up the quiet lagoon. The great thing was to remain hidden until that happened.

With the pistol in his pocket and the rifle in his hands, he made his way to the old ruined wall where the fig trees grew. As the result of his previous depredations the crop was now greatly reduced, and such fruit as remained was far from ripe. But after much searching he gathered enough for a meal, though they looked far from appetizing. Sitting in the warm sunshine he slowly demolished them, and prayed for the future welfare of his internal economy. The scene on either hand was ravishing. The incredible clarity of the atmosphere enhanced all the rich colouring, and even the patches of ugly grey rock had a beauty impossible to describe.

Far away he could see points of land — islands he thought — and a few smoke trails. Somewhere out there was Trieste and civilization; hot baths and probably rump steaks. He wondered whether it was safe to risk a bathe, which he badly needed, and finally, after climbing a rock, and having a look round, he decided to do so. Leaving the rifle under the nearest suitable rock, he spread out his still damp clothing in the sunlight, and then took the plunge into a deep pool. It was so delicious he stayed submerged for quite a long time, and finally came out and lay beside his discarded soiled white garments. Within a few minutes his body was bone dry, and tingling with heat. The clothing too was dry, but the outer garments were dreadfully creased. Dressing in leisurely fashion, he made his way to the point where he could look up the lagoon. On reaching the spit of sand where Donkin had landed him he was surprised to see a white craft anchored off the jetty. It signified that the launch mentioned by Lombroso had returned during the night. Quickly he made away from the spot lest someone on board should possess a telescope.

It seemed to him that the cave was the best place to while away the hours, since it afforded him a restricted view of the sea in the direction from which help would come, and at the same time made it almost impossible for him to be taken by surprise. There would be shade there too from the sun which was getting quite unpleasantly warm.

But on drawing near to the cave he was suddenly surprised by coming across a series of footprints, which quite obviously led to his objective. They were so small as to leave no doubt in his mind that they had been made by a woman, and as he stood there hesitating the person who had made the footprints came to view on his left. It was Greta.

She gave him one glance and then turned and fled. In a moment the seriousness of the situation was clear to him, and he went after her in flying leaps across innumerable rocky obstacles and deep pools. She had the advantage of being on flat sand, but her tight little skirt and high-heeled shoes were not conducive to such antics, and very soon he gripped her by the arm, and swung her round, gasping for breath.

"Let me go!" she panted.

"I'm afraid that's out of the question.

It's no use struggling. You'll only hurt yourself."

Greta, swiftly becoming aware of that fact, ceased her violent movements.

"Where did you come from?" he asked.

"From the house."

"Alone?"

"Yes."

She put her hand to her left cheek, and McLean noticed a definite crimson weal across it.

"Who did that?" he asked.

"That's none of your business."

"No. I suppose it isn't. If I let you go, will you come with me quietly?"

"Where to?"

"To the cave, where I think you have already been."

"What for?"

"Because I want to avoid being seen. You can understand that, can't you?"

"Yes I can. You're a spy — just as Enzo said. You're not Mr. Ward, but Mr. Hudson, the man I met in London, and who told me all sorts of lies. I can see it now."

"I won't deny that," said McLean. "Will you come quietly and save me a lot of trouble, and yourself a lot of discomfort?"

"I suppose I must."

"Good! I don't want to linger here."

He set a fast pace, and Greta lagged a bit, but made no attempt to repeat her former antics. In a short time they reached the cave, Greta gasping from the furious exercise.

"They told me you were dead," she said, after a pause.

"Who told you?"

"Enzo and Doctor Roy."

"Well, you know the answer to that. I may be a little off colour, but I am far from dead."

"Not very far," she said, "if I know anything."

"That again is a matter of opinion. I'm afraid I shall have to hold you for a short time."

"What do you call a short time?"

"Some hours — possibly until evening,

by which time I think some friends of mine will arrive."

Greta shook her head. She had been thinking hard and the situation was becoming clearer to her.

"There's something you don't know," she said. "Lombroso believes you were on that motor-boat, but now I realize you couldn't have been. You never left this island?"

"I did not."

"Your friend never got as far as Trieste," she said, regarding him more in sorrow than in anger. "He's back here, imprisoned somewhere."

"Who told you that?"

"I know. Lombroso sent a wireless message to the *Stella* — his launch, and the motor-boat was intercepted and sunk. The man who was guarding it was drowned, and your friend led Lombroso to believe that you were drowned with him."

McLean's face did not reveal the full depth of his bitter disappointment. It was possible the girl was lying, but somehow he knew she was not.

"I shall still have to hold you," he said.

"Why?"

"So that time can prove your statement."

"I'm not lying. If you hold me long Lombroso will send out search parties. It's no use, Mr. Hudson — you've lost in this game, as you were bound to do. You're up against superior brain-power. Their organization is perfect."

"And that organization includes you?"

Greta ground her white teeth together.

"No. I hate them. They dragged me here against my will. All I dream about is escape, but escape is as far from me as it is from you. Shall I tell you something? I wish to God your friend had got to Trieste, and brought the help you expected. Then I should be free."

This surprising statement caused McLean to ponder. Could it be true, or was this synthetic beauty merely attempting to pull wool over his eyes? Greta was shrewd enough to read his thoughts.

"You've got to believe me," she said. "Lombroso hates me for falling in love with his brother Hendryk, and undermining his interests in the organization."

"You mean Hendryk Stein?"

"Yes. Lombroso's name is also Stein — Jacob Stein. I think he used an Italian name in order to buy, or lease, this island. I never saw the place until I was brought here a few days ago, and Hendryk never once mentioned it. All the time it's been a tug-of-war — me trying to get Hendryk interested in the life which I love, and Lombroso and the others dragging him the other way."

"What others?"

"I don't know. There are others high above Lombroso, and Roy, but they remain always in the dark. Hendryk knows them, but he has always refused to talk about them."

"Did you know a man named

Banner?" asked McLean.

Greta hesitated.

"I think I have heard the name before," she said. "But it means nothing to me."

"Do you know where Hendryk is now?"

"Yes — in prison. But I don't know why. He isn't a bad man — not at heart."

"Tell me the truth — was he your lover?"

"Yes. We would have married but Hendryk has a wife in a mental home. You know about Hendryk, don't you? You know why he is being held."

"Yes, I know."

"Well, I've been frank with you, why can't you be frank with me. Why is Hendryk in prison?"

"He is involved in the death of the man I mentioned — Joseph Banner, in a house called 'Leylands' on the southern outskirts of London. It's possible you may know that place."

"I have heard of it. Hendryk went

there to stay with an old friend of his named Balding or something like that."

"Not Balding — Baldock."

"That's right. It was after we left Venice. He left me in Paris, and later we both went to London."

"There was no Mr. Baldock. That house was rented by Stein, under the name of Baldock. Doctor Donkin — my friend — was called there by Stein. He found a dead man, and was kept a prisoner lest he should report the matter. The gang got away, but later Stein was arrested, he was about to be identified by Donkin when Donkin was kidnapped and brought here. Now I think you understand the situation."

"Yes I do — all but one thing?"

"And what is that?"

"Who are you?"

"I am a friend of Doctor Donkin, and of his sister, who is also a prisoner. My hope was — and still is — to rescue them and see that justice is done."

Greta shook her head disconsolately.

"You were clever to trail them all this way," she said. "But it's quite hopeless now. No ships ever come this way, because of some bad reefs, and it doesn't lead anywhere. Once they know you are here they will get you and lock you up for ever, if they spare your life. Keeping me won't help you, but merely shorten your existence, because they are bound to look for me."

"I admit the situation is a little difficult," said McLean. "But nothing is ever quite hopeless. When the Israelites were in the desert Manna fell from Heaven."

"The only things that fall from Heaven these days are bombs."

McLean laughed at her grim humour, and took out his cigarette case and lighter. On opening the case he found his few cigarettes ruined by water.

"I thought as much," he muttered.

Greta opened her hand-bag and drew out a slim case in gold and platinum.

"I can help you there," she said.

McLean accepted a cigarette, and

Greta took one for herself. Surprisingly the lighter functioned, and they sat on a rock and smoked reflectively. Again McLean's glance went to the weal across her cheek. She saw it and instinctively stroked the place with her slim fingers.

"A little horseplay on the part of dear Doctor Roy," she now admitted. "We quarrelled, and I had the last word. He didn't like that word, and acted true to pattern."

"He looked that sort of person. You certainly move in strange company."

"Yes, they're strange," she ruminated. "There must be twenty or thirty men here all told, and there's a kind of underground workshop, which is out of bounds to me. The men live there. Then there's another place called the 'Glasshouse'. It's a new building and looks out to sea. There's always a guard on duty, night and day. Sometimes Lombroso and Roy go there, but they never say for what purpose. It's all mysterious and sinister, and I wish to

God I were a thousand miles away."

McLean never missed a word, although he refrained from displaying any intense interest, and all the while he watched for some inconsistency on Greta's part, but finally he came to the conclusion that she was either telling the truth, or was the most consummate actress he had ever met. One thing was certain — that to hold her for any length of time was as dangerous as letting her go.

"Would you like to do a deal?" he asked.

"What sort of deal?"

"I'll let you go, if you promise to keep quiet about my whereabouts."

"Would you really accept my word of honour?" she asked.

"Yes, I think I would."

She gave a little trill of laughter.

"Strangely enough I am rather enjoying sitting here talking to you. I might, at a pinch, agree to stay the night."

"That might be very unwise. But

seriously, will you do that?"

"Yes I will. There's something else too. This evening, just before sunset I'll try to bring you a parcel of food. But that must depend upon circumstances."

"Naturally."

"Look, take the cigarettes," she begged. "I've got a box of them at the house."

McLean removed the cigarettes from her case, and thanked her. A few moments later she was moving across the sand and over the rocks. At the summit she turned and waved her hand.

McLean sat there for some time, astonished at the way things had developed. The crushing disappointment of Donkin's recapture was mitigated to a small extent by Greta's revelation of her hatred for Lombroso and his gang and her promise of food. In the changed circumstances he dared not move far from the cave in daylight, in that tell-tale white suit which could be seen a mile away. But when darkness came down there would come the opportunity to make himself more acquainted with the island west of the jetty, where the mass of buildings appeared to come down to the sea itself. Somewhere he might find a small row-boat.

The long dreary hours passed without incident. The sun at noon was tremendously hot and penetrated the shallow cave, so that it became difficult to find a yard of shade. To kill time he cleaned his two weapons with his handkerchief, and checked up the ammunition. There were eight rounds in the rifle and five in the automatic, and both weapons were working beautifully.

Watching the sea produced no hope in that direction. He could see occasional ships at a distance, but nothing came within many miles, and that smooth, colourful ocean became a mockery. He even dallied with the notion of swimming, but was soon brought to realize that such a venture would be plain suicide. No, his best hope was still a ship, and given sufficient food that miracle might happen one day.

But what of Valerie and Donkin? What lease of life had they. The thought was most painful.

By late evening McLean was as hungry as a wolf, for the fruit he had eaten had no lasting benefit. In addition his throat was parched. Greta had said nothing about drink, but he hoped she would realize his need for that. One thing seemed certain. She intended to keep her promise, otherwise something would have happened before now.

The sun was very low when suddenly he saw her coming over the rocky ridge. She had changed her clothing since he last saw her, and was carrying an out-size hand-bag, which looked as if it contained the answer to his prayers. A minute or two later she was at the cave entrance, breathing heavily.

"Did you think I wasn't coming?" she asked.

"I did not."

"Thanks for the compliment. Well, here's your nose-bag. I had to be careful, because Marco mounts guard over the kitchen as if it were a gold-mine."

She commenced to unload the hand-bag, dumping tin after tin on the sand. McLean checked off the items as they appeared.

"Bully beef, ham, sardines, bully again. Oh, this is marvellous! Butter, and home-made rolls. And a knife equipped with a tin-opener. Greta, you're a wizard. Is that the lot?"

Greta laughed and then with a flourish produced the final item. It was a large bottle of lager beer, still deliciously cold.

"It was all I could carry," she said modestly.

"It's far more than I dared hope for. Do you mind if I make a start?"

"Of course not. You must be famished."

McLean soon had the handy knife in operation, spreading out his coat to serve as a tablecloth. The rolls were new and the butter excellent. Greta smoked calmly as he made the rolls into sandwiches, and ate as one eats whose stomach has been rudely insulted in the past.

"I have been trying to find out something about your friends," she said, after a long silence. "But without success. Lombroso is in a bad temper about something. I don't know what. He was furious with Walther — who runs the launch — about something he had left behind. I thought he said 'birds' but perhaps I was mistaken. Anyway he said that Walther would have to go back and get them."

"Birds!" mused McLean. "It might be birds. Have you ever heard any birds — pigeons, for example?"

"No. I don't think there is a single bird on the island, except a few seagulls. Now will you tell me something?"

"That depends. What do you want to know?"

"Was it by accident that you knocked

my drink over on that night in London?"

"Do you think I did it purposely?"

"Yes. I don't think you are a clumsy man. Far from it."

McLean hesitated. Was this a trap, or was she impelled by nothing more than feminine curiosity?

"Why should I deliberately knock your drink over?" he asked.

"Perhaps to find out something about me — and Hendryk."

"Are you still in love with that man?"

"No. I was at first — genuinely. But we had a violent quarrel in Venice, and it changed everything. I realized that Lombroso had a hold over him that I could not break — that the organization still held him in their power. Sometimes he left me for weeks on end, and was never able to explain what he had been doing. I'm sorry he is in prison, because he was really a kind man. Now will you answer my question?"

"Yes. I wanted to find Hendryk Stein, because I had good reason to believe he was the man who called himself Baldock, and who rented that house where the dead man was found."

"Then you — you must have told the police?"

"You are not far wrong. Listen, Greta. I believe that murder was done in that house, by some subtle means. I believe that Hendryk Stein was not directly responsible, because otherwise he would not have begged Doctor Donkin to come to the house. Clearly he wanted to save Banner's life. But someone else may have had different ideas. Banner was a danger to the organization as you call it. His mouth had to be closed, and it was closed very effectively. Can you blame the police for taking the action they did?"

"No. I am beginning to understand. It was a bad day when I met Hendryk, and yet I thought it was the best day of my life. All I want now is a chance to get away from these dreadful people.

But somehow I know I won't. No one ever gets away. Always — always they have the last word."

"Never give up hope. What was that?"

It was the deep throb of a marine engine, in the direction of the lagoon, and very soon it was clear that the craft was moving away from them.

"Walther going back for the birds he forgot," said McLean. "He's German, of course?"

"Yes. Most of them are German, but there are a few Italians, and some mixed nationalities. Oh, there's one thing I forgot to tell you. There's an aeroplane here."

"I know."

Greta seemed surprised at this admission, but she said nothing.

"Is that how you came here?" asked McLean, still not willing completely to disclose all he knew.

"Yes. I was rung up that night at the hotel, after Hendryk had gone, and told to pack and wait for a car to pick me up. At first I refused, but I was told that if I didn't the police would arrest me. I asked who was speaking and was told it was Max. I had met Max previously, and knew him to be a friend of Hendryk. He used to be a pilot in the *Luftwaffe*. Finally I decided to do as I was told. The car called late at night. It contained Max and two other men. We motored through the night for hours to a lonely house not far from the sea, and the following evening I was driven in the car to a hangar where the aeroplane was concealed. There were four of us aboard, and we left one man behind us. Max piloted the plane."

"Was Doctor Donkin on that plane?"

"No, only members of the organization. But they were all strangers to me except Max."

"There was baggage, of course?"

"Oh yes — quite a lot."

"Any big item?"

"Yes. There was a long box, which took two men to carry. Oh, I see what you mean."

"Did you leave the hangar when you got here?"

"No. We went up a lot of steps, and through some rooms into a building at the rear of the villa. The men came afterwards with the box. You — you think that Doctor Donkin was in the box?"

"Yes. I'm almost certain of that, although he remembers nothing about it."

Greta sat for a few moments gazing in reflection at the fast-setting sun. The last doubt was removed from McLean's mind. Everything she had said convinced him that her contempt for the gang was no less than his own.

"I had better go now," she said. "It would not do to cause them to get suspicious. I'll bring you some more food tomorrow about the same time."

"Thank you," he said. "But be careful for your own sake. Just one thing more — have you seen a boat of any kind on the foreshore near the buildings?"

"Yes," she said. "There is a small boat drawn up on the beach near the new building which they call the 'Glasshouse'. I walked round there but was shooed off by the sentry. It didn't look very seaworthy, and was half full of water."

"Any oars?"

"I can't remember."

"All right. I'll look into that."

"Oh, don't go without me," she begged. "If it's possible to make a bid for freedom, give me a chance."

"I will, but don't bank on that. I can't think they would leave a seaworthy boat lying about. I'll tell you about it tomorrow."

"Yes — yes. But mind the sentry. He'll shoot if he sees you."

"I'll take care. Thanks for everything."

Greta held out her hand, which he gripped for a moment. Then she went hurrying across the sand and rocks, leaving him to his cogitations. Here he was, back again at the boring business of killing time. The business of the row-boat intrigued him, but it would be sheer lunacy to go prowling round the buildings on the headland until such time as most human beings would be in their beds. That meant hours yet, and even then there was that vigilant sentry to be taken into account.

In the ordinary way a few hours of lonely meditation wouldn't have come amiss, but meditation is not a pleasant occupation when the mind is troubled. He could not dismiss Donkin and Valerie from his mind. Bad as his own predicament was, theirs was infinitely worse. He imagined them in some dark and airless chamber, suffering the torments of hunger and thirst, and perhaps building false hopes on his ability to end their torture. It was natural that the image of Valerie should dominate that mental picture, for he knew that her doctor brother had the stamina of an ox. But Valerie was different. There was indeed nothing soft about her, but it was horrible to contemplate what might conceivably happen to her at the hands of the lawless gang who at the moment controlled her destiny.

The minutes and hours passed, and the bright stars and planets moved across the heavens. He recalled what Greta had said about the 'birds' and concluded that they were carrier pigeons used in emergency to take messages to the mainland. It was just another bit of evidence that the organization left nothing to chance. Then there was the mystery of the guarded 'Glasshouse'. That had a significance, but what?

Finally he decided to start on his quest. The half-moon was a blessing, for his electric torch was now almost exhausted and in danger of dying on him. Hiding the rifle in the cave, he took the pistol and moved in the direction of the buildings, and the foreshore on their farther side. His immediate objective was the row-boat which Greta had mentioned. In that was centred his sole hope.

On reaching the built-up area he avoided what appeared to him to be the more used passages and crept through narrow alleys and broken-down courtyards until he suddenly emerged on a narrow sandy beach, which went curving away in front of the big building, with its many windows, which he took to be the 'Glasshouse'. These windows were high above the heavily buttressed base of the building, and in two of them were lights, facing seawards. As he came under these he could hear the sound of music from above him, and he recognized it as 'Siegfried's Journey to the Rhine', played at full blast by a powerful radiogram. It was music much to his own liking, but he was surprised that anyone should choose the early hours of the morning in which to play it.

He saw now that immediately under the lower lighted windows there was a narrow gallery which appeared to go round the whole building, and suddenly at the left end of the gallery a man appeared shouldering a rifle. Instantly he dived under the shelter of the lower wall, dreading for a moment that he had been seen. But to his great relief nothing happened, and he could hear the sentry's footsteps between the blasts of the music, growing louder and then slowly fading away.

As yet there was no sign of the row-boat, but the end of the building cut across the curving beach and restricted his visibility to a hundred yards or so. Cautiously he made his way round the bastion, and a little later he came upon the boat, lying up close to the wall, and in a position where it was not likely to be seen by the perambulating sentry above him. It was a diminutive craft, built for but one pair of oars, and these were absent, as well as the metal rowlocks in which they worked. There were a few inches of water in the bottom of the boat, and this was all to the good since it had the effect of keeping the timbers water-tight. The music ceased and again he heard the footsteps of the sentry. Taking no chances he pressed his body close to the wall, and waited for the sentry to pass him.

Then again the music blared out. This time it was the 'Ride of the Valkyries', magnificently performed but loud enough to wake the dead. But he scarcely heard it, for his mind was now occupied with nautical possibilities. He had no doubt that the small craft was seaworthy, but what could one do without oars and rowlocks? As a substitute a narrow plank might suffice to get some forward movement on the boat, using it as one used a canoe paddle. If the calm weather held one might possibly make some point on the mainland, by dint of the most strenuous effort.

Finally he decided to leave this danger point, and go in search of a suitable plank. He waited for the sentry to pass again, and then hurried round the building, and continued along the beach, until he reached the jetty. Here he made his way through the arch where he and Donkin had waited prior to making their assault on the motor-boat. From the direction of the 'Glasshouse' there came the strains of the radiogram, otherwise all was silence and darkness, save where the moonbeams filtered through narrow spaces. But nowhere could he see a single piece of wood which would serve his purpose, and his sense of frustration grew apace.

Then suddenly he remembered the packing cases which he had seen in the room up the subterranean passage, close to Donkin's late prison. They were made up of just the right length of boards for his purpose, and he had no doubt he could wrench a couple of them apart.

Half an hour later he was climbing the steps which led to the chamber, with the torch now really at its last gasp. To his great relief the cases were still there. He chose two stout slats that were free of knots and blemishes, and quickly knocked them free with the muffled butt-end of the automatic pistol. Then, removing the nails, he made his way back through the hangar and out into the open air.

Back in the cave, with his improvised paddles, he worked out his programme. Much as he would have liked to get away at once, logic was against such a proceeding, for it wanted but a few hours to sunrise, and in that short time he could not hope to get far enough away from the island to avoid being seen, and overhauled. No, the attempt must be started immediately darkness fell, giving him seven or eight hours of sailing time before the all-revealing sun rose. There was, too, the question of food. Greta had promised to bring him a further supply, and if she still wished to go with him that was all to the good, for two paddles were preferable to one. There was the sentry to be considered, but he believed that if the boat were launched immediately the fellow had passed it, there would be time to get the boat round the point and out of his view before he completed his circuit.

Yes, the following night, half an hour after sunset would be zero hour, whatever the upshot. With that resolution fixed firmly in his mind he went to sleep, and did not awake until the sun was well up in the sky. He made a scanty meal, leaving a portion of the remaining food against the possibility of Greta being unable to keep her promise. Now the urge to get going was almost irrepressible. So many things could happen in the next few hours to spoil everything. That calm sea might be whipped up into ugly waves by a change in the weather conditions, or someone might take it into his head to remove the boat. Never in his life had his nerves been so much on edge.

13

THE sun had already dipped below the watery horizon when his doubts about Greta were banished. As before she carried that large handbag, bulging with the necessaries of life, and she waved her hand as she came into view, and almost ran across the intervening sand.

"Sorry I'm late," she gasped. "But I had to watch my step. I think Marco missed the rolls yesterday, so I had to leave them out of the menu. There you are — help yourself."

She passed McLean the heavy handbag, and sat on a rock while he examined the contents. They were much as before, including another bottle of lager.

"Have you eaten?" asked McLean.

"Yes — enormously. But you go ahead. You must be famished."

"Any news about the prisoners?"

"No. I don't know what's happening. They tell me nothing, and if I ask any questions I get no answers."

"Is the launch back?"

"Yes. It must have returned during the night. Aren't you going to eat anything?"

"No. All I want is a drink. Last night I found the rowboat."

"And the oars?"

"Unfortunately no."

"Then — then there's no chance of getting away?"

"A slender chance, but it involves some risk. The sentry is the danger. Are you still keen to leave?"

"Yes. I hate this place. But how can you leave without oars to row the boat?"

McLean reached behind a rock and produced the two wooden planks, the top parts of which he had cut away with his knife to fashion rough handles.

"Substitutes for oars," he said. "Have you ever paddled a canoe?"

"Yes. Oh, this is marvellous."

"Not so marvellous. Even if we get clear of the island we can't hope to make more than about two miles an hour, and the nearest point on the mainland must be twelve miles at least. If we should run into bad weather there is no knowing what might happen. It's dangerous, and it might be better if I went alone."

"No — No. You promised. Two of us could make twice the speed of one."

"Are you ready to come as soon as darkness settles down?"

"Yes. I don't need to go back to the house, as I've brought my jewellery with me. It's inside the pocket of the handbag. I was hoping this might happen. Look, it's getting dark already."

McLean nodded as he stared at the wonderful evening miracle in the western sky. Already the stars were appearing in the darker portion of the sky, and over all there hung a great and almost painful silence.

"Are you perfectly certain you want to take this risk?" he asked.

"Absolutely."

"Very well. We'll say no more about it. I propose to go round the south side of the island. I don't like that launch being in harbour, but I think the jetty will prevent our being seen by anyone on board. The sentry at the 'Glasshouse' is our chief problem. He perambulates round the narrow gallery about once every three minutes, and we have to get the boat afloat and round the point in that time if we want to avoid being seen and fired upon. That is the most ticklish bit of the whole programme. But I think it can be done, if we put every ounce into it — "

Suddenly Greta caught him by the sleeve, and pulled him farther inside the small cave.

"I — I thought I saw someone," she whispered. "Over there on the rocks — the way I came."

McLean peered round the rock in the fading light, praying that Greta was the victim of hallucination, but a few moments later his worst fears were realized, for over the rocks swarmed not one lone man, but half a dozen, spread out in line, and all carrying weapons.

"They must have followed you," he said grimly. "There's only one thing to do. Go out now, and pretend you have merely been taking a walk. Otherwise everything is lost. Try to meet me by the boat in half an hour's time. Go on — quick!"

"Must I?" she pleaded.

"It's our only chance. Please do as I say."

Greta hesitated for a moment, and then tipped the provisions from her handbag, and walked out into the open. The oncoming men stopped and waited for her. There was an altercation, but McLean could hear nothing of what was said. He did not believe that Greta would get away with her story, for the man who was arguing with her had snatched the handbag, and was looking inside it. It was significant, too, that all of them were armed. Why should they arm themselves against a single woman, unless they had reason to believe that she was engaged in aiding and abetting their enemies?

The outcome of the altercation was surprising. Suddenly Greta snatched the handbag and came running towards him at great speed. A rifle was raised, but lowered again on a shouted command. Greta, breathless, burst into the cave.

"It's no use," she gasped. "They — they wanted to know what I had done with the provisions. They mean to come here. Give me the pistol."

McLean shook his head as he picked up the loaded rifle. It was ironical to reflect that the little cave which had served him so well now looked like being his death-trap. Probably he could stave them off for a bit, for they could have no idea that he was armed, but it would merely delay the end. The light was still good enough for him to see all the oncoming men in detail. At about fifty yards distance they stopped and then two of them came forward, with small sign of trepidation.

"Keep behind me," he whispered to Greta. "I shall have to show my teeth."

"Where's the pistol?" she asked.

The two men were now far too close for his liking, and he aimed between their shoulders, and pressed the trigger of the rifle. The report in the enclosed space was terrific and the two men jumped like scalded cats, and then fired wildly into the cave. The bullets smashed themselves against the rock with savage howls. Then he felt Greta's hand in his side pocket, and the next moment the automatic pistol was in her hands.

"Put that back!" he said. "Don't be a fool. If you should hit one of them they'll kill you."

"They'll kill me anyway," she panted. "They told me so. That's why I ran back. You're not going to surrender, are you?"

"Not yet, anyway. Look out!"

A rain of bullets now entered the cave, and a small piece of metal struck McLean on the cheek and drew blood. It trickled down on to his white coat, and the sight of it brought a cry from Greta's lips.

"It's nothing," said McLean. "For Heaven's sake keep out of the line of fire, and put that pistol down. I may need it later."

Greta obeyed the first part of the order, but she still clung obstinately to the automatic, and McLean was far too occupied to take it from her by force. He expected another rain of bullets, but instead the party began to withdraw, and finally reached the cover of the rocks.

"Why have they done that?" asked Greta.

"I don't know. Possibly regard for their skins, but more likely to work out some better plan of campaign. Now I'll take that pistol."

Greta sighed as he took it from her

and put it back into his pocket. She then took McLean's handkerchief and wiped the blood from his cheek.

"Just a little scratch," she said. "I thought it was a bullet. When it gets a little darker couldn't we make a dash for the boat?"

"We might try. But at the moment it would be hopeless. There are half a dozen guns trained on us, and they can't all be bad marksmen. I think I'd like that bottle of beer. Will you open it?"

Greta did so and poured the contents into a mug which she had brought. McLean took it from her and drank deeply. Greta herself took what was left. Little by little the darkness came down, and then suddenly the cave was lit up by a long bright ray of light which came from the distant rocks.

"Damn!" he muttered. "I might have expected that. No sneaking away in the darkness now. Hullo, what's this?"

A lone figure was coming towards them, unarmed and waving a white handkerchief. As he drew nearer McLean recognized Lombroso. He stopped at about thirty yards distance.

"Listen, Ward!" he shouted. "Throw out your gun, and come outside. You haven't a dog's chance. If you refuse I'll blow you both to bits. Do you hear?"

"I hear," replied McLean.

"Then what's your answer?"

"I'll tell you in the morning. I need time to consider the proposition."

"I'm not prepared to give you any time."

"And I'm not prepared to give you my answer now."

"I'll give you ten minutes and then I'll come and gather up what's left of you."

McLean made no response and Lombroso went back to the rocks and disappeared from view.

"Was that just bluff?" asked Greta.

"I don't know. You should know Mr. Lombroso better than I. Is he given to bluster?"

"He's cunning and clever."

"I can well believe that. Ten minutes isn't long. I believe he means what he says. It's nearly dark too. Will you take a chance?"

"Is there one?"

"A slender one, as I said before. I believe he means to project a grenade or mortar shell at us, and the result might be horrible. That searchlight must be about a foot in diameter, and the distance is point blank."

"What are you talking about?"

"We'll take a chance. If I'm successful snatch up those two paddles and follow me. Bring that handbag too, and some of the provisions. Now stand by!"

He knelt down and rested the barrel of the rifle on a small projecting rock ledge, taking careful aim at the searchlight. Then he pressed the trigger and a heavy report reverberated through the cave. But the light still shone. Swearing under his breath he took a second aim. There was another shattering explosion and instantly the light went out, plunging everything into darkness.

"Come on!" he cried. "Got the paddles?"

"Yes."

Catching her hand he almost jerked her out of the cave, and then ran with all his speed well away to the left where there was temporary cover. From the direction of the rocks came flashes and explosions, and from nearer at hand the whine of bullets. Reaching the cover he stared into the darkness and saw before him an open space for about a hundred yards. Beyond that were frequent and considerable outcrops of rock, among which they could doubtless thread their way to the place where the boat lay.

"Once across that open space things will be easier," he whispered. "They're still shooting at the cave, which suggests they think we are still there. Ready?"

"Yes."

"Here goes!"

Off they went, Greta trying her best to cover up that revealing white suit with her darker attire. At every moment McLean expected bullets to start whizzing, but none came, and finally they were under cover again.

"So far so good!" he gasped. "I must have busted that searchlight completely. No more talking now. This way."

At that moment there was a bright flash away to their right, followed by a loud report and then, after a matter of seconds, a louder and quite different kind of explosion.

"What was that?" whispered Greta.

"That, I think, was Colonel Lombardo carrying out his threat. It's just as well we left that cave."

There was silence now as they made their way forward, broken only by a few sporadic rifle shots at a distance, and soon these ceased entirely, causing McLean to conclude that their escape from the cave had been discovered. Keeping up a rapid pace the couple were soon in the region of the citadel, and McLean hesitated a moment before he took the final perilous dive through the alleys which led to the little beach. Another enemy was threatening them now — the rising moon. Greta was breathing heavily — glad of a momentary respite, but in a very short time McLean was off again amid the ruins. He was within fifty yards of the beach when suddenly a man emerged from a doorway, and stood blocking the narrow passage. His mouth opened to utter a yell, but the butt of the rifle projected forcefully into his large stomach reduced the yell to a pitiful whimper, and he measured his length on the rocky ground. Greta gave a little gulp of horror as McLean caught her arm and almost swept her off her feet.

"Touch and go now," he whispered. "At the end of the passage we must watch out for the sentry."

In a matter of seconds they were at this point, with the beach before them, and the 'Glasshouse' in full view. The row-boat was where McLean had last seen it, but the little gallery around which the sentry did his turn of duty was empty, so far as he could see.

"Can't we go?" asked Greta.

"Not yet. We must wait for the sentry. I think I can hear him."

The rather slow footsteps grew louder, and then the sentry came into sight. All his movements were leisurely — obviously a different man from the one McLean had last seen. He even stopped at one point, and scanned the beach in both directions. McLean's nerves were on edge. How long would the fool stay there? At any moment he expected to hear a commotion in his rear, as evidence that the corpulent man had recovered from the effects of the rifle butt. Then at last the sentry continued his tour.

"Now for it," whispered McLean. "We have to get the boat in the water and round that point in a few minutes. Here comes the damned moon!"

They rushed at full speed towards the row-boat, and on this occasion Greta did not lag. The small craft was turned on its side and the water tipped out. Then, tugging on the stern, they dragged her down to the sea.

"Get in," whispered McLean. "I'll follow."

The moment Greta was aboard, he gave the boat a final push and then scrambled inside. The two improvised paddles were put into action, and the boat moved out to sea at fair speed. But the moon had now lifted from a low-lying cloudbank, and the headland which promised them shelter seemed farther away than before. McLean prayed that the leisurely sentry would find something to hold his attention at the rear part of the 'Glasshouse', but while he was still a hundred yards from comparative safety the fellow appeared. Glancing over his shoulder McLean saw the sentry unsling his rifle.

"Get into the bottom of the boat," he said to Greta. "Go on. He's going to open fire. I'll try to get out of range."

But Greta behaved as if she were

311

stone deaf, and used her paddle at even greater speed. McLean saw the sentry's rifle go to his shoulder, and instantly he grabbed Greta and pulled her to the bottom of the boat. There came a succession of flashes from the rifle, and two or three of the bullets smashed through the side of the boat. Then the sentry, having used up his whole magazine, began to reload. McLean put down the paddle and picked up the rifle which was close to his hand. The sentry was in full moonlight as he got the sights nicely aligned on his shoulders. McLean pressed the trigger, and the sentry staggered, dropped his weapon and fell backwards.

But this was only the beginning of the trouble, for as McLean laid down the rifle and picked up the paddle, two of the large windows above the parapet sprang into light, and over the ledge of one of them there appeared the unmistakable barrel of a machine-gun. It opened fire with a terrific tattoo, and in a matter of seconds the bows of the small boat were reduced to matchwood, and the water came inboard with a swirling rush. Greta, who was still crouching low, turned her head to McLean. It was agonized, and in the bright moonlight he saw the cause. She had been shot through the neck.

"My God!" he cried. "Greta — !"

The machine-gun was silent as the boat heeled over, and disappeared from view. McLean saw Greta quite close to him. She was incapable of physical action and was sinking when he grabbed her under the arms, and commenced to swim towards the beach. Before he could reach it four men came running to the point for which he was making, and the moment he was in shallow water two of them ran into the sea, and took the mortally wounded Greta from him. The remaining two waited until he stepped on dry land and then grabbed him roughly, cursing him in voluble German, only part of which he understood. He was not permitted to see what was happening to Greta, as he was booted and propelled to the path down which he had come, with the business end of a pistol pushed into his back.

It was all over. His little spell of liberty was at an end. Luck which had served him so well had now deserted him completely. The 'organization' was on top again, and looked very much like remaining in that enviable position. It was soon fairly obvious that he was being taken to the villa, and he had good reason to believe that his reception there would be far from cordial.

14

IN the lounge at the villa Lombroso had just returned from the unsuccessful operations at the cave. Roy, who was useless in such situations, had been drinking heavily, and was slightly incoherent.

"What happened?" he asked thickly.

Lombroso made no answer until he himself had taken a long drink of neat whisky.

"He was hidden in the small cave with that bitch," he growled. "It looked a simple enough matter, but the swine had a rifle and approach was difficult. Finally I decided to blast them out and I sent a man back for the small mortar, and a couple of shells. But before we could open-up Ward put the searchlight out of action with a well-aimed shot."

"Well?"

"They slipped away in the darkness, and the men are still searching for them."

"Well, it's only a matter of time. But where did he get the rifle?"

"That's clear enough now. He was never on that motor-boat with Donkin. When Donkin went for help he must have landed his companion somewhere along the lagoon, armed with Luigi's rifle. All this time he's been lying up, probably hoping to attract some passing craft."

"And our charming little Greta met him, and decided to join forces with him?"

"You needn't rub it in," said Lombroso. "When I lay hands on her I'll make her pay for this treachery. What was that?"

"I heard nothing," mumbled Roy.

"You wouldn't. You're half drunk. That was a rifle shot, and there it is again."

He hurried through one of the casement windows, and stood listening on the veranda. There came another shot, and then silence.

"Something is happening over by the 'Glasshouse'," he said.

Roy, walking unsteadily, came and joined him. For a time there was no sound, and then suddenly there came the rattle of a machine-gun.

"Funny!" mutttered Roy. "The only machine-gun we have is in the 'Glasshouse'."

Lombroso hurried to the internal telephone, and moved a switch.

"What's happening over there?" he bellowed.

Roy watched his face as he listened, and then Lombroso hung up the receiver, and gave a little sigh of relief.

"We've got 'em," he muttered. "They were trying to get away in a small row-boat that was lying on the beach. Who the hell left that thing lying about I should like to know?"

"But what happened?" asked Roy.

"The boat was sunk and the occupants are swimming ashore. They will be brought here. Leave that whisky alone, you old soak. We are about to enjoy a pleasant reunion. Some black coffee will do you good."

He pushed the bell and Marco entered the room.

"Strong black coffee, Marco," he said.

"*Si, Signore*. Did you hear the shooting?"

"Of course I heard it. Hurry!"

Marco brought the coffee with commendable promptitude, and at the same time he brought an English newspaper.

"What's this?" asked Lombroso.

"Walther gave it to me. He brought some papers back in the launch. There is something in it which is interesting. This picture. It is very like Mr. Ward, isn't it?"

Lombroso gave one look at the reproduced photograph, and then uttered a cry of astonishment.

"Look at that!" he said to Roy. "Who is it?"

Roy shook his head foolishly.

"It's Ward, without his little moustache, and side whiskers. But his name isn't really Ward — nor Donkin. It's Chief Inspector McLean, of Scotland Yard."

"What!"

"Listen. It says underneath that the C.I.D. is perturbed by the strange disappearance of one of its most famous officials, Chief Inspector McLean, some days ago, while engaged in an important investigation. That's enough to make your hair curl, isn't it?"

Roy caressed his almost bald scalp, and cackled amusedly, not at his companion's attempt at wit, but at this quite extraordinary piece of news.

"Scotland Yard has every — hic — reason to be perturbed," he said. "And what liars they all are. Quite shocking when you come to think of it. What exactly do you propose to do with this luminary of the British Police?"

"I don't know. Actually it isn't for me to decide."

"So the matter goes to a higher court?"

"It has to — now that they know. I wanted to keep the whole thing quiet, but there's no hushing it up now. After all it was they who brought about the kill."

"You mean *will* bring it about. Well, thank God the affair is at an end. Now we shall be able to resume our quiet but pleasant life. Good coffee this. Marco is to be congratulated."

There were now sounds from without, and then from within. Lombroso sat down in an arm-chair, facing the door, and after a short rat-tat the door opened and into the room came McLean, with a guard on either side of him. He looked a sorry figure in his dirty, drenched, bloodstained suit, and Lombroso grinned maliciously as they came face to face.

"Good evening, Mr. Ward, or should I say, Inspector McLean?" he said. "You seem to have had the worst of some adventure."

"I congratulate you upon the extent of your knowledge," replied McLean. "Your intelligence service must be good."

"Better than you know. Where is my sister-in-law, who aided and abetted you?"

"She should be here in a few moments."

"Good! It will be interesting to hear what she has to say about this matter."

"It might be if she could say it."

"What do you mean?"

"She is dying, if not already dead."

Lombroso turned to the two guards, and questioned them in rapid German. They could do no more than corroborate McLean's statement. Then he turned to McLean, and wagged an admonishing finger.

"I hold you responsible," he raved. "If she should die then you will be held accountable. And that is not all. There is Luigi who was drowned, and also the sentry at the 'Glasshouse' who is seriously wounded. You will be tried for your crimes and punished accordingly."

"And who are to be my judges?" asked McLean. "You and Doctor Roy, I presume? You will at least afford me the services of a competent lawyer, I hope?"

"I think if I were in your position, Inspector," put in Roy, "I shouldn't indulge in cheap facetiousness. This is not a place where such stuff is appreciated."

"Then why practise it yourselves, with your amusing talk of trials. You're not concerned about the death and wounding of your hirelings, nor even of the sad fate of Greta. What you are concerned about is the reason for this strange set-up, and the fear that what you are doing may be discovered. Let us at least talk sense."

Lombroso brandished his fist, but was prevented from making any rejoinder by the arrival of another party. It comprised Greta and three men, one of whom was Walther, the thick-set captain of the launch. Two of the men who were carrying Greta laid her on a couch. Her eyes were closed, and a scarf had been wrapped round the wound in her neck. Roy, now apparently quite sober, pushed past Lombroso, and untied the bloodstained scarf. He gave a little grunt, and felt for Greta's pulse.

"Hopeless!" he said.

"Not — dead?" asked Lombroso.

"Within an ace. There's nothing I can do. Nothing anyone can do."

"Is she conscious?"

Roy rolled back one of Greta's eyelids, and to his obvious surprise the pupils of both eyes came to view. They stared strangely for a few moments until they found a focus on Roy's cadaverous face, and then the lips began to move.

"What's she saying?" asked Lombroso.

Roy shook his head, and Lombroso winced as blood suddenly flowed through the parted lips of the dying woman. Then came a sound that was like the sighing of a fitful wind, and

McLean, watching the lips, knew what she was trying to say.

"No escape — Robert. They — always — win. Tried — help — Oh — where are you?"

The final despairing cry brought McLean close to the couch. One of the guards made to grab him, but Lombroso waved him back almost fiercely. McLean put the scarf round the horrible wound in her slim little neck, and gripped one of her hands.

"I'm here," he said.

For a moment consciousness was present in her eyes, and the lips trembled. But it was her last earthly moment save one — that curious rattle in her throat that McLean had heard before in his life. That last little smile stayed on her dead face. McLean placed the limp hand across her breast and turned away. Roy quickly took his place and satisfied himself that life was extinct.

"That's all," he said, and closed the staring eyes.

Lombroso shrugged his shoulders, and did not look again at McLean.

"Take him away," he called. "Lock him up with his friends, and put a guard on the lower door. I want no more accidents."

Instantly the two men closed in on McLean, and he was escorted out of the house and through devious pathways that were unfamiliar to him, since he had taken care to avoid that part of the citadel. His mind was full of the tragedy which had overtaken Greta who had done so much to ease his predicament during the last two days. Then suddenly he saw before him the ancient basilica, with its lovely dome and soaring tower. The lower part was in shadow, but the tower stood out clear in the moonlight. Soon he realized that this was the objective of his guards, and he remembered Lombroso's reference to 'his friends'. It meant that Valerie and her brother were alive, and that a reunion was at hand. There was joy in that thought, mitigated by the sense of his own futility on their behalf.

They entered the building by a side-door and, when the keys had been found, ascended the spiral staircase to the lofty belfry. Here the door was unlocked and opened, and he was unceremoniously projected into the dark room, where he caught his foot in some projection and fell heavily, while the door clanged behind him to an accompaniment of raucous laughter from his late guard.

"Mac!"

He looked up from his prone position, and saw a vague face hovering over his own. He could see none of the details but the voice was unmistakable.

"Valerie!" he said. "Not a very graceful entrance I'm afraid."

"Are you all right?"

"Yes — but a trifle battered. Is Ian there?"

Donkin put out his hand and gripped McLean's warmly, helping him to his feet.

"I'm very much here," growled

Donkin. "Your eyes will get adjusted in a few moments. It's always damnably dark here until the moon gets round a bit. What's the worst news?"

"The worse news is that I've failed. Tonight I made an attempt to get away in a small row-boat, but they got a machine-gun working and shot the boat to bits."

"You — you didn't get hit?" asked Valerie anxiously.

"No; but my companion was killed."

"Companion?" asked Donkin.

"Lombroso's brother's mistress. By the way his name is not really Lombroso, but Stein. His brother is the gentleman who called on you on that memorable evening and induced you to visit that dying man."

"Baldock!" said Donkin.

"Yes — Baldock, who is now in prison waiting for you to identify him."

Donkin gave a short laugh.

"I've a notion that that appointment is going to be indefinitely postponed," he said.

"But tell us about the woman," pleaded Valerie.

"Didn't you meet her?"

"No."

"She was brought here when Stein was arrested, in order that she should not be interrogated. She liked Lombroso no better than we do, and he hated her for winning his brother away from him. So she and I had a mutual desire — to get away from this place as quickly as possible. It was she who put me on to the row-boat, but it had no paddles, and so there was a delay. I fabricated some paddles from slats of wood, and tonight we made the attempt. It ended in tragedy. I had disposed of a sentry and we were rounding the 'Glasshouse' when a machine-gun was brought into action through one of the windows. Greta was shot through the neck and the boat sunk. I managed to get her to land, but she died in the villa while I was being questioned by Lombroso."

"We heard the shooting," said Donkin, "and wondered what it was all about."

"What was she like?" asked Valerie.

"Fairly young — about thirty. A genuine blonde, but a trifle synthetic, due probably to having acted in films. But she was a brave woman — and not mixed up in this strange business. All she wanted was to be a film star."

"What do you mean by the 'Glass-house'?" asked Donkin.

"It's a big building, facing the sea, with many large modern-type windows. An armed sentry is on duty there day and night. It is, in my opinion, the key to the mystery of this island."

"Couldn't the woman tell you anything about it?" asked Donkin.

"No. She was not allowed to go near it, but I gathered that Lombroso and that villainous Doctor Roy are not the top men in the outfit. They take their orders from their superiors, who I believe live in the 'Glasshouse' and are protected by a murderous bodyguard."

"And you have no idea what is taking place here?"

"No. Whatever the secret it is most

carefully guarded. Greta invariably referred to the gang as the 'organization' and it appears to have a number of agents. They use a launch to run between here and the mainland, and they seem to have established a pigeon post for urgent and vital messages."

"Yes, there are pigeons," said Valerie. "You can hear them early in the morning — not far from here."

McLean, whose eyes had become adjusted to the gloomy chamber, was now able to take in the details of the place.

"Pretty grim," he said. "No place to rest, except the floor, and that none too sanitary. What can you see from the window?"

"Only a courtyard. The view seaward is almost completely obstructed by those buildings higher up the hill. But look for yourself."

McLean found that he could just see through the window, with its single iron bar. There was room on either side of the bar to push his head through.

It was, as Donkin had said, a very restricted view, except in one direction where he could see a long corridor of moonlit sea, in the direction of the mainland, across which, with better luck he and Greta would now be making their way.

As he gazed about him the moon breasted the buildings across the courtyard, and shone obliquely into the room. A full hundred feet below he could see the stone-flagged courtyard, with absolutely nothing between him and the ground except a narrow ledge which seemed to go round the tower, for no particular reason, but merely an æsthetic effort on the part of the original builder.

When he turned away it was to find the chamber well-lighted and his two companions equally well illuminated. What he saw shocked him. Donkin's eyes were sunken and bloodshot, and his normally muscular and robust figure drooped visibly. Valerie was in no better condition. Her wonderfully fresh complexion had vanished, and the smile that had been so wont to play about her fine mouth was no longer in evidence. Her cheeks were pallid, and she was leaning against her brother as if for physical support.

"What's this?" he asked. "Are you both ill?"

"Man, have you never seen starvation at work?" asked Donkin. "We've had no food since we were brought here. Only a jug of water each day. What about yourself? There's blood all over you."

"That's nothing. Some came from a scratch on my cheek, and some from Greta's wound. Why are they starving you?"

"Because we weren't prepared to talk as much as they would like. They wanted to know too much."

"About me, perhaps?"

"Yes," said Donkin. "I had to pretend that you were my brother. That seemed to save a lot of explanation, but it was clear that Lombroso never believed it. Valerie, of course, backed me up. But still they had doubts."

"Well, their doubts are settled. They know who I am. It was in a newspaper. Somebody at headquarters slipped up and gave the news of my disappearance to an enterprising journalist, who lost no time in getting my photograph. I saw the newspaper lying on a table when I was taken to the villa."

"That must have shaken them," said Donkin.

"Not much. They are now so sure of themselves."

"No — not dead sure," said Donkin. "What is troubling them is just how we came to be here. They suspect a serious leakage in their organization, and want to know who is responsible, and how far it has gone."

"And you told them nothing?"

"Of course not. We thought that so long as they believed others might know of the existence of this island they might refrain from doing us, and you, any serious injury."

McLean shook his head. The injury was being done. A few more days of starvation would reduce them to utter helplessness. Valerie was looking at him, waiting for his observations on the situation.

"First things first," he said. "And food is the first thing so far as you two are concerned. There's nothing to be lost now by concealing anything. I propose to do a deal with Lombroso. It's possible he may accept."

"What sort of deal?" asked Donkin.

"I'll undertake to tell him by what means I came here, and also by what means Valerie knew where to come, on condition that he gives us a square meal first."

"Do you think he'll fall for that?"

"He'll have to if he wants the information. Is anyone likely to come here again tonight?"

"No. The water supply is usually replenished early in the morning," said Valerie.

"Then we'll wait until morning. Let's

sit down and try to get some rest."

They sat on the dirty floor huddled together, Valerie between the two men, with her head inclined towards McLean, and it was strange that despite the wretchedness of their position, and the hopeless outlook before them, McLean was aware of a thrill of satisfaction. Perhaps it was because Valerie's warm hand had fallen upon his own, and showed every intention of staying there.

15

IT was about seven o'clock the next morning that footsteps were heard coming up the staircase.

"The guards!" said Donkin. "They're bringing the water."

McLean rose to his feet, gently pushing the sleeping Valerie towards her brother.

"You stay and rest," he said to Donkin. "I'll deal with them. Do they speak English?"

"Yes — one of them."

From outside came grumbling voices, in Italian, about having to climb the blasted staircase, and then the door opened, and into the room came a man with a large jug of water, while the other stayed near the door.

"I want you to take a message to Colonel Lombroso," said McLean to the man who carried the water.

"I take no messages," he growled.

"You'll take this one," said McLean, "or the Colonel will deal with you when he hears about it. It's a message he wants to receive. Tell him Inspector McLean has important information for him, and that it is urgent. Is that clear?"

"Yes," growled the man.

"Repeat the message."

The fellow repeated it, word for word, but with some trouble over the surname.

"Good enough!" said McLean.

They watched the heavy door being closed on them, and heard the working of the key in the lock. Then came retreating footsteps, and silence. Valerie, who was now fully awake, was doing her best to improve her appearance with the aid of various toilet articles contained in her handbag.

"It's a difficult problem even to look human," she complained. "Mac, have you had a look at yourself recently?"

"No, and I'd rather not."

"Oh, but you must. Come on — be brave."

She handed him her little mirror, in which he gave one look, and then turned his head away with a grimace. Valerie took the mirror from him, with a little laugh of amusement, and continued to wrestle with her mass of hair.

"I thought food was the most pressing question," she said. "But I'm not sure that I wouldn't place a hot bath and a hair 'do' first. This comb will soon be as toothless as a newborn infant."

"What about a drink?" asked Donkin. "We have only one mug. Most unhygienic. Or shall we wait for the coffee and repast which may arrive later?"

"You don't think Lombroso will accept my proposal?" asked McLean.

"I wouldn't care to bank on it. Valerie, for heaven's sake, stop breaking up that comb. Mac and I may need it later."

Valerie shook her hair at him, put the comb and other things back into her handbag, and then stood up. She would have fallen had not McLean gone to her assistance.

"Steady!" he said.

"I'm all right. Just a bit weak at the knees. Mac, lift me up to the window. I'd like to have a look outside."

McLean did as she asked, and she pushed her head between the central iron bar and the wall.

"Glory!" she said. "It's a long way down. But what wouldn't I give to be down there, out of this filthy cage. Couldn't we tear up our clothing or something and make a rope. This old bar wouldn't take much removing."

"And what would you do when you got down?" asked her brother.

"Just run around for a bit, until I was recaptured. It would certainly be a change."

"You wouldn't run far," said McLean. "There's an armed man down there, although you may not see him. How much longer am I to hold you up here?"

"No longer. You can rest your poor muscles."

McLean let her down to the floor, and then borrowed the mug which Donkin had been using. He found the water cold and delicious.

"Now me," said Valerie. "I don't place much faith in coffee, and eggs and bacon."

But she had scarcely finished drinking when from below there came sounds which caused Donkin to go to the door.

"There's someone coming up," he said excitedly. "More than one person."

McLean could now hear the footsteps, which rang hollow in the enclosed space of the spiral staircase, but what they portended was yet in doubt. A minute or two later the door opened and into the room came Lombroso, Roy, and the two guards whom they had seen before. The two hirelings stayed near the door, but Lombroso and Roy advanced a yard or two.

"So you got my message?" asked McLean.

"I did," replied Lombroso. "But I cannot imagine what valuable information you can have for me. Perhaps you will be a bit more explicit."

"Certainly. But in the first place I should like to know whether it is your intention to starve me and my friends to death?"

"I did not come here to discuss my intentions. Don't waste my time. Say what you have to say."

"We need food — and we need it badly. Are you not anxious to find out how we discovered this island?"

"Not now. It was different while you were at large, but the circumstances have changed."

"In what way have they changed?"

"Until a short time ago you were a pseudonym, but now your identity is beyond dispute."

"Does that ease your mind?"

"It satisfies my curiosity."

McLean laughed and shook his head.

"I don't think so, or you would not be here, and we should not be in danger of starving. Even condemned criminals are given meals."

"Our food here is limited. I do not see why it should be wasted on people who have caused us so much trouble."

"Then you don't wish to hear what I have to say?"

Lombroso looked at Roy, but Roy did not appear to be so disinterested as his companion, and McLean felt that he was very close to swallowing the bait. Roy gazed at Lombroso over his glasses as if to say, "Don't be a fool. Hear what the fellow has to say."

"All right," said Lombroso. "What is the proposal?"

"Send us up some food — plenty of it — and I'll tell you exactly how I got here, despite all the precautions you have taken to keep this place secret."

"All right. Go ahead."

"Oh no. The food first — the information afterwards."

"Why should I trust you?"

"No reason at all. But those are the terms. If you carry out your part I give you my word of honour I'll carry out mine. One would imagine I am asking for the moon."

Lombroso looked again at Roy, and Roy inclined his head.

"Very well," he said. "But if you break your promise, I'll find a way to make you regret it."

"It's a deal," said McLean. "But get the food here quickly, please. Then come back in an hour."

Lombroso nodded and he and his party then departed. Donkin laughed and clapped McLean on the back.

"It worked," he said. "But he'll be disappointed with the information he gets. He's looking for a traitor when there isn't one, and he'll feel he has been tricked."

"Who cares what he feels once we

have the food? But actually he may feel relieved to know that there has been no treachery. Perhaps I should have stipulated the kind of food we expect to get."

"You're a hard man, Mac," laughed Donkin. "Oh Lord, I've almost forgotten what food tastes like."

"I haven't," said Valerie. "I'm going to eat till I bust — against future emergency."

Half an hour passed, and then came the familar sound of approaching footsteps. This time it was Marco from the villa and another man. Marco carried a huge tray, on which was a vast assortment of food — rolls and butter, a big plated dish which was half full of fried sausages, and slices of ham, some fruit, and three plates with knives and forks. The second man carried a smaller tray on which was a very large coffee-pot, and three cups.

"Where's the sugar and milk?" asked McLean.

"Sugar and milk very short," replied Marco.

"Well, we must make do."

"I brought more than I was told," murmured Marco. "A man must eat."

McLean took this as an invitation for some kind of a tip. The only money he had was drenched English pound-notes, which previously he had removed from his own clothing. He took three of these and handed them to Marco.

"Two for you — one for your friend," he said.

"*Gratzie, Signore!*" said Marco, with a grin.

He was departing when McLean called him back.

"Five more notes when you come again, Marco," he whispered.

Marco nodded and then went out with his companion.

The feast began without a moment's delay. With nowhere to put the tray and coffee, they squatted on the floor in Japanese fashion, and within a quarter of an hour every atom of food and drink vanished.

"Not wise to eat so big a meal after a long fast," muttered Donkin. "Hope it stays down."

"Don't be beastly!" said Valerie. "Oh dear, I'm so tired. I think I'll have a little nap. Thanks, Mac, for the most wonderful meal I've ever had."

"Don't thank me," said McLean. "Thank Marco. That astute gentleman was out for a tip."

Valerie was asleep in a few moments, and McLean and Donkin made their combined coats into a pillow, with Donkin's drier garment next to her head. She did not wake while this was being done.

"Poor kid!" said Donkin. "What would I not give to get her safely out of here. Mac, what's your opinion of the situation?"

"I wish I could say something soothing, but I'm damned if I can see any way out of it. It isn't simply a case of escaping from this room, but of escaping from the island. We've made two attempts and failed. The odds against a third attempt succeeding are greater than ever."

"But where can it end?"

McLean looked at the sleeping form of Valerie.

"It could end in a firing squad," he said in a low voice.

"You think they would go as far as that?"

"Why not? Dead men tell no tales. Looked at from their point of view it is the only sensible thing to do."

"Then why didn't they do it at once?"

"I can think of two reasons. The first is that they were intent on finding the flaw in the organization which permitted me to get here — not guessing that it was due to pure chance."

"Until you tell them it was? Isn't that a mistake, Mac? Once they know they are safe won't they finish the whole thing the way you said?"

"I intend to leave them in doubt."

"Ah, I thought so. What's the second reason?"

"Lombroso holds me responsible for the death of Greta, and dropped the hint that I might be tried for my crime."

"What damned nonsense!"

"Yes, but there have been such nonsensical trials staged for no other reason than to salve someone's conscience. It's happening in a great number of countries."

"But here they can have no jurisdiction. It would be the cheapest and most transparent farce. Lombroso doesn't look that sort of idiot to me. If he wants our blood all he has to do is stick us up against the wall, and no one would be any the wiser."

"He lacks the authority. There is someone behind him who finally calls the tune, and it is that mysterious person, or persons, who will decide our fate. I have an idea that decision will not be long delayed."

It was not often that McLean expressed himself with such grimness, and Donkin, casting a glance at his sleeping sister, bit his lip at the dismal outlook.

"The condemned men ate a hearty meal," he quoted. "Do you think we shall get another?"

McLean had no reply to that. Never before in his life had he been in such a sorry plight, and he felt his ignominy acutely. He could have borne it better but for the presence of Valerie, for his career had been such as to embrace a large element of danger, and on more than one occasion he had taken his life in his hands, but never had the tables been turned on him more completely. Nor had he paused to examine the close relationship between himself and the sister of his best and oldest friend, in whose company he was always happy, and whose qualities were such as to arouse his deepest admiration. The love of another woman, which had come to nothing, had had the effect of damping down the amatory fires of his youth, and he had succeeded in persuading himself that in his work he would find all the excitement and satisfaction he needed. But now that illusion was being blown sky-high. Valerie was no less attractive and enchanting than that other woman, and even more courageous. Why had he taken so long to realize that fact? Stealing a glance at the sleeping figure he inwardly cursed his folly in not jerking himself out of the deep rut of his own digging long before this. If he and Donkin were put to death what would become of Valerie, if, as he thought, she should be spared? Unconsciously he uttered a little groan, and Donkin stared at him.

"Did you say something, Mac?" he asked.

"No. I was just thinking — and thinking doesn't get me very far."

"Nor me," said Donkin sombrely.

A full hour was to pass before Lombroso put in an appearance, and by this time Valerie had finished her doze, and looked the better for it. As before Lombroso was accompanied by Roy, and two of the guards.

"Well, you've made a nice clearance," he said, with a glance at the empty dish. "Now, Inspector, we'll have the facts. No inventions, please."

"I've no need to invent anything. I promised to tell you how I got here. Well, it's quite simple. I came with some of your hirelings on the plane which left Tadmarsh Manor, with Greta on board, and Doctor Donkin, too, I think."

Lombroso looked at him incredulously.

"That's a lie," he said. "It was an impossibility."

"Oh no. I was in the luggage compartment, and I had to hang on to the door to prevent a man named Max from putting the luggage in it. Finally, he came to the conclusion that the door was jammed, and the luggage was dumped outside."

"I don't believe it."

"I think he is telling the truth," said

Roy. "Max told me about the jammed door, and went to attend to it the next day. He was surprised to find the door in fair order."

"If so, then tell me how you came to know about Tadmarsh Manor?" said Lombroso.

"Your brother gave that away," said McLean. "Oh, not deliberately. In the hotel where he stayed he kept a typewriter, and was always careful to write letters to you in code. But he made the mistake of using the machine to type the address, and it was recorded on the carbon ribbon. I found that ribbon, and went to Tadmarsh with some assistants. There I found the plane, and was trapped in it. Now you know the truth."

Lombroso was silent for a few moments while he cogitated over McLean's statement.

"It doesn't explain everything," he said. "What about Miss Donkin? She could not have been with you on the plane. By what means did she get here?

Who gave her that information?"

"I did," said Donkin. "After your gang kidnapped and doped me, I was taken to a house from which I managed to escape for a short time. I got as far as a telephone box and telephoned my sister."

"Telling her you were being brought here?" asked Lombroso.

"Yes. I had overheard a conversation to that effect, and wanted it passed on to McLean."

Lombroso turned to Valerie, who had been listening intently.

"Was that information ever passed to McLean?" he asked.

Valerie saw the warning in McLean's eyes, and did exactly what he hoped she would do.

"I left a message at Scotland Yard," she said. "But McLean never got it. He was already on his way to Tadmarsh."

"A written message?"

"Yes — the message as received from my brother."

"You're lying!" snarled Lombroso.

"Very well. You are not bound to believe it. I don't care whether you do or not."

"If you are telling the truth why has no action been taken by Scotland Yard? In the newspaper it said that Scotland Yard was puzzled by the Inspector's disappearance."

"My dear Colonel," said McLean. "Do you imagine that Scotland Yard is in the habit of confiding in newspaper reporters? I think you will shortly be able to check Miss Donkin's statement. Anyway, that seems to settle our bargain."

Here Doctor Roy gave a little titter, as if he were greatly amused.

"Did you say something?" asked McLean icily.

"No, I never make important pronouncements, but I think the Colonel has one to make."

All eyes now went to Lombroso.

"Yes," he said. "I am instructed to inform you that you are all charged with trespass, espionage, and murder, and that you will be tried at three o'clock this afternoon."

At this solemn statement Donkin burst into mocking laughter, which caused Roy to peer at him as if he doubted his sanity.

"Forgive me, gentlemen," said Donkin. "But just whom are we supposed to have murdered?"

"Luigi Costello, by shooting him, and Greta Borch, who died as the result of her abduction — "

"Really, Colonel," remonstrated McLean. "I expected something a little less idiotic from you? Are you scared of what may possibly happen in the near future that you must find infantile excuses for your conduct. Where is this little farce to take place, and who will conduct the orchestra?"

"That you will soon discover. I, personally, do not find this a laughing matter, but the mad English seem to have a sense of humour all their own."

"And that includes the Scots," put in

Roy. "Colonel, I think that takes care of everything."

Lombroso nodded, and the party then left the chamber.

"The swine!" muttered Donkin. "I suppose they're in earnest?"

"It looks very much like it. It would be foolish for us to think otherwise."

"But this rubbish about a trial — I still don't understand it. Can there be some catch in it? Do they imagine that they may wring some last-minute confession from us?"

"About what?"

"I don't know, but they may have something in their minds. And by whom was Lombroso instructed to deliver his droll pronouncement?"

"That will probably emerge this afternoon," said McLean. "Valerie, that wasn't true what you said about leaving Ian's message at Scotland Yard?"

"No. I thought, from your expression, that you might want me to say that."

"I did, but I didn't think you would read my thoughts."

"Not often," she replied with a smile. "Mac, I suppose this fake trial will go against us?"

McLean hesitated.

"No fibbing," she begged. "Treat me like a grown-up. Actually I've never believed that we should get away from here, so I'm prepared for anything."

"We are bound to be found guilty — at least, Ian and I," said McLean.

"And I may be acquitted?"

"Oh, for heaven's sake let's not anticipate — " interrupted Donkin.

"Why not?" asked Valerie. "I don't like having things rushed on me. Perhaps, after the trial. I may be taken from you. I want to think things out calmly — in case the worst happens."

"What do you mean?"

"I mean if you and Mac are found guilty and killed, and I am acquitted. I don't want to be acquitted — not in those circumstances. Don't you understand?"

Donkin came and took her firmly by the shoulders, gazing intently at her.

"Listen, Val," he said. "I won't insult your intelligence by trying to pretend that our situation isn't desperate. For Mac and I they may be worse than desperate. They have it weighed up for us — for me because I might be able to identify Lombroso's brother, and for Mac because he is what he is. But you have done them no harm — "

"That's what I'm saying. Because of that I may be acquitted, or sentenced to stay here alone, at their pleasure, or for their pleasure. I don't want life at that price, and I won't have it. You must tell me what to do, while there is a chance — before they part us, as they may do when the trial is over. You've got that sharp little penknife. If you showed me how to — how to — "

She stopped as Donkin turned his head away from her, so overcome that he was afraid of the dark earnestness in her eyes. McLean, scarcely less affected, came and took her away.

"Steady!" he murmured. "Things are never quite as bad as our imagination may make them. We should still be thinking of life, not of death. There is just a slender chance that my people may be taking action. It's just possible that Sergeant Brook may have made some arrests at Tadmarsh, and that some of the gang may be induced to talk. Failing that one of us may have a brain-wave which might save the situation."

"You mean — *you* might, because both Ian and I are bankrupt in the ideas department. Oh, Mac, it's terrible to think that the two people I love most in the world — "

She stopped as McLean's lips quivered a little.

"I should have said 'liked'," she corrected. "Oh no, it's true. I like hundreds of people, but love so few. Do you wonder that I should find life intolerable when those are gone?"

"But they haven't gone — not yet. You have been so splendid through all this — as I knew you would be. Shall I tell you something?"

"What?" she asked huskily.

"I've always regarded you as the bravest and most self-reliant girl I ever knew. I've watched you grow up from a long-legged schoolgirl to an attractive, beautiful woman, always cheerful and delightful to be with. You have a moral and spiritual courage that, in my opinion, is beyond all other virtues; and I have it on my conscience that knowing these things I have never had the courage to tell you so."

"You've got the picture all wrong, Mac. That isn't me at all. It's some other woman you are thinking of."

"It was for a time but it faded and died, even though I tried to keep it bright for ever. It's incredible how stupid a man can be when his nature, like mine, is fundamentally a stubborn one. I had resolved that work and sweet memories were enough to sustain me and for a time it seemed to work, but — "

"But what?" she asked, with her eyes gleaming.

"Lately I have been sorting myself out, and it's quite surprising what a huge vacuum I have discovered — a vacuum which, had I been wiser, and less stubborn, I should have made some attempt to fill. Do you know what I'm driving at?"

"No. You are most oblique."

"What do you imagine I have missed most in life?"

"I don't know enough about your private life even to guess."

"It comprises three rooms, a house-keeper, a concert or theatre occasionally, re-heated meals in a restaurant, and over all a kind of grey monotony. Never a real home, nor the sound of a beloved voice calling me to account. Freedom galore until it becomes as irksome as yesterday's rehashed food. It should never have been like that, and perhaps never would if I had dwelt less in the past and more in the present. And the days go by, and a voice within whispers, 'Hurry! It is later than you think'. Now perhaps it is too late. But

I must tell you all the same, while there is a chance to say it. I love you, Valerie, and have loved you for a long time. No obliqueness about that, is there?"

Valerie shook her head speechlessly, and a bright tear gathered in one of her eyes, and trickled down her pale cheek. Then she pulled down his head and kissed him on the lips with a curious little sigh.

"Not too late," she whispered. "Oh Mac, Mac — you've made me so happy. At least nothing can alter this."

"Nothing. And now, no more gloomy anticipations. This is the here and now. What does the poet say? 'Gather ye rosebuds while ye may'."

"What are you up to?" asked Donkin, from the end of the room.

"Strictly private and personal," laughed Valerie.

16

IT was a quarter to three when, with a thudding of footsteps the armed escort arrived. It consisted of four men, wearing a semi-military uniform, with a German type of headgear. The leader was a morose fellow who gave all his orders in German. He and his men split up into two parties, with the prisoners between them.

"Now for the great pantomime," said Donkin, as they finally stepped out into bright sunshine.

"No talking!" snapped the leader.

"Why the hell not?" retorted Donkin.

The butt of a rifle in his back answered that question, and as the party advanced McLean looked back at the basilica. It showed two sides of the square belfry, the nearer side being the room from which they had just come, with its iron bar at the narrow window. To the left, and round the corner, was a similar window, exactly like the other one, but minus the iron bar. It was a thing to remember.

Soon they were making through alleys in the direction of the 'Glasshouse', and it looked as if that was their objective. Valerie, with her arm linked in McLean's, was pale but self-controlled. She looked up at McLean and smiled as they approached the entrance to the big building, at which a sentry was now posted.

"The 'Glasshouse'," whispered McLean. "But the glass is all on the seaward side."

"Stop that talking!" howled the leader.

They passed through the wide door, then along a corridor, and finally into a long room, of quite exceptional interest. The seaward side of it was furnished with enormous windows, through which the bright sunshine struck at an angle, illuminating a dais which was part of the architectural design, breaking the room into two parts, divided by long plush curtains, which were now partially open, revealing a long table on the edge of the dais, behind which were four high-backed chairs, at the moment vacant. Facing this, in the lower part of the room, were the normal furnishings of the place — many luxurious antique chairs, and several settees, arranged in two groups, so as to leave a wide corridor between them. But what took McLean's attention was the array of paintings on the longer windowless wall. They were atrocious in their colouring and subject matter, ranging from hideous large breasted nudes to what might have been either landscapes or seascapes, according to one's fancy. No nightmare ever yielded more fantastic representations of reality, and McLean sensed the mind of a lunatic behind them.

He was still staring at them when he, and his companions, were ushered into three seats to the right of the corridor, and the guards ranged themselves on either side of them. McLean, finally switching his gaze elsewhere, located a huge radio, and by the side of it some shelves packed with volumes of records. He realized that it was from this room that he had heard the loud nocturnal music on his first visit to the strip of beach below. And it was from here that the machine gun had put an end to his escapade with poor Greta.

"Did you ever see such a set-up," grunted Donkin. "Why should we tolerate such damned nonsense?"

"Because we must," muttered McLean. "S-sh!"

The warning was just in time, for the guard nearest Donkin was about to induce a respect for the court with the butt-end of his rifle. For a few minutes nothing happened, and then into the room filed a number of men, in varied garb, who quietly occupied chairs on the farther side of the corridor. They were, presumably, witnesses for the prosecution, for McLean identified Marco, also the Captain of the launch and two of the men who had taken him into custody. To his surprise there was a little ruddy-faced man with a clerical collar amongst them.

"A clergyman!" whispered Valerie, in his ear. "What on earth is he doing here?"

"Window dressing," McLean whispered back. "It looks as if they want to make the whole sickly farce appear respectable. Ah, here come two old friends."

They were Lombroso and Roy. The former had a dossier in his hands, but Roy carried nothing. Lombroso took a special chair slightly removed from the witnesses, but Roy mounted the step to the dais, operated the curtains so that they swung away out of sight, and then took one of the chairs behind the long table. He looked very ominous as he sat there, with his egg-shaped head thrust forward, and his eyes staring over his glasses, and McLean reflected that if they had one friend in that place it certainly wasn't Doctor Roy.

Then at last came the judges, and Donkin gave a little hiss as he saw them, for their appearance was calculated to produce surprise. There were three of them, and they were all dressed alike in loose black robes, and all heavily masked in black crêpe from their noses to well below their chins. They walked like automatons, two of them less firmly than the third man. Instantly Lombroso stood up.

"The court will rise," he said in English.

"That means us, too," whispered McLean. "Come on, Ian, let's join this little game."

They rose as did everyone else, and in a few moments the judges were seated along with Doctor Roy. At a sign from Lombroso everyone in front of the bench sat down, with the exception of Lombroso himself. It was now clear that he was to be the Prosecutor, and that it was not intended that the prisoners should have any legal or other aid. Then the whole ridiculous travesty really started.

Lombroso started to read from the document in his hand. It was in English, and he read it very deliberately and clearly. McLean noticed that the younger of the three judges translated this in a low voice for the benefit of his two colleagues, who evidently had small knowledge of the English language. The charges against the prisoners as framed were utterly without foundation. Donkin was charged with the deliberate murder of Luigi by shooting, and McLean of the murder of the sentry, also by shooting. Valerie was charged with conspiracy.

Then came the witnesses, none of them being sworn first. McLean, who had been used to real courts, could have laughed had the circumstances been less grim. He knew what had really happened to Luigi, who had been but slightly wounded, and had had his wound dressed by Donkin, and, in his own case he was certain that he had hit the sentry in the shoulder, and that the fellow was now well on the road to recovery.

But what interested him far more than this travesty was the three masked judges in whom was vested the powers of life and death. Only the man who interpreted the evidence showed any signs of animation. The other two were as silent and rigid as a couple of corpses. They fascinated him as they did Donkin.

When the last lying witness was finished with, Lombroso addressed the prisoners, informing them that they could now recall any of the witnesses if they so desired. Doctor Donkin would take precedence. All eyes were turned on Donkin. He did not rise to his feet, but spoke from a sitting position.

"I've nothing to say," he said, "except that this so-called Court has no competence to try even a stray cat, and that all the charges and evidence are a pack of black and damnable lies."

"Order!" shouted Lombroso.

"Order yourself, and to hell with you!" said Donkin.

The little padre turned and stared at Donkin. He seemed to be shaking with nerves.

"Inspector McLean!" called Lombroso.

McLean squeezed Valerie's hand and then stood up.

"I'm sure it would be useless recalling any of the witnesses," he said. "They have learnt their pieces far too well. I confess I have lost interest in this strange rigmarole, but as a patron of the arts I should very much like to know who perpetrated those atrocities yonder."

He pointed across to the wall, turning his head away from the ghastly daubs, as if their lewdness offended his eyes. There came an enraged cry from the direction of the bench, and the masked judge on the left of the translator, now seemed not to need the linguistic aid of his colleague. He staggered to his feet, brandishing his left arm, while he held the right one rigidly to his

371

side. He started to say something and then collapsed and was caught by his near companions. There was a hushed murmur as Roy went to him, and held a small bottle to his lips. Finally they got him into his chair again, where he sat silent as before, with staring black eyes.

"My goodness!" muttered Donkin. "That stung him hard."

McLean sat down, and after a pause Lombroso called "Miss Donkin!"

"Say nothing," whispered McLean.

"I must," she murmured. "I must."

She stood up, tossed back her mass of hair, and stared at the figure behind the table.

"I have harmed no one," she said. "I came here to be with my brother. But if they are guilty then I am guilty too, for my heart is with them in all they have done."

Then she sat down and McLean enfolded her slim warm hand.

"You shouldn't have done that," he murmured.

"It's the way I want it. Oh, God, I hope they won't part us."

Lombroso then became seated, and it was obvious that the judges were about to consider their verdict. It did not take them long. There was some muttering, and then the interpreter wrote something on a sheet of paper, and Lombroso went forward and took the paper.

"The verdict of the court," he said slowly, "is that the two male prisoners are guilty of murder, and the woman prisoner guilty of being an accessory. The sentences are death for the two men, and two years imprisonment for the woman. The executions to be carried out within forty-eight hours."

Valerie gave a little choke, and McLean drew her closely to him.

"Courage!" he said. "We agreed on that, didn't we?"

"Yes. But forty-eight hours!"

"It can be made into an eternity."

"If — if we stay together."

"That may be possible."

Lombroso ordered everyone to rise, and then the Judges retired, and Roy came down to join Lombroso. When they and the other persons had gone McLean and his companions were marched out, and back to the Basilica, where, to mitigate Valerie's great sorrow, they were left in their old quarters. Valerie then flung herself into McLean's arms, while Donkin did his best to appear singularly unobservant.

"You needn't look so embarrassed, Ian," called Valerie. "We're just making up for lost time."

"Don't mind me, my children. But what a situation! And what a triumph for Lombroso and company."

"Scarcely for Lombroso. He's only a willing tool. Those people in the 'Glasshouse' are the bosses. What happened to the fellow who nearly collapsed?"

"Heart, I think. Roy evidently expected it, for he had the temporary remedy in his pocket. You evidently hit the nail on the head when you were rude about the paintings. Hadn't we better get down to brass tacks?"

"Meaning what?"

"Well, I don't feel like sitting still waiting to be either hanged or shot. We may not be able to leave the island, but if we could manage to get out of this place we might be able to give them a run around. I suppose if we tore all our clothing into strips we shouldn't have enough to reach the ground?"

"No. There's no hope that way, but there's another possibility."

"What?" asked Valerie eagerly.

"Don't place much reliance on it. But when we went to the trial I noticed that the window round the end of this face of the tower has no bar, and the bar at this window isn't any too secure."

"But there's no way of reaching the other window," objected Donkin.

"There is. It is only a narrow coping, about a foot wide, but it might be possible to get round it — sideways."

Valerie stared at McLean in astonishment.

"Why, it's hardly wide enough for a cat to walk along it," she protested.

"Oh, it's not so bad as that," said McLean. "If one walked with his face to the wall, and shuffled along he might succeed."

"But there's the corner to get round," said Donkin.

"Yes. That would be tricky, but still — "

"No," said Valerie. "It would be suicidal. If one fell it would be the end."

"Let's have another look before we discuss it further," said Donkin.

He went to the window and thrust his head through the narrow space.

"Just about a foot wide," he muttered. "Lord, what a ghastly operation!"

He withdrew his head and turned to McLean, who went to the window and had another look at the cat-walk.

"Well?" asked Donkin.

"I still think it's possible, provided

we can move this bar."

"Let's assume that we can, and that one can get through the other window. What good will it do?"

"No good, unless that other door which leads to the staircase is not locked, as ours is."

"And if it isn't?"

"In that event we — you and I — might creep down the staircase at a suitable time, and get possession of the sentries' rifles. I believe there are two of them down there, and one of them would probably be asleep."

"Go on," said Donkin, his eyes gleaming.

"We could get the keys and release Valerie, then make our way to the villa and take possession of it. So far as I know the only persons there are Lombroso, Roy, and a couple of servants. They could speedily be dealt with, and then we could move all the food supplies to a suitable room, and hold it for a considerable time."

"By Jove, it's an idea!" said Donkin.

"At the very least it would give us an extension of life. What do you think about it, Valerie?"

"It sounds promising except for the acrobatics," said Valerie. "Ian, you may be, and are, as brave as a lion, but you know you're no good at heights. I remember years ago in Switzerland you had bad vertigo — "

"I wasn't under sentence of death on that occasion. That makes a hell of a difference."

"As a matter of fact, it isn't absolutely essential that both of us should go along the ledge in the first instance," said McLean. "If there's no outlet from the other room then the scheme is dead. I could go first, and if I made the staircase I could rap softly on our door, and then you could follow."

Donkin stared at him suspiciously.

"Trying to let me out of it?" he asked.

"No. But there's no sense in your making that effort if the plan proves to be impossible."

"Then why not let me go first?"

"Must I tell you the painful truth? Your girth isn't in your favour for the job we have in mind. Now don't be an idiot, and let me have my way."

"He's right, Ian," pleaded Valerie. "Oh, but I don't like any of it. Mac, is it wise? Are you sure you won't fall and be smashed to bits?"

"It's a reasonable risk when you consider what is at stake. Believe me, I have every reason to want to live a bit longer, more reason than I have ever had before."

"Me, too," she said, with a forced smile. "When — when would you make the attempt?"

"Not in broad daylight."

"But in the darkness it would be far, far more dangerous."

"Yes. I think the early morning is the best time. We could try to get rid of the bar in the darkness, and be all ready by first light. What do you think, Ian?"

"Yes, you're right. I suppose we can't make a start on that bar forthwith?"

McLean shook his head.

"There's always the risk that someone may come here before evening. No, we must wait."

"What we need is a lever of some kind. I'll have a look round for a beam or something that can be removed."

17

WHEN night finally fell all of them were in a state of great nervous tension. Donkin and McLean had already removed a piece of quartering from its seating. It was a six-foot length of 'four by two', which they reckoned would form a lever powerful enough to remove the bottom of the iron bar from its crumbling seating, and this they hid in a corner.

It was midnight before they tackled the first obstacle, and within a matter of minutes the bottom of the bar was loose. There was no need to remove the bar completely, for Donkin found it was wrought iron, and could be bent aside without much difficulty.

"We'll leave it as it is for the time being," he said. "But before we make the attack I'll wrench it clean out. Nice little weapon for the subsequent job.

What are we going to do about the two sentries, presuming we disarm them?"

"Lock 'em in here."

"Fine!"

Since nothing further could be done until the appointed time, the trio tried to snatch some sleep, but it was soon obvious that they were far too strung up to capture that elusive phantom.

"I'm trying to forget that I'm hungry," murmured Valerie in McLean's ear. "Even the effects of that colossal breakfast have passed away. It would certainly be nice to capture the villa and get a square meal again."

"It would," agreed McLean. "But do try to get some sleep, darling."

"Darling!" she mused. "It's the first time you have ever called me that. Was it much of an effort?"

"Not much — and don't fidget."

"Can't help it. I seem to be tingling all over. I believe there are fleas in this place."

McLean laughed, and then for a long time there was silence, broken only by an occasional cooing from close at hand. It looked as if the pigeons were not sleeping as well as they might. Suddenly Donkin gave a loud snore and woke up.

"Hell!" he muttered. "I was actually asleep. Why don't those damned pigeons settle down?"

"Why don't we?" asked McLean. "I expect we disturb them as much as they do us. Valerie, what are you doing?"

"Scratching," replied Valerie. "I'm sure there are fleas on this floor."

"Nonsense!"

"Well, let's talk. We're just wasting time."

"What is there to talk about?"

"Millions of things. Suppose by some miracle we got out of all this trouble — what would you do?"

"Marry you, I suppose."

"You suppose? So there's a doubt in your mind?"

"You know quite well there isn't."

"What then? Where should we live?"

"Where would you like to live?"

"In the country — but not too far from town. I've always lived in the country, and should die cooped up in some London flat."

"Very well. The country it shall be. A small period cottage, with bottle-glass windows, oak beams and inglenooks, but modern plumbing and main services. A place perhaps, with a garden that has a stream running at the bottom, with fish in it, so that when we quarrelled I could take a fishing-rod and go and sulk with the fishes."

"I can almost see it," said Valerie. "Not one of those black and white places — too many of them. I'd prefer good old English brick of mellow colour, and interspersed with oak timbers. One with a little front garden, and a gay porch overrun with roses or clematis. You only need about six thousand pounds and the thing is yours."

"Is that all?"

"You didn't expect to rent one did you?"

"Why not?"

"Because it isn't done."

"Who says so?"

"I do."

"Well, you are wrong in this case."

"What case?"

"My case. I know a man who has such a cottage — empty. He offered it to me for rent, because he knew I was tired of flat dwelling. Curiously it has the stream too — a tributary of Old Father Thames — with a boat-house and a punt."

"Mac, you're not serious?"

"Never more serious. The thing is still on offer."

"Mac! Darling! This is the most wonderful thing that ever happened. Where is it?"

"Not very far from where you live — on the River Wey."

"What are you two gassing about?" asked Donkin. "Why don't you go to sleep?"

"We were only whispering," said Valerie.

"Whispering my foot! You were shouting the odds. Now you've woken up those infernal pigeons again. Mac, can't you keep her quiet?"

"I can — and will," said McLean.

Valerie sighed as she snuggled up closer to him, and very soon she looked as if she were asleep, but McLean knew she wasn't, from the quick rhythm of her breathing. He hoped she was dwelling on that doubtful picture of the future which he had dangled before her eyes, and not on the perilous business which was part and parcel of his plan. He had certain misgivings about his own ability to make the passage of the narrow ledge, but in Donkin's case the situation was even more grim, for Donkin's great girth was against him, apart from the alleged tendency to vertigo. Yet it seemed to him desirable that he should have help in overcoming the guards, so that the pair of them could be attacked simultaneously, and silenced immediately.

Sitting there in the increasing darkness

before the dawn a rush of thoughts passed through his mind, and none of them pleasant, until suddenly there came, like a gift from Heaven itself, the germ of an idea. It jolted his half-awake brain into intense activity, for it ran in harness with the plan of escape, but had wider implications. It had many 'ifs' about it, none of which could be answered at the moment, but at least it was sound enough to make the future just a little less inevitable.

He decided to say nothing about this, for fear of arousing false hopes. Already his companions had hoped for more than had been in his power to accomplish. No, he would say nothing — at least until he had had a chance to investigate that other chamber.

When at last the first dim light of dawn smote through the window it found him ready — almost eager for the ordeal. Valerie needed no waking, and was on her feet as quickly as he. Donkin came to them with serious face.

"Now?" he asked McLean.

"Yes. No reason why we should wait a moment longer. Let's get that bar out of the way."

Donkin needed no help in that matter. His powerful hands bent the bar across the top of the window in one steady movement.

"All clear," he said.

Valerie came close up to McLean and linked her arms round his neck, regardless of her brother, who, in fact, was well aware of the state of affairs as between these two. He turned his head away for a moment.

"Can — can you do it?" she asked in a hoarse whisper.

"I think so."

"Oh my darling! If anything — "

He put his finger on her lips, and she smiled.

McLean slipped off his shoes, and went to the window, where Donkin was staring down at the narrow ledge.

"Not a soul about," said Donkin. "Are you going now?"

"Yes. If all is well I should be at the door in about five minutes. Stand close to it so that you can hear what I have to say."

"I'll be there. Do you want any help here?"

"Yes. It's a bit awkward getting out. Your back should make it easier."

Donkin kneeled down, with his hands on the floor, and McLean stood on his broad back, got his head and shoulders through the window, and then felt down with one leg. A few moments later he was standing on the ledge, facing the window.

"Have a care, old chap!" said Donkin, in a curiously weak voice.

McLean nodded, gave one look at Valerie, and then commenced to move sideways along the perilous ledge. Foot by foot he made his way towards the turn in the masonry, with his hands spread flat against the wall. He tried to forget the hundred-foot drop beneath him, but there was no forgetting that terrible corner which loomed closer and closer to him. At last his left hand went round it and he stood still for a moment, literally hugging the stone blocks. Then on again, but inch by inch now. His knees began to ache, owing to his inability to bend his legs, and perspiration began to trickle down his forehead. The footing was most tricky. One mistake and all would be over. Finally he took the step which brought his left leg round the corner, bringing his body in the most awkward position. To follow up with his right leg and still keep his balance was a matter of the most extreme difficulty. Putting up a silent prayer, he made the effort, and so accomplished the worst part of the journey.

A minute or two brought him to the open window, and after a brief rest he drew himself up and clambered through it. There was barely room to do this, for just inside was a large pigeon coop, with an alighting board stretched between a trap-door and the window-sill. Inside he could see about half a dozen carrier pigeons, all in a state of excitement at this invasion of their domain.

In their rear was a door exactly similar to the one in the room from which he had come, and to the right of the door was an old desk. The first thing he did was to go to the door, and to his great joy it was not locked. He opened it quietly and saw the neighbouring door and the staircase. The way was open but now he was confronted with difficulties. The first was insurmountable. Donkin, with all his courage and strength, would never make that passage along the ledge. Vertigo or no vertigo his physical girth was too great. To attempt it would be madness. It meant that he would have to tackle the two guards alone, and this was not pleasant to contemplate. True, one of them — if indeed there were two — might be taking his spell of sleep, but all the same it was a most venturesome business. But it was that or the admission of failure. He decided

391

to lose no time in putting the position to Donkin, and tip-toed to the locked door. Two or three gentle taps were enough to bring Donkin to the door, speaking through the keyhole.

"So you made it, Mac?"

"Yes. But you can't. There isn't a hope. In fact I wouldn't make the journey back for anything on earth."

"But I can try."

"No. Stay where you are, until I get the key."

"But you can't — "

"There's no other way. Promise me you'll do nothing."

"All right — if that's how you want it."

"No more. I've got a job to do before I tackle the guard."

McLean then crept back to the pigeon loft. It was soon clear that the pigeon post was in regular use, for in the desk he found some tiny celluloid cylinders, intended to be used as envelopes for messages, and each equipped with a split ring to enable them to be attached to the ring on the bird's foot, and in a cubby-hole he found a supply of narrow message forms, which, when rolled up fitted the cylinders. There was also a ball-pointed fountain pen, full of green ink.

Delving into the wastepaper basket, close to the desk, McLean found an old spoiled message. It was written in the same green ink as in the pen, and the text was Italian. McLean had no difficulty in translating this into English, for Italian was his best foreign language. It said:

Communicate N.A.D. Bremen deal is off. Launch will be at Trieste 23rd instant to bring him here. E.L.

McLean was not greatly interested in the message, but he was interested in the handwriting and the signature. There seemed little doubt that E.L. stood for Enzo Lombroso, and that the persons at the unknown destination were members of the organization and used to receiving such messages. Taking the pen he began to experiment with it, writing many copies of the message in order to get familiar with Lombroso's calligraphy. Finally he was satisfied that he could write another sort of message that would look genuine. But what message exactly?

It would be dangerous to attempt to get a message to Scotland Yard, for that address was rather too well known. But a message to Sergeant Brook would serve the same purpose, for Brook would lose no time in getting such a message to the right quarters. Brook would know it was genuine if it were in the code which he and Brook had used on previous occasions. He decided to operate on those lines, and then carefully wrote his message.

Telephone following message immediately to Brook, 29499 Mayfair, London. E.L.

This was written in Italian, but the message which followed was done in code.

Am prisoner on Delbros island, near Trieste. Great danger. Armed help needed in strength. Mac.

He sat and looked at this result of his labour for a few moments, comparing it with the spoiled message. There was no reason why it should be suspect, and if, as he prayed, the recipient acted on instructions it was possible that the whole situation might be saved. Rolling it up he slipped it into one of the cylinders, and then went to the cage, opened the door in the rear, and brought out one of the birds. It took but a few seconds to attach the cylinder to its ringed foot, after which he went to the window, and put the bird on the wooden board. It stood still for a second, then waddled to the end of the board, and almost instantly spread its wings. He saw it make a circle in the air, and then fly off in a straight line out to sea.

"Good luck to you, birdie!" he muttered.

He went back to the desk to remove all signs of his handiwork, and while doing so he disturbed a glass phial which was lying under some papers. It was about five inches long, and contained a cloudy kind of fluid. The open end had obviously been hermetically sealed by heat, and round the phial itself was stamped the letters C.F.X. Realizing that time was now of the utmost importance, he slipped the phial into his pocket, and looked round for anything which might serve as a weapon. The only thing he found was a large paper-knife made of ivory with a long, wide, sharp blade. It was a poor enough weapon, but heavy in the hand and quite capable of causing serious injury if used on a human head or neck.

With every nerve in his body tingling, he crept out of the door, closing it behind him, and then commenced to descend the spiral staircase in his stockinged feet. It seemed an interminably long way down, but finally, at the last bend, he saw the little entrance hall just below him, with one of the double doors slightly open, and revealing part of the sitting form of one of the guards, with rifle across his knees. He was so still that McLean concluded he must be asleep. His companion — if he had one — was not visible. But as McLean hesitated there drifted across the open doorway the blue smoke of a pipe or cigarette, as evidence that the second man was close by, and very wide awake.

McLean was working out his exact form of attack when suddenly his gaze fell on something which caused his heart to beat faster. Just inside the half-open door, hanging on a nail, was an enormous key, and he recalled that the key had been on that nail when he was brought to his late prison, and taken from it by the man in charge of his escort. This discovery eased the problem considerably. He had but to get the key to bring to his aid the worthy Donkin.

In dead silence he descended the remaining steps, and then crept up to the wall, without bringing himself into view of the smoking man. The next moment the key was his, and swiftly and silently he made his way up the staircase, to arrive at the prison door almost breathless.

The lock turned easily, and he entered the chamber, with finger on lips to enjoin silence, while he closed the door behind him. Valerie ran to him, and threw her arms round his neck.

"What has happened?" whispered Donkin. "You can't have — "

"No. I was about to cause a rumpus when I saw the key hanging up just inside the door. There are two of them, but one is asleep. Two of us are likely to be more successful than one."

"By Jove — yes!" said Donkin. "Want your shoes?"

"Not yet. You'd better remove yours too, and we can put them on when we come back here with our prisoners — presuming we are successful."

"We're going to be successful," said Donkin grimly. "Thank God you saved me that cat-walk. What about Valerie?"

"She'd better stay here until this business is settled."

"Not I," retorted Valerie. "I may not be trained in Commando tactics, but I can be useful in a scrimmage."

But here McLean was adamant. The least slip-up and there would be bullets flying. Donkin was of the same opinion, and finally Valerie sighed and held her peace.

"Ready now," whispered Donkin. "No, wait. I'll take that iron bar."

He went to the window, and in a short time wrenched the bar from its top seating. He and McLean then straightened it between them, and a few moments later they were creeping down the staircase.

"The sleeping man is to the left of

the door," whispered McLean. "The other must be away to the right."

"You take the sleeper," whispered Donkin. "I'll deal with the other one. Okay?"

McLean nodded, and now they went on in dead silence until they reached the spot where McLean had halted before. The situation seemed unaltered, and there was still smoke drifting across the half-open door. A momentary halt and then McLean nodded his head, and they descended the few steps and crept towards the door. Suddenly McLean descended on the sleeping man, and simultaneously Donkin dived to the right, where the smoking man made an attempt to get his rifle into use, but the iron bar fell across his outstretched arm, and the next moment the rifle barrel was pushed into his chest, with Donkin's cold eyes behind it.

"Make one sound and I'll shoot," said Donkin. "Get up!"

McLean's bewildered man was now on his feet, holding his hands above his head, while the rifle barrel was pushed into his back.

"Up the stairs!" said McLean.

Donkin repeated the order in German, and the two prisoners obeyed with alacrity. McLean was pleased to find that his own prisoner was the same man who had projected him into the room with considerably more force than had been necessary, and when finally the door was opened by Valerie, he did the same thing with identical results. Donkin followed, and then the door was closed.

Here the rifles were examined, and found to be fully loaded, but in addition both men carried ammunition bandoliers, each of which contained thirty rounds. These were taken from them, and they were searched for any other hidden weapons, without result. Donkin and McLean put on their shoes one at a time, and discarded their now useless clubs.

"Listen, you two," said Donkin to the sullen prisoners. "There's a way out of this place — along the parapet outside and into the next room. If you feel like having a go you're welcome. Ready, Mac?"

McLean nodded and the trio left the room, and locked the door behind them. When they stepped out into the clear morning air it was still only half-past five, and nowhere was there any sign of activity.

"Now for the villa," said McLean. "There are several ways, but the longest one is safest. Some of these people may be early risers, and I should prefer not to meet them. This way."

They walked rapidly through the unfrequented old alleys into which the low rays of the sun had not yet entered, and finally they emerged quite near the villa, which was bathed in glorious sunlight. McLean chose the terrace as the quickest and easiest means of entry and when they reached the casement windows of the lounge, he pushed the butt of his rifle through one of the panes of glass, and then put his hand through the orifice and slipped back the catch.

"Upstairs!" he said to Donkin. "Valerie, you had better stay here."

"Not I," said Valerie. "I'm going into the kitchen to investigate the larder."

What followed was greatly to Donkin's liking. Lombroso was roused from sleep to see Donkin standing over him with a rifle in his hand.

"What the — !" he exclaimed.

"Morning, Colonel!" said Donkin. "As you will perceive there has been a slight change in the situation. Keep your hand away from that drawer. I'll get whatever there is inside it that appeals to you so much."

He opened the drawer of the side-table and took out a big automatic.

"You're certainly a man who believes in precautions," he said, as he put the weapon into his pocket.

There was a noise outside, and into the room came Doctor Roy, almost foaming at the mouth with rage, and still in his very shabby pyjamas, with

McLean following up.

"Hold them!" said McLean. "I want Marco, and anyone else who may be here."

"Nothing more to my liking," said Donkin. "Be seated, Doctor Roy. I hope you spent a pleasant night."

"Very smart!" sneered Roy. "But where do you think this will get you?"

"Honestly, I don't know," replied Donkin. "But it can't be to a worse spot than was arranged for us. Sit down and make yourself at home."

18

MARCO was no less surprised than his masters to be rudely awakened and to look down the barrel of a rifle. He gave a gasp of horror, and pulled the bedclothes around him.

"It's all right," said McLean. "Do as you're told and nothing will happen to you. Get into some clothes — quick!"

Marco was inside his trousers and shirt in a few moments. He pushed his feet into some slippers and looked at McLean for instructions.

"Is there anyone else sleeping in the villa?" asked McLean.

"No, *Signore* — only me, Colonel Lombroso and Doctor Roy."

"Is there some connection between this villa and the hangar?"

"Yes. A passage which goes from the wine-cellar."

"What is upstairs?"

"Only a long room, full of lumber."

"And where is that clothing you took from me?"

"In the kitchen — the cupboard opposite the larder?"

"Is the larder locked?"

"*Si, Signore.*"

"Give me the key."

Marco produced some keys from the dressing-table and McLean took them, after Marco had indicated the larder key.

"Any firearms in the villa?"

"The Colonel has a pistol, but not the Doctor."

"Then where are the rifles kept?"

"I don't know."

"You mean you won't tell."

"No. I swear I don't know, but I think they come from the 'Glasshouse'. I'm not allowed in there. I am only a servant here, and know nothing — "

"All right. We'll go into that later. Now, come with me up to the next floor. Hurry!"

Marco led the way up some narrow stairs to the room which he had mentioned. It was, as he had said, nothing but a storeroom, and it possessed only a series of grills for ventilation. The door was of sound construction, and one of the keys fitted it.

"This is your temporary home," said McLean. "Your employers will shortly join you, so you will have company."

Locking the door McLean hurried down to the next floor, to find Donkin guarding his two prisoners. Lombroso had been permitted to leave his bed and was now nearly dressed, but Roy was still looking baleful in his pyjamas.

"I'll get you some clothing, Doctor," said McLean. "I hate to see you looking so forlorn. I won't be a minute, Ian."

McLean brought back an armful of garments which he had found in Roy's room, and flung them at him.

"No time to put them on," said McLean. "You are both going to fresh quarters. Come on!"

They were marched up to the attic room and there locked up with Marco.

"End of Act One," said Donkin. "Where do we go from here?"

"A defensive position, and without delay, for those two fellows in the belfry will yell their lungs out until somebody hears them. Then there will be action. What is it to be — this floor or the lower one?"

"The lower one I should say. We could be trapped up here. Let's go and have a look."

Valerie met them at the foot of the stairs. She had found what she believed to be the pantry, but the door was locked. All she could do was to put a kettle on the electric stove.

"Here's the key," said McLean. "Open up the pantry while we find the telephone."

"Oh, I've seen that. It's in the lounge, near the righthand window."

McLean and Donkin went into the lounge, and promptly put the telephone out of order. Looking round the room

McLean came to the conclusion, that despite certain disadvantages, it was on the whole the best defensive point, for on the garden side it had an uninterrupted view of the terrain, while on the opposite side there was but one window, outside which the land sloped away in a series of unscalable rocks.

"This is the place," he said. "Let's hope we are permitted to have a quiet meal before the storm breaks. Now come and help shift the provisions. We can't run the risk of being cut off from them."

The pantry was only what might have been expected in a house remotely situated. It contained almost everything that the most thorough-going gourmand could desire. There were pyramids of canned luxuries, whole sides of bacon, some cooked hams, and fruit in abundance. Valerie was sucking a nectarine when McLean and Donkin found her.

"You cheat!" said McLean.

"Couldn't resist it. It's like the

interior of Fortnum and Masons. I'll have some breakfast dished up soon. What happened to all the inmates of this place?"

Donkin pointed above his head, and then commenced to fill a basket with tins and rolls, explaining the position to Valerie as he did so. McLean disappeared for a few minutes, and then was met in the hall by Valerie, who gasped as she saw him, for in those few minutes he had scraped the beard off his face, and got back into his own clothing, which Marco had creased with considerable skill.

"My hat!" ejaculated Valerie. "Are you a quick-change artist? Ian — where are you?"

Ian emerged from the lounge, and blinked at the apparition. Then he laughed amusedly.

"You might be in Bond Street," he said. "But that popgun ruins the picture. Anyway, where's that razor?"

"Later," begged McLean. "Let's get this transport job over. Your suit is quite respectable. Mine was an offence. It smelt of Colonel Lombroso."

Very soon they had transferred all the provisions they were likely to need, and then McLean found the wine-cellar, and also the door which led through the tunnel to the hangar. He bolted it and ascended to the ground floor with three bottles of wine in his arms.

"Beautiful sight," said Donkin.

"Where's Valerie?"

"Getting some breakfast. Mac?"

"Yes."

"How long are we likely to hold this place?"

"Long enough — I hope."

"Long enough for what?"

"For help to arrive."

"Isn't that completely out of the question?"

"Not completely. Ah, here comes Valerie."

Valerie brought in a huge tray packed with delicious things. McLean took the heavy load from her and dumped it on a low table, which was near enough to the central windows for him to have a long view across the terrace towards the 'Glasshouse'.

"I'll be mother," he said. "Ian, did you look at the front door?"

"I did. It's bolted top and bottom, and that goes for the kitchen door, too."

"Good! We're safe for the moment. Now, my children, you may eat."

While the meal proceeded McLean scarcely took his eyes off the scene which the windows framed, across which he believed the attack would soon come. What troubled him was his ignorance of the weapons which might be brought against them. There was at least a machine-gun and a light mortar, and there might be others even more destructive, but upstairs he thought he had the answer to anything really overwhelming — Lombroso and Roy. As a last resort he was prepared to use them as hostages — anything to afford Sergeant Brook more time to take effective action. Looking round the room he took note of the three full bookcases on the rear wall.

"Too much window space here," he said. "If we can shift those bookcases in front of the windows they would be almost as effective as sandbags. All we need is a small firing aperture."

"Good idea!" said Donkin. "I was just thinking the same thing."

"Let's try."

While Valerie replenished the coffee cups McLean and Donkin dealt with the bookcases, and found they slid easily on the parqueted floor once the rugs were rolled up. Within a few minutes the windows were almost completely blocked, leaving but two narrow spaces. To prevent the cases from being blown backwards some furniture was piled against them. Valerie watched these proceedings with anxious eyes.

"Now come and finish breakfast," she begged.

McLean still had a long view between the bookcases, and all he could see was a vacant landscape backed by the sunlit citadel.

"Mac, we made one mistake," said Donkin.

"Only one?"

"I mean we should have tied up those two prisoners in the belfry, and gagged them. Then we might have had hours of respite."

"I should have done had there been rope available, but there wasn't, and time was precious. Also I wanted to make sure that Lombroso and Roy were not in a position to oppose us. I don't think we've done so badly. Oh, here's something I meant to show you. I found it in the room where the pigeons live."

Donkin took the phial, held it up to the light, and then shook it.

"Looks mighty like some kind of culture," he muttered.

"That's what I thought. You'll notice the tube is stamped C.F.X. I suppose that doesn't convey anything?"

Donkin shook his head.

"Do you mean bacteria, Ian?" asked Valerie.

"Yes, of course!"

"Germ warfare!" said Valerie. "Doesn't that stick out a mile? It would explain everything. Mac, you told me that some sort of industry was being carried out below ground. It could be a big laboratory, couldn't it? And the presence of Doctor Roy backs up that possibility. Ian, you ought to be able to tell us what it is."

"My dear child," said Donkin, "what do you think I am — a magician? Or do you expect me to swallow some and wait for results? It might be some harmless vaccine. I simply don't know, and am not likely to know without a good microscope. But I agree, it makes one think. Can I keep this, Mac?"

McLean nodded, and then gave a little start, and reached for the rifle. Donkin, staring in the same direction as his companion, saw what occasioned the start. In the distance was a group of armed men, making straight for the villa.

"It's come," he said.

"Yes," said McLean. "Valerie, never mind about taking those things to the kitchen. That part of the house will be out of bounds for awhile. Better go up by the fireplace."

"Aren't I in this?" asked Valerie.

"No, but you can run and bolt that door, and push the couch up against it. Ian, you take the left firing point, but don't shoot until I tell you. We can't afford to waste any ammunition. We must try to keep them on the farther side of that lower wall."

Donkin nodded grimly and took up his position. Valerie, having made the door safe, came back and gave one look at the oncoming men.

"Now go, darling," pleaded McLean. "This is a state of war — real war, and it isn't going to be nice."

She kissed him, then with a little sigh went to the fireplace which offered better shelter than any other place in the room.

"They're getting near," said Donkin. "Making for the little gate."

"Fire over their heads as they try to enter. Just one shot."

The two foremost men reached the gate and were about to enter when McLean pressed the trigger of his rifle, and a bullet sailed within a few feet of the two men. Donkin's rifle rang out almost simultaneously. The two men ducked, and those behind them scuttled to the shelter of the low wall.

"That settles all their doubts," muttered Donkin. "Suppose they decide to rush us — what then?"

"You know the answer to that. It's the only answer if we are to remain alive."

For awhile there was complete silence, and then suddenly half a dozen rifles appeared above the low wall, with heads behind them.

"Look out!" said McLean.

He took cover for an instant, and a

hail of bullets shattered the window glass, and knocked a number of books from the shelves of the bookcases.

"They're coming!" said Donkin.

McLean needed no information on that point. Four of the men were already over the wall and running hard for the veranda. He picked off the leader, and saw him fall sideways, while the man behind him sank to his knees as Donkin opened fire. The remaining two hesitated, and then turned and vaulted over the wall.

"First blood!" muttered Donkin. "I don't imagine they will try that again."

McLean took advantage of the temporary lull to replace the damaged books in the bookcase, and then Donkin did the same on his side.

"What are they cooking up now?" muttered Donkin. "Oh, there goes a man back to the 'Glasshouse'. Shall I stop him?"

"No. You'd probably miss him at the speed he's going, and we may need that bullet for strictly defensive purposes."

"But he's probably gone for reinforcements."

"They'll arrive anyway. What a bloodthirsty fellow you have become."

"I've always been that way where rats are concerned. Mac, there's something I want to ask you?"

"What is it?"

Donkin left his firing point, and came across to McLean, who was watching the wall for any sign of a fresh rain of bullets.

"Why were you so long in that pigeon loft?" he asked in a whisper. "What were you up to?"

"I was looking for a weapon, and found that heavy ivory paper-knife."

"That wouldn't have taken you all the time you used up. Are you holding back on me, Mac?"

"To some extent. I had a kind of brain-wave before I went in there, and the circumstances were such that I was able to put it into operation. It was just a chance, and it may fail."

"But you think it may succeed?"

419

"Who says so?"

"You said so — a little while ago. You suggested it wasn't impossible that help might come if we held out long enough."

Valerie, seeing their heads together, crept across to them from the fireplace, ignoring her brother's signal to stay where she was.

"I refuse to be left in ignorance of any dirty work that is pending," she said. "What is all this whispering?"

McLean gave a little sigh.

"I didn't want to tell you," he said. "I know what it is to have one's hopes raised only to have them dashed again. You are driving me into a corner."

"I knew you were thinking up something," said Valerie. "Is it good or bad?"

"Nothing is either good or bad, but thinking makes it so," demurred McLean.

"Never mind your quotations," said Valerie. "Let's have the truth, whatever it is."

"Very well, but for heaven's sake keep it in perspective."

Quickly McLean explained what had kept him engaged so long in the pigeon loft, and when he had finished Valerie flung her arms round his neck.

"You're marvellous, Mac!" she said. "So simple too, and yet it never occurred to me that the pigeons might be used to our advantage. Ian, say something."

"There's nothing to say, except that I wish I had thought of it. But Mac's right. We mustn't build on it. At this moment the gang may be considering means to blow us all into eternity."

"If they do they'll blow Lombroso and Roy there as well," said Valerie. "I wonder if they know that?"

"I intend that they shall know before anything like that happens," said McLean.

"By jove, yes," agreed Donkin. "Mac, you've given us just a gleam of sunshine. Let's be satisfied with that. What we have to do is play for time.

How fast does a carrier pigeon fly?"

"Forty miles an hour, or more. But keep your thoughts off that pigeon. He may have to go two or three hundred miles. Valerie, you'd better go back. It's not safe just here."

"Do you think I want to be safe?"

"Don't you? I do," said McLean with a smile.

"Yes, safe together, but not otherwise."

McLean gave a sharp cry of warning and pulled Valerie to his rear, as two bullets, accurately aimed, passed through the gap between the bookcases and embedded themselves in the wall opposite. Valerie gave a little gasp and scuttled across to the fireplace.

"They don't intend to give us much rest," muttered Donkin. "The next time a fellow puts his head up I'm going to have a pot at him."

McLean raised no objection, since a little success in that direction might put an end to the snap shooting. The two wounded men in the garden were making an attempt to crawl towards the wall, and as they drew nearer to it a white flag was hoisted on the end of a rifle from the other side of the wall.

"They want to pick up the casualties," said McLean. "At least we'll observe the decencies. If you've got a handkerchief wave it."

Donkin did this, and instantly two men clambered over the wall, and the injured men were removed one by one. Then the sporadic shooting started again, but never from the same spots. A rifle and the top part of a head would appear, and before appropriate action could be taken the bullet was away, and the head gone.

But this happened once too often. McLean had his sights aligned nicely on the top of the wall when a head appeared only a few feet away from his point of aim; swiftly he adjusted his sighting and fired. The bullet actually hit the rifle at the point where the supporting hand gripped it, and the weapon was sent flying as the head disappeared.

"You got him!" said Donkin. "That must have been a most unpleasant surprise for him."

"It was intended to be."

Followed complete silence, which was maintained for quite a long time. Then suddenly McLean saw the inevitable. Three or four hundred yards away there appeared four men. Two of them carried rifles, and the other two the parts of a machine-gun. Donkin turned his grim face to McLean.

"What do we do about that?" he asked.

"Keep them at a distance. But be careful with the ammunition. Ready?"

"More than ready. I don't like machine-guns."

"All right. Let them have it!"

A couple of rounds from each rifle dropped all four men flat on their chests. None of them appeared to be hit, for they were soon wriggling along the ground to the nearest bit of cover. Behind a low rocky ridge, on which a few stunted cacti managed to subsist, they got the machine-gun ready for action. McLean could see the end of the barrel projecting through the spiky leaves of the plants.

"Things are getting warmer," he muttered. "Look out for yourself, Ian!"

He had scarcely spoken when the machine-gun opened up. The first shots were too high, and shattered some windows on the first floor, but quickly the gunner altered his sights and a terrific fusillade of bullets swept the lower windows, and entered the room, ripping through the bookcases and cascading the heavy volumes. While it lasted McLean and Donkin lay flat on the floor, while Valerie, pale with inward terror at this new and dreadful experience, stood like a statue by the fireplace, with her hands clenched.

"Ian, can you see the end of the gun?" shouted McLean, above the din.

"Yes."

"When there's a break shoot at the gun — five rounds. I'll do the same. We may be lucky enough to put it out of action."

"Okay!"

The stuttering devastating weapon was silent at last, and the two rifles then opened fire, each shot carefully aimed. McLean could see some of the bullets raising dust from the rock that was within a few inches of the gun, and then suddenly the gun barrel disappeared from view.

"Have we got it?" asked Donkin, wiping his sweating forehead.

"I don't know. But now is the time to plug some of the holes in our defences. Warn me if you see that gun again."

He moved with great rapidity, gathering up the damaged books and stuffing them into the bookcases. The general damage was now considerable, and the floor was littered with broken ornaments and wood splinters. Valerie was coming to help him, but he drove her back almost fiercely.

"Get down, Mac!" shouted Donkin, and McLean slid to the floor beside his rifle.

Again the machine-gun opened up, with its nerve-shattering clatter, and again things cracked and splintered. How long they would be able to withstand such concentrated fire was problematical.

"The gun has been moved," said Donkin. "It's now about two yards to the left of where it was. They've pulled some stuff round it and it's difficult to see it at all, except by the flashes. I saw them when they opened up."

McLean took one perilous peep and saw the steady flickering at the gun muzzle. He fixed the spot in his mind and waited for the din to finish.

"Same tactics as before!" he shouted to Donkin. "But five rounds only."

When the gun ceased the rifles started up, with what result it was impossible to say. This time Donkin attended to the bookcases while McLean kept watch. He expected at any moment to hear the gun again, but a long time passed and nothing happened. Donkin had plenty of time to finish his job, even to go to Valerie and have a few words with her. After that infernal din the silence was almost painful. Finally he came back to his post.

"Can't see any movement over there," he muttered. "Oh yes — there are two men running for home. Mac, I believe we've done it. They've left the two riflemen behind. Phew! that would be a bit of luck. They may not have another gun."

McLean was relieved but was far from cheering. He, unlike his companions, knew of one thing they had, which for some reason they had not yet produced. It was the mortar, which Marco had sworn was not in the villa. Presumably they had imagined that they could gain their ends without causing extensive damage to the villa.

But now they might change their minds and bring that more terrifying weapon into use.

"No counting chickens, Ian," he said. "While there's comparative peace I want to tell you something. If we can't hold this place there's a way of retreat open to us. Not a permanent retreat, but one which might serve us for a time. The entrance to it is down in the wine-cellar, and it leads to the hangar. You came that way when you arrived here, but you didn't know it because you weren't conscious. If we have to go we must take some food and ammunition with us. And here's something else in case I should be unlucky."

He passed a folded sheet of notepaper to Donkin, on the outside of which was written 'Last Will and Testament of Robert McLean', and Donkin stared at it for a moment.

"Just a precaution," said McLean. "I wrote it while I was upstairs just now. It needs witnessing. Better do it now if you have a pen, and then pass it to Valerie if — if things shouldn't go in our favour. Yes, you can read it."

Donkin gave a little cough as he read the very brief document. Then he found his pen and signed it, using a book as a backing.

"Oughtn't there to be another witness?" he asked.

"I think it would pass."

"We're getting a little morbid, aren't we?"

"Merely realistic. I have a sister, but she is married and well provided for. Put it away now or Valerie will wonder what the devil we are up to."

Donkin stuffed the document into his pocket, and then both of them resumed their vigil. Time passed and there was no resumption of the attack.

"It's curious — this silence," said Donkin. "Why don't they get on with it?"

"They may think it better to wait

until dark, when their prospects would be far more hopeful. That reminds me — we shall need an electric torch if we have to make that retreat. Have a look round and see what you can find. If any shooting starts, come back here at once."

While Donkin went on this quest Valerie came across to McLean, kneeling down just behind him.

"What happened?" she asked.

"I think we damaged the machine-gun."

"Thank goodness! Are they likely to have another?"

"If they had I think it would have been in action by now."

"You don't think they will make another open attack, with more men?"

"I think it's doubtful — in daylight. We could knock them off quite easily."

"But — after dark?"

"It wouldn't be so easy to hold them. Still, the hours are passing. So in a sense we are succeeding. If we should have to leave here in a hurry we must take food with us, so keep a supply ready in the basket."

"But where should we go?"

"Underground. Don't ask any more questions now. So much depends upon what the enemy do next, and that we are not likely to know until it happens."

"I won't be a nuisance, darling," she murmured. "Shall I prepare another meal? It will soon be due."

"Yes, but no trips to the kitchen. Make shift with what we have here."

"We have plenty here — even a corkscrew to open a bottle of wine. May I look through the window?"

"Just a quick glance. But why?"

"The room is gloomy and I want to see the sunshine."

She projected her head forward over McLean's shoulder, and uttered a little sigh as her eyes took in the gay sunlit scene. Then McLean pulled her back.

"Life could be so wonderful if men were not such wild animals," she mused. "I should like to be out there, walking on the edge of the sea — with you."

"That may yet happen."

She stole a kiss from him and then went back to the fireplace and began to prepare a meal.

19

DURING the afternoon and early evening there were a few shots fired from behind the low wall, but none of them did any harm, and now as the light began to fade the thing which McLean expected happened. From the direction of the citadel came half a dozen men, armed with small weapons and transporting other items.

"The mortar," said McLean, "and shells for it. I imagine they'll keep out of range until the light fails, and then get closer in and give us hell."

"It doesn't look very big," said Donkin.

"Quite big enough to bring down this place about our ears. Valerie had better get down to the cellar at once. Take her, Ian, and I'll try to hold them where they are."

"I hear you," called Valerie. "But I'm not leaving without you. If you insist you'll have to carry me."

"That's not difficult," said her brother. "Come, Valerie, don't be foolish. There's no sense at all in taking unnecessary risks."

But Valerie was absolutely adamant on this point, and Donkin looked at McLean appealingly.

"Never mind," said McLean. "I'm going to get either Lombroso or Roy down here. You hold those fellows at bay for a bit. I won't be long."

He fired a couple of shots before he left the position, and Donkin took over.

"Stay where you are," he called to Valerie, and then went out and up the stairs to the top room.

When he unbolted and opened the door he found the three prisoners, sitting on an old chest looking disconsolate. Lombroso jumped up at once and stared down the barrel of a rifle.

"What fool's game is this?" he snarled.

"What indeed? We didn't start it."

"It serves no purpose. In the end you will all be killed — even the girl."

"Not to mention you three," replied McLean. "Have you any control over those men, or do they take their orders from someone else?"

"Of course I've some control."

"Then if you want to save your lives one of you had better come with me. They have brought up that mortar, and will soon have it in action."

"Good God! Don't they know we are here?"

"Perhaps they don't care."

"I'll make them care. Come on, before it is too late."

But McLean shook his head.

"To achieve any success you would have to speak to them — have a meeting in fact. I should stand a very good chance of losing you, and I don't want to lose you just yet. I think Doctor Roy would do just as well."

"He has no authority," protested Lombroso.

"You over-rate yourself, my dear Colonel," said Roy. "I think I could persuade them not to use the mortar against the villa. What do you say, Inspector?"

"Very well," said McLean. "Come with me — and quickly."

He stood aside and Roy rose and passed him. Immediately McLean closed and bolted the door, and then followed Roy down the stairs. As they reached the lounge Donkin let off another shot.

"What's the position?" asked McLean.

"They're standing off — not far from where they had the machine-gun. How do, Doctor Roy!"

Roy paid no attention to the sarcastic greeting. He was looking at McLean for instructions.

"I will let you out by the front door," said McLean. "There is still light enough for them to recognize you. Go to the place where the mortar

437

is sited and warn them that Lombroso is here. I shall hold him as a hostage if they use that gun. Is that clear?"

"Perfectly clear, but I can't promise that they will not continue the attack by other means."

"I don't want you to promise anything. Just tell them the position — that's all."

"I am ready."

McLean took him out into the hall and then unlocked the front door and let him out. He was back in the lounge in time to see Roy go across the garden, with his hands up. After he had passed through the gate he was lost to view for a few moments, but again he came to view hurrying towards the spot where the mortar was hidden, until finally he disappeared from view.

"What now?" asked Donkin. "Will he succeed?"

"I don't think so. But it was worth trying."

"Why don't you think they will listen to him?"

"Because the powers that be — those fellows who masked their faces — probably hold Lombroso responsible for all the trouble we have brought them, and don't care two hoots whether he gets killed or not. But we shall soon know. In the meantime, keep your eyes skinned for any movement. If they attempt to bring the mortar any closer under darkness we must beat a retreat."

For a long time they lay staring into the gathering gloom, and then McLean saw two or three men taking a zig-zag course towards the garden wall. They were carrying nothing but rifles.

"Don't shoot!" he said to Donkin. "Waste of ammunition. This, I think, is the prelude. They'll probably use the mortar against us prior to a ground attack. Yes, they're bringing up the gun now."

"I can see them," said Donkin, in a strained voice.

"Fire a couple of rounds," said

McLean. "And then off we go. Valerie, are you ready?"

"Yes."

Four separate shots rang out, and these were immediately answered by shots from the lower wall. Then the three passed through the hall and along the passage which led to the cellar. Valerie, sandwiched between them, carried a basket full of food, and as they passed along the wine bins she snatched a couple of bottles of wine, and added them to the food. McLean led the way to the door which communicated with the hangar, and opened the heavy door. Close by the door was a switch, and on pressing this a wide well-built tunnel came to view. It had a gentle downward slope and terminated at another big door.

"I'll take the food now," said McLean. "It must be a pretty heavy load."

Valerie was quite agreeable to this, and the party advanced to the second door. They were very close to it when there came the sound of a terrific explosion which put out all the lights and caused the gound under their feet to tremble. Valerie grabbed McLean in the darkness.

"My goodness!" ejaculated Donkin. "It sounds as if the whole villa has collapsed."

"I think it has," said McLean. "Most of it was jerry-built with cement."

"What an escape!" muttered Valerie. "If we hadn't left when we did — "

"Anyway, it's in our favour," mused McLean. "The entrance to the cellar is probably blocked with debris, and for awhile, at least, they will presume we are dead."

"Until they dig for our remains."

"That will take a time. But let's get on. There is still the hangar to be crossed. Beyond that there is quite a good hiding-place."

On passing through the second door, which was bolted on the inside, McLean recognized the room where he had found the empty crates, but these were no longer present.

"Like to see your first prison?" he asked Donkin.

"No thanks. I'm not yet in a sentimental mood."

They were soon passing down the steps which led to the hangar, aided by the two torches which Donkin had previously found. The hangar was in complete darkness, with the big doors closed, and the plane looked fantastic under the moving lights.

"Don't we go through the doors?" asked Donkin.

"No. The way I took you before."

Valerie looked back at the aeroplane when they had passed it.

"If only one of you two could fly it," she sighed.

When they reached the rock wall McLean took the lead, and carefully picked his way upwards, and finally they all reached the gap.

"Wait here while I go forward and make sure that the other end is closed," he said.

He was back in a minute or two, looking slightly dishevelled from his trip.

"All right?" asked Donkin.

"Yes. I think we'll stay where we are, because we can hold an attack here better than anywhere else. Valerie, we can now delve into that basket."

By the light of a torch they sat and satisfied their hunger and thirst, which in the anxiety and tension of the past hours they had neglected.

"Sixteen hours since you dispatched that message," mused Donkin. "I wonder where it is now?"

"Perhaps it's as well we don't know," said Valerie. "Mac, if everything went as planned where would it most likely be at this moment. I know it's only a childish game but let's play it."

"It's too dangerous a game. I rather wish I hadn't told you."

"You don't," said Valerie. "Because you know that it gave us something to live and hope for. There's no other hope, is there? Be honest."

"For heaven's sake, Valerie — " protested Donkin.

"It's all right," said McLean. "I'll play. If the gods are with us, and Lombroso's agents acted on the instructions, Brook must have got that message hours ago."

"And then?"

"He would know it to be genuine because of the code I used, and would take the matter to the Chief Commissioner."

"Go on."

"The Chief would at once get in touch with the Italian authorities, perhaps the Yugo-Slavian also, to find out who has jurisdiction over this island, and then swift and effective action would be taken."

Valerie drew in her breath with a long sigh, and McLean knew what she was seeing in her vivid imagination, for he too had visions of the same kind, although he was well aware that all yet remained in the balance.

"You've played your game," he said

444

to Valerie. "Now get some sleep. Ian and I will take watches in turn."

"Yes, I'm tired," she admitted. "Thanks, Mac darling, for everything."

McLean took her soft kiss in silence, and in a matter of minutes she was fast asleep, leaning heavily against him. Donkin, finishing the last drop of wine from the bottle, looked across at McLean.

"I suppose I ought to congratulate you two," he said, "But in the circumstances it wouldn't ring very true. Still you've made her very happy — come what may. Like me to take the first watch?"

"Just as you wish."

"All right. You get some sleep. I'll wake you in about four hours. No need for that light, is there? We ought to keep some juice in reserve."

McLean switched off the torch, and drew the sleeping girl very close to him. In a few minutes he, too, was asleep. It seemed only a very short time afterwards that he was awakened by a touch on his arm, and the darkness was so intense he could not see the hand which had awakened him.

"Anything wrong?" he asked.

"No. I've done my turn. It's been as quiet as the grave. But we need some air. It's suffocating in here."

"You're right. I think I'll go along the passage and open up the entrance. That should ventilate the place."

He took the torch with him and soon reached the end of the passage. The loose rock which blocked it was pushed aside, and he crept through the opening into the cool night air, under the blazing stars. He climbed a rock and looked across to the villa. It was enshrouded by a reddish halo, against which he could see ascending smoke, and now and then a little spurt of flame, which flung into relief the bulk of the building. It was little more than a pile of ruins. That one mortar shell had brought down the roof and blown out the upper part of the unsubstantial walls. As he listened he could hear metallic noises, like the impact of steel against cement. The search for bodies was still going on.

He made his way back to his companions, and explained his long absence to Donkin, who was now sitting beside Valerie, blinking his tired eyes.

"Poor old Lombroso!" he yawned. "He must have become very unpopular with the big bosses. Glad it wasn't us. You've certainly let in some fresh air. The place is almost tolerable. Call me when breakfast is ready."

20

IT was some time after daybreak when Valerie stirred, but in the tunnel it was impenetrable darkness, for the big entrance doors to the hangar were so well fitted as to permit no light to enter the cavern.

"Mac!"

It was Valerie's voice, and McLean switched on the electric torch, to see her startled eyes.

"Oh, I thought we were still in the belfry," she said. "What's the time?"

"I don't know. My watch hasn't gone since I was in the sea. But you should know."

She looked at her wrist-watch.

"Half-past six! So — so nothing happened?"

"Nothing at all. But I went to the end of the tunnel last night and looked out. The villa is a wreck, and was still burning."

"How ghastly! Why, there's quite a breeze here!"

"I opened up the end of the tunnel. The place became insufferably hot. How are you feeling?"

"Filthy. I'd give anything for a bathe, but I suppose that is impossible?"

"Absolutely."

"Then I had better make myself useful, and get some food ready. It will help me to forget my insanitary state. Shall we let Ian go on sleeping?"

"Yes. He needs all he can get."

"I suppose daylight never penetrates this place?"

"Not while the big doors are closed. Let's see what we have in those cans."

They were selecting the most appealing canned items when McLean heard a sound, and immediately he switched off the torch. Valerie had heard it too, and maintained a dead silence. Then there came, as from a distance, the unmistakable sound of human voices, and suddenly it became light enough for them to see each other, and the voices grew louder. The light was artificial and when McLean crept to the spot from which he could look down into the hangar, he was dumbfounded to see four armed men descending the steps on the farther side, lighted by a big hand-lamp.

The situation was clear enough. The gang had worked all night searching for their bodies, and having failed they had removed the debris which had blocked the cellar door, and were now relentlessly seeking them. Two men went forward to the large doors, presumably to examine them, and then came back again. A spot-light was brought into use, and began to search out likely hiding-places.

"Wake Ian!" whispered McLean to Valerie, who was now close behind him.

In a few moments Donkin was also peering round the rock, and then the moving finger of light began to approach the opening inside which they stood. McLean leaned back and the light stayed focused on the cleft. There was low conversation, and McLean had no doubt what it portended.

"They're coming up here," he whispered.

"What do we do? Fight here?"

McLean hesitated, for the situation had developed much quicker than he had anticipated. There was much to be said for making a stand where they were, but there was always the risk that some member of the gang knew of the existence of that old passage, and a simultaneous attack from the rear would be horrible. Yet a decision had to be made.

"You and Valerie go to the other end of the passage," he whispered. "If things get too hot here I'll come and join you, and we'll make a break for the cave. Take the food with you."

Valerie was most unwilling, but Donkin saw sense in the suggestion, and almost dragged her away. By this time the two foremost attackers were at the foot of the steep climb, while the other pair stood by with weapons ready. He now had a close view of the weapons through a narrow slit, and saw that they were not ordinary rifles but automatics. It boded ill for the future.

The two foremost men commenced the climb, while all the time the spotlight remained focused on the gap. Up and up they came, one about three yards before the other. Then for a second or two he lost sight of them, but soon they came right into his line of vision through the narrow slit.

"Halt!" he yelled. "Go back!"

Immediately the two weapons of the men on the ground opened fire with a deafening roar, and bullets poured into the passage, whining as they ricocheted against the rock, splintering it into dangerous flying pieces. The climbers retreated out of sight, but McLean had a clear view of one of the tommy-gunners. He pressed the trigger of the rifle, and saw the man spin round and

452

collapse. The second tommy-gunner dashed for the shelter of one of the aeroplane's landing wheels, and then one of the climbers came to view for a split second and lobbed something forward and upwards. It fell with a thud somewhere near McLean, but he was unable to see it. Fortunately his brain reacted swiftly. Without question it was a bomb, and every second was vital. He turned like a hare and ran up the passage. Within five seconds there was a blinding flash and a roar like thunder. The blast brought him to his knees, but he quickly regained his feet and blundered on in the darkness until a ray of daylight showed the extreme low-ceilinged end of the passage, where Valerie and Donkin were anxiously waiting.

"What was it?" asked Donkin.

"Hand grenade. Nothing I could do against them. Have you looked outside?"

"Yes. No one about."

"Well, we can't stay here any longer.

The cave is our only chance now."

Donkin nodded. He could not see that the cave would shelter them for long, for he could not forget the mortar, and what it did to the villa. But life was no longer amenable to long-term planning. One had to be content to be alive — that and no more.

McLean led the way, climbing to the high ridge to make sure the way was open. Then he came down and the party proceeded to crawl through the maze of rocks which led to the more open ground. The basket of food was an encumbrance, but could not be abandoned. Finally they came out on level sand, and McLean pointed to a little cave which could just be seen away to the right.

"I'll go first," he said. "If all is clear I'll wave to you. Then come as fast as you can."

He took the basket, and with the rifle slung over his shoulder, he went off at a good pace, reaching the cave without incident. From there he had a better view of the surroundings, although the citadel was now out of sight. Seeing nothing but sand and rocks he waved and Valerie and her brother swiftly joined him.

"It's quite lovely here," panted Valerie. "Miles better than that horrid tunnel. And the air! Wonderful!"

Actually it was far less lovely than when McLean had last seen it, for the mortar shell had smashed great pieces of rock from the entrance, and had brought down some of the roof inside.

"Better get under cover," he said.

The basket was dumped inside and McLean began to move some of the debris from the sandy floor. A slight wind had got up, and it brought with it the smell of burning.

"I wonder how long we shall remain in possession?" mused Donkin.

McLean shook his head at him, but Valerie turned in time to see the movement.

"You can be honest, you two," she

said. "We are at the end of things, aren't we?"

Donkin, counting his remaining cartridges, looked at McLean.

"You can answer that one, Mac," he said quietly.

"No, Mac, you needn't," said Valerie. "I know they're bound to come here soon, and unless we surrender they will bring up that terrible mortar. We've put up a good show so far, but all things must come to an end."

McLean took her into his arms, and looked at her intently.

"Things are bad," he said. "I had hoped there might have been some sign of aid before this, but now I think it would be better if we placed no reliance on that. The pigeon may have met with some accident, or the message may have given rise to suspicion, and not been forwarded. All we can do is — "

He stopped for a moment and listened, then released her and ran outside the cave. In the sky was an aeroplane coming from the direction of the mainland, and as it approached it lost height rapidly and went round in a wide circle until it was no more than a thousand feet above them. Frantically he waved his arms, and Valerie and Donkin came and joined him, and followed his example.

"R.A.F. machine!" said Donkin. "I could see the markings. Oh, he's going away. It's a jet. Just look at his speed!"

"Do you think he saw us?" asked Valerie.

"I think so," replied McLean. "But — it doesn't follow that it is the answer to our prayer. Now get inside."

They obeyed and he was about to follow them when a small piece of charred paper moved across the sand under a gust of wind. He picked it up and saw that it was the latter part of an old discoloured letter. There were but two lines written in German followed by a signature. The writing was execrable, and on entering the cave he handed the scrap to Donkin.

"Something borne by the wind from the villa during the night," he said. "Can you translate that, Ian?"

"Filthy handwriting," muttered Donkin. "Yes, I think I've got it. It says:

'— it is of the utmost importance that we have a meeting this evening, same place as before. I will contact M.B.

Rattenhuber.'

McLean wrinkled his brows. The text was of no importance but the name of the writer rang a bell in his mind.

"I've heard that name," he said. "Or seen it in print. Rattenhuber! Yes, I'm certain of it. But it was a long time ago. I suppose it conveys nothing to you?"

"Not a thing," said Donkin. "But why worry? What is vastly more important is that aeroplane. You know it could be — "

But McLean wasn't listening. He

was delving into his prodigious memory for the unusual name, for he had the feeling that it had been associated with some important event. But it persisted in eluding him, and he left the matter for his subconscious mind to deal with.

"Oh, you're awake again, Mac?" said Valerie. "Why should you worry about this Mr. Rattenhuber? He's nothing to us — or is he?"

"He could be, but we'll let him rest for the moment."

"You'll have to," said Donkin, grimly. "Because unless I'm suffering from hallucinations our old friends have caught up with us again."

McLean swung round to see Donkin pushing cartridges into the magazine of his rifle.

"Where?" asked McLean.

"I swear I saw a human head behind that ridge."

It was the same ridge from behind which the previous attack on the cave had been made, and as McLean peered at it from behind the rock, the head appeared again for a brief moment.

"Yes," he muttered. "They must know we are here."

As he spoke the muzzle of a gun was pushed over the ridge, and about three inches of a human head became visible. He drew Valerie behind him as the weapon spat forth a torrent of bullets.

"The tommy-gun again," he muttered. "Trying to draw our fire, but we're not quite so silly. Every round is very precious now."

The rain of bullets ceased, and for a few minutes there was dead silence.

"Think they'll make an open attack?" asked Donkin.

"They may — provided they can muster enough men. I wish I knew what was happening behind that ridge."

"How about turning the tables on them, and rushing the position? We might be able to capture the tommy-gun."

"Why commit suicide? Our task is

to play for time. Look out!"

Again the tommy-gun appeared and instantly the cave was full of flying bullets, and bits of rock. Donkin suddenly gave a little cry and gripped his left forearm. McLean looked and saw that his arm was covered with blood.

"Are you hit?" he asked.

"Yes, but not direct. A bit of lead, I think. Nothing to worry about."

Again there was silence, and Donkin removed his coat and rolled up his left shirt-sleeve. There was a superficial jagged wound which was bleeding copiously. Valerie took his handkerchief and made a rough bandage, after which he swore he felt perfectly fit.

"But I do hate being a sitting target," he muttered. "Why the hell don't they come?"

"Waiting for reinforcements," said McLean.

He spoke calmly enough, but underneath his outward calm was the feeling of despair. He and Donkin had enough ammunition between them to make an all-out frontal attack very costly, but the end was inevitable. The aeroplane might possibly have some significance, but he believed that capture would be followed by swift execution. Yet there was nothing to be done but see it through to the end.

Valerie sidled up close to him, and in her eyes he read an appreciation of the position. The hand which she placed on his was as hot as fire, and trembled a little. The other hand she held behind her in a curious manner.

"This may be the end, darling," she said, with a wan smile. "There may be no time — or opportunity — to say goodbye later. Let's say it now."

He lowered his head and kissed her inviting lips, rather than argue with her. Then he drew her other arm forward, and saw that she had a pistol in her hand.

"Where did you get that?" he asked.

"It was in Ian's coat pocket. He took it from Lombroso's bedroom."

Donkin, with a little cry of surprise, made to take it from her when the whole situation changed. A terrific fusilade of bullets poured into the cave, and through a small orifice McLean saw at least twenty men leap over the ridge at intervals of about five yards, and advance under cover of the automatic.

"Wait!" he shouted to Donkin. "That tommy-gun will be silent in a few moments."

The converging arc of men were within fifty yards of the cave when the chattering gun ceased. Instantly McLean and Donkin got their rifles into action, lying flat on their stomachs with only their heads visible to the attackers. For a few dreadful moments everything was in the balance. Man after man dropped under the rapid but accurate fire of the two defenders, while bullets kicked up the sand within inches of their heads. Then one man rushed at McLean while he was in the act of reloading, and Donkin was engaged with another assailant. McLean saw the butt of a rifle about to smash his head when there came two reports from behind him, and the man held his stomach and dropped on the sand. He turned his head for a second to see Valerie, wild-eyed, with the pistol in her hand, and the next moment what were left of the attackers were running wildly for the ridge.

"Beat it, you scum!" shouted Donkin, firing after them.

"Steady!" gasped McLean.

Donkin stood up mopping his brow.

"Miraculous!" he said. "We ought to be dead, and we're still kicking."

"At least I ought to be dead," said McLean. "Valerie, I owe you my life."

Valerie gave McLean the pistol weakly and burst into tears.

"I — I didn't want to kill anyone," she sobbed.

"Thank God you did," said Donkin. "It was the turning point. They won't try that again. We've got eight of them — without a casualty."

But the long pause which followed, while being most welcome, was not calculated to change McLean's earlier opinion about the final result. The attackers had acted unwisely in trying to take them by storm, but it was folly to imagine that they might sit and do nothing but waste small arms ammunition. What he had dreaded from the first soon became a fact. There came a loud explosion from behind the ridge, and the eerie sound of a projectile overhead. It fell about forty yards from the cave and dead in line with it, throwing up a great cloud of sand that obscured everything for a few moments. Valerie gave a little moan of terror, and Donkin cursed under his breath. Then came another, McLean actually saw it in flight, and judged that it would finish up in the cave itself, but it struck the rock wall above it, bringing down huge pieces. Above the ridge he could see the barrels of several weapons, ready to snipe them if they attempted to run.

"It's all over, Ian," he said. "We've got no reply to that murderous thing. The next one may come inside. I'm going out. Can you spare that handkerchief?"

"You mean surrender?"

"Yes. Anything else is madness."

Donkin nodded glumly and tore the bloodstained bandage from his arm. Before McLean could tie it to the end of his rifle the third shell came whistling down. It fell but ten yards from the cave entrance, and the sand was driven in with tremendous force. McLean, half-blinded, staggered into the open and waved the improvised flag. Donkin joined him, and flung his rifle on the ground.

"Not a very gallant end," he grunted.

"It's time we need — not glory," replied McLean. "Yes, they are coming, and look who is leading them."

"Doctor Roy!" muttered Donkin. "He always was a bird of ill-omen. I should like to wipe that smug grin from his face."

Roy stopped within two yards of them, and the men who accompanied him pressed closer while McLean handed over his rifle.

"Search them!" he rasped. "And the cave."

The searching was roughly and quickly done. McLean had nothing of interest to them, but from Donkin they took a very small penknife and the phial of C.F.X. Roy took the phial from the searcher, and glared at Donkin.

"Where did you get this?" he demanded.

"What does it matter where I got it? I suppose there are thousands like it on the island."

Roy struck him savagely across the cheek, and for a second McLean thought Donkin would drive his big fist into Roy's lean jaw, and meet instant death. But Donkin merely smiled, and held his peace.

"Take him away," snarled Roy. "The others will follow."

Donkin was marched off, and Roy

turned to the man who had been to the cave and brought back the basket of provisions, and the two electric torches.

"All right," he growled. "You can take them away."

Valerie had now joined McLean, and was standing beside him with her handbag clutched in her hand. Roy looked at her balefully.

"Come here!" he said.

Valerie made no movement of any kind, but the fist of the armed man behind her propelled her towards Roy. McLean sprang at the fellow like a tiger, but came up against a gunbarrel.

"Careful, Inspector!" said Roy. "Orders were to take you alive if possible. Don't make it impossible."

He turned to Valerie, who was still feeling the effects of the punch in the back, and snatched the handbag from her. He opened it and took out the automatic pistol.

"I heard there was a third weapon in operation," he sneered. "Really, Miss

Donkin, I'm surprised at you. At the trial we assumed you to be an innocent young woman. Curious how one can be misled by a pretty face. You may have your bag now, but there will be scant opportunity of using the contents. All right. Take them away!"

The ensuing ignominious march to the citadel took them past the ruined villa, and McLean gave a glance at the mass of debris, through which a path had been driven during the night. They were passed by some men carrying stretchers, all of whom regarded them with hateful glances, and finally they were flung into a filthy old dungeon, which possessed but one barred window, and this less than nine inches square. Standing at this window was Donkin.

"Thank God!" he said. "At least we are together. No breaking out of here I'm afraid."

McLean was bound to agree, for the walls were of solid stone and the door iron. The chamber was completely bare

469

except for an old table in the centre.

"What's going to happen now?" asked Donkin.

"We are all to die," replied Valerie. "And very soon."

"Not you — "

"Oh yes. Doctor Roy made that quite clear. Isn't that so, Mac?"

"The powers of life and death may not lie with Doctor Roy. He takes his orders from others as all of them do," demurred McLean.

It was only a few minutes later that the door was opened noisily, and into the room stepped the short little cleric who had surprised McLean by being at the fake trial.

"I — I thought you might like to see me," he said, quite meekly.

"Why?" demanded Donkin.

"It is customary to allow condemned prisoners to see Ministers of the Church before sentence is carried out."

"Very kind of you," said McLean in a non-committal voice. "But are you really a clergyman?"

470

"I am."

"Then what on earth are you doing in this murderous community?"

"I have duties to perform. It is not for me to withhold the comfort of Religion to any soul who desires it, least of all at the moment when they face Eternity."

"But you know that the people here are engaged in illegal operations, that my friend here, Doctor Donkin, was kidnapped and brought here, that both of us have been falsely accused of murder. Do these things square with the tenets of your religious faith?"

"My faith lies deeper than the foibles of human beings. Before the war I was a poor pastor in Austria. During the war I ministered to the sick and dying in Buckenwald camp. It is not for me to judge men but to comfort them."

"I want no comfort," said Donkin, nursing his injured arm. "It's a poor substitute for justice."

"Justice is not of this world. Is there nothing you would wish me to do?"

"Yes," said McLean. "How long have we got before they shoot us?"

The Pastor looked sincerely embarrassed.

"The sentence has been altered," he said. "You are not to be shot — but hanged."

Valerie uttered a little gasp, and Donkin gave a growl of anger.

"When?" asked McLean.

"When the necessary preparations have been completed. Perhaps half an hour."

"You mean — all of us?"

"No. The young lady's former sentence still stands. She is to be confined here as a prisoner."

"I will not!" cried Valerie. "You can't do that to me. I demand to be murdered with my brother and fiancé."

The Pastor looked from her to McLean.

"I'm sorry," he said. "But there is nothing I can do. I had hoped you might like to make your peace with God — "

"Please go," interrupted Donkin. "You are merely upsetting my sister."

"Very well!"

He was nearing the door when McLean called him back.

"There is one last request I should like to make," he said. "I and my fiancée would like to be married. You have an old church here, and the ceremony could take place there. Will you try to get that concession on our behalf?"

The Pastor hesitated a moment and then nodded.

"I will do my best," he said.

"Thank you!"

Valerie and Donkin stared at McLean until the door closed with a clang, and then Valerie went to him.

"More time-saving?" she asked.

"Yes. He will have to go and get permission. That will take time, and if it is given the service will use up more time. Valerie, why are you staring at me like that? Oh, you silly goose. I'm not only concerned with wasting time.

I really do want to marry you without regard to any other consideration. Now smile and be sensible."

A smile and a kiss closed the slight breach, and they waited impatiently for the Pastor's return. He came back in about a quarter of an hour, and by the expression on his face McLean knew that the unusual request had been granted.

"It's all right," he said, beaming as if the prospect of a marriage service appealed to him very much. "I have asked for some water and towels to be brought here, so that you can make yourselves presentable. But at the church you must part. I will come back for you in half an hour."

The aids to ablution were brought in very soon afterwards, and these included a comb and brush, but not a safety razor as McLean had hoped. The reason for this omission was fairly obvious. He and Donkin talked in low whispers in a corner while Valerie brought back some of her natural beauty. Then McLean set to work on himself. He was brushing his hair into shape when suddenly he made an ejaculation.

"Eh?" asked Donkin.

"Rattenhuber! I've just remembered. He was captured by the Russians after the fall of Berlin, with another man whose name I can't remember. He was a top-ranking Nazi, along with Martin Bormann. Nothing more was heard of him after the brief announcement of his capture. He may have died, or he may have escaped."

"Well?" asked Donkin. "Where does that get us?"

"I think it gets us partly to the solution of the mystery of this island. In that note which we found Rattenhuber referred to M.B. Those are the initials of Martin Bormann, whose body was never discovered. Remember the ghastly paintings in that room at the 'Glasshouse', and the man who almost threw a fit when I insulted the person responsible?"

"Yes — of course."

"Whom do you think he might be?"

Donkin was just beginning to see the light, but he stared at McLean incredulously.

"No, it's impossible!" he gasped.

"Is it? Why were our judges so keen to cover their faces? Clearly they were all well-known people who might be recognized. And didn't you notice that it was the third man — the paralytic — to whom the others deferred?"

"That's true," agreed Donkin. "But they might be ordinary criminals using this island as a hide-out, and at the same time experimenting in germ culture for illegal use."

"They might, but think of all the trouble they have gone to to keep secret their whereabouts and their activities. I believe that the germ culture is merely a side line. They could easily carry on that business in the back room of a country house, but they chose to come here and live in isolation for years under the covering wings of

476

the so-called Colonel Lombroso, who was himself a German. If two of those three beauties are indeed Rattenhuber and Bormann, than it's highly probable that the other is their chief, being kept in cold storage for a future attempt at world domination."

"I don't know what you two are talking about," pleaded Valerie. "And what a time to start an argument. Ian, aren't you going to clean yourself up?"

"Perhaps I had better. Mac, you've got me all hot and bothered. Why did you have to spring that amazing theory on me, at a time when the proof of it is impossible. All right, Valerie, I'll make myself pretty."

While Donkin splashed about in the bowl, Valerie drew McLean away. He believed she understood full well the gist of the argument, but considered it of no real importance in view of what was pending.

"How do I look?" she asked, attempting a smile.

"As lovely as ever. You've never looked anything else in my eyes."

"When did you begin to love me?" she asked.

"Ages ago, but you were such a child then. It never occurred to me that the disparity in our ages would become negligible as time passed. Can you forgive me for being so blind?"

"All is forgiven. Now tell me one thing — do you believe there is a future life?"

"Yes, for those who love deeply. You know, some of the greatest truths in the world can be expressed in very simple language. One of these is that 'God is Love'. It seems to me that Love is the greatest force in the universe, and it has a dozen other names — cohesion, magnetism, gravitation — a gathering together of particles, atoms, individuals and even stars. It is in itself creative and eternal. What we call 'death' is merely change. Never doubt that we shall endure, my darling, and that the best is yet to be. If I have to wait for you a little while I can bear it, and you must bear it too."

"I'll try," she said huskily.

There was a noise outside the door, and then the Pastor appeared, followed by four armed guards. Valerie caught her breath, and Donkin, who was still titivating, growled his displeasure.

"You must hurry," said the Pastor. "These men won't wait."

Donkin flung down the hairbrush, and for a moment it looked as if he were going to make a disturbance, but Valerie's appealing eyes calmed him.

"Ready," he said.

Two guards went first, followed by Valerie on McLean's arm, and then came Donkin, alone, with the other two guards and the Pastor bringing up the rear. As a wedding procession it was surely unique, and to add a note of grim irony to it, the route to the church passed within a few yards of a newly-erected rough scaffold, around which were gathered nearly a score of men in mixed garb. Some of them jeered but others stood glum and silent. McLean felt Valerie wilt on his arm.

"Courage!" he whispered.

She revived as soon as they had passed that grim reminder, and within a minute or two they were climbing the steps which led to the main door of the ancient building. Normally McLean would have been interested in the wonderful painted ceiling and the frescoes on the lower walls, but now the painful pressure of events was overwhelming. The place was bare of any sort of furnishings, and the old mosaic floor was cracked and dirty. But the Pastor had had the good sense to close the door on the men who had followed the procession, and only the participants and the armed guard were finally present.

"Oh, the ring!" ejaculated Valerie, as they approached the chancel steps. "I've forgotten the ring."

"So have I," said McLean.

But the Pastor hadn't forgotten. He passed a plain metal ring to McLean, and McLean held it very awkwardly.

The service which followed was the orthodox Anglican one, which the Pastor spoke clearly, with but the slightest accent. Donkin moved uneasily when having given his sister away he heard her responses in a voice that was near to breaking point. Everything else had seemed a mockery, but not this. McLean dropped the ring when he made to slip it on Valerie's finger. It rolled a yard or two and one of the guards picked it up, and handed it back. Finally the Pastor blessed them in tones which did not lack sincerity — and then it was all over. McLean had dreaded this moment, but when he took his wife into his arms her eyes were unnaturally bright. A long embrace and he turned to the Pastor.

"What now?" he asked.

"You must go — you two men. But your wife may stay here a little while if she chooses."

"Yes," said Valerie, with a little choke. "I should like to do that."

The guards gathered round the two men. Donkin kissed his sister fondly, and whispered something to her, and then he and McLean were led away, side by side. Outside the little crowd tagged itself on to the procession, and soon they came in sight of the scaffold.

"This is it," muttered Donkin. "I'm damned if I'll be hanged like a common felon — "

He stopped as he saw McLean's figure tighten up in a queer way, and his gaze go towards a gap between two tall buildings. Looking in the same direction he saw the open sea, but not empty as usual. Some miles away there was a large low vessel coming at terrific speed, and throwing up great columns of water. But the stolid guards appeared not to notice it, and the next moment the vessel was out of their line of vision.

"Mac, could it — ?" gasped Donkin.

The butt of a rifle silenced him, but one look at McLean's face was enough. There was new hope in McLean's eyes.

"*Halte!*"

The party stopped, close to Doctor Roy, who was obviously in charge of the proceedings. He came forward a yard or two, and regarded the two prisoners with his deep-set, hateful eyes.

"Is there anything you wish to say before the sentence is carried out?" he asked.

"Quite a lot," replied McLean. "But I should like to say it in the presence of Lombroso, whom it chiefly concerns."

"Lombroso is not in a position to attend this regrettable ceremony."

"You mean he's dead?"

"Shall we say as good as dead. But I will pass on any loving message you have to give."

"Oh no. It is for him personally. I do not mind your being present, for it concerns you as well as him. I suggest you take us to him."

"He is unconscious, so it would be quite useless."

"Then give me a sheet of paper and a pencil, and I will write it."

"My dear Inspector, there is nothing you can say or write that is of the slightest interest to Lombroso or myself. But say what you want to say now, or let it remain unsaid for ever."

"Very well. Be prepared for a surprise."

"Go on — hurry! The hangman is waiting."

"Listen! Can you hear anything?"

"I can hear nothing — except the hum of the generating plant."

"You are getting old, Doctor, and your hearing is defective. That hum is not your generating plant. If you disbelieve me send a man to look out to sea — "

McLean stopped as from the direction of the 'Glasshouse' there rose the piercing note of a siren, and at the same time a man came running into the square, shouting hoarsely in German.

"My goodness!" whispered Donkin. "He says there's a warship approaching. It's happened, Mac. It's happened. Hullo, what's this?"

484

There suddenly arose the increasing whine of a plane, and almost instantly a jet fighter dived out of the blue, missing the tops of the buildings by a matter of yards. Almost everyone fell flat, expecting a rain of bullets, and that was McLean's opportunity. He fell on the nearest guard, and wrenched away his rifle, while Donkin acted similarly. The third man turned to shoot, but was bludgeoned into unconsciousness by Donkin, and the fourth man left his rifle and ran for his life. Again came the plane, putting everyone to flight, except the two almost hysterical prisoners. Donkin shot off a few rounds without caring where they went.

Now they could hear the powerful engine of the approaching craft, and McLean concluded that it was making for the entrance of the lagoon. The pair of them ran to the gap between the buildings and looked down into the lagoon. The launch must have left during the night, for the lagoon was now empty, but across the spit of land they could see a smart M.T.B. packed with men in uniform, racing for the entrance.

"Oh Glory — what a sight!" sighed Donkin. "Come on. We can just get to the quay in time."

But McLean had other thoughts in his mind. Leaving Donkin to have his bit of fun he ran to the church and opened the wide doors. Valerie was sitting on the chancel steps, staring towards him. He waved the rifle and hurried to her.

"Mac!"

She rose to her feet, with tears streaming from her eyes, and the rifle clattered to the floor as she was caught up in his arms.

"It's all over," he said. "Help has come. A small armed vessel full of men. Wake up, darling. It's no dream. If you don't stop crying I shall join you."

"But Ian — where?"

"Ian is safe. He wants to be in at the kill. Ah, that's better!"

Valerie was now smiling through her tears.

"Was it the pigeon?" she asked.

"I imagine so. But it was the devil of a near thing. If I hadn't put into execution a little more delaying action we might be hanging up on that ghastly beam at this moment. That's the ship coming up the lagoon."

"Will there be a battle?"

"I don't think the gang will put up much of a resistance against trained troops."

"Are they soldiers, then?"

"I don't know. They may be Marines. Let's go and see. It will be safe enough down by the quay."

McLean picked up the rifle and led her out of the church. Not a living soul was met on their way to the quay, and when they reached it the rakish-looking Italian vessel was at anchor and well-equipped Marines were coming ashore, and lining up on the jetty under the command of a smart young officer. Ian was chatting to a broad-shouldered man in plain-clothes, who had his back towards McLean, but McLean knew that back.

"Hey, Brook!" he called.

Sergeant Brook swung round, and his big face beamed with joy, as McLean went forward and wrung his hand.

"So you got my message, Brook?" said McLean.

"I did, sir, and what a commotion there was. How do you do, Miss Donkin!"

"So Doctor Donkin hasn't told you?" asked McLean.

"Told me what, sir?"

"The lady you are looking at is Mrs. McLean."

"Good Lord!" gasped Brook. "Oh I beg your pardon. I meant congratulations Miss — Madam, I mean."

Valerie laughed, and then the young officer, having got his men lined up, came along and was introduced. He spoke quite good English, and wanted to know the position of the enemy.

"I don't know where they are," replied McLean. "When they saw you coming they scuttled. But that big building yonder is their headquarters. There are three men there whom I am most anxious to see under arrest. But the place is — or was — well guarded, and I know they have a machine-gun — or had."

"We'll soon deal with that. I think, Inspector, you and your friends had better stay here until we see what sort of opposition there is. Perhaps — "

He did not finish his remarks for there suddenly came the sound of a terrific explosion, and the sky became black with smoke and flying debris. Immediately there came another, and another, nearer at hand, and while everyone scuttled for the shelter of the jetty wall, the debris came down like rain, and some great pieces of rock narrowly missed the ship.

"That's the end of the 'Glasshouse', and probably of those underground workshops," said Donkin. "They've blown up the whole show, and decamped."

The young officer now got his men moving, and McLean watched them fanning out along the quay, and finally through the various passages until they all vanished from sight.

"I wouldn't mind betting that they're planning to get away on the aeroplane. It could carry almost all of them at a pinch."

"No," said McLean. "That isn't possible."

"You're wrong, sir," said Brook. "I can hear the engines. Look there she is — taking off!"

McLean stared into the distant sky and saw the machine rise up at a steep angle. Within a minute or two it was well out to sea.

"I don't understand," he muttered.

But he did the next moment, for suddenly the right wing dipped steeply, and then the tail came up and the machine dived at terrific speed. There was a great surge of water, and then rising steam, followed by a low booming sound, and silence.

"No use sending rescue craft," muttered Brook. "She's gone for ever. Didn't you bargain for that, sir?"

"No. I took steps to prevent the machine from taking off. I thought I had succeeded, but apparently I was only partly successful."

"Successful enough," said Donkin. "But it's a pity in a way, because now you'll never be able to settle that little matter of Herr Rattenhuber and his two friends."

"There may be some survivors, and at least there is Mr. Stein, languishing in jail."

"You can wash him out, sir," said Brook. "He died in prison most mysteriously two days ago, without uttering a word."

21

FINALLY the Marines came back, with but a handful of sullen prisoners, none of whom had put up any resistance. They denied all knowledge of the occupants of the 'Glasshouse', and swore that they had been engaged in the laboratory where a vaccine against Foot and Mouth disease was being perfected.

"They know," said McLean. "But I doubt if they will ever talk. Let's have a look round before the ship leaves."

The damage done by the series of explosions was enormous. There were mountains of rock and rubble everywhere, to clear which would have taken weeks of toil. But in a lower room at the villa an important discovery was made. It was Colonel Lombroso, bandaged from head to foot, and clearly on the point of death. Donkin made a quick examination, and shook his head.

"It's a miracle he is still living," he said. "But he can't last much longer, and his jaw is broken. Couldn't speak if he wanted to."

"Is he conscious?" asked McLean.

"Yes."

McLean went to the dying man and put his important questions about the late occupants of the 'Glasshouse', but Lombroso simply stared at him blankly. Whether he really understood or not was very much open to conjecture. He died while he was being carried on a stretcher to the ship, and with him died the last hope of substantiating McLean's theory.

That evening the vessel sailed for Trieste, across a beautiful opalescent sea, while Brook told his own story from the time when he reached the Norfolk farmhouse, only to find McLean missing, and the place deserted. Subsequently he had found the hangar, and the evidence that a plane had left recently. But he had not considered the possibility of McLean being on that plane, and the next day the whole district was thoroughly searched for McLean's corpse.

"What a to-do!" he said. "We had Stein on the mat and he swore he knew nothing about the place. Nothing would shift him. We tried to keep it out of the Press, but somehow they got hold of it, and that started more trouble. Then I heard that Miss Donkin was missing! Lord, I wished I was dead."

He took a long drink from the tankard of beer which had been provided for him.

"You can imagine my surprise when I was rung up by someone who wouldn't give his name. Had a voice you could cut with a knife and asked me if I was Mr. Brook. I said I was, and then he read me out that message very slowly, so that I had time to write it down. It made no sense until he gave me the final letters 'M.A.C.'. Then I knew it was genuine, and that it was our code. I nearly had a fit when I decoded it. Well, you can guess what followed. Long telephone calls to Rome and Trieste — time wasted because the Italians would insist that the island was completely uninhabited, and didn't want to do anything. They swore it belonged to Italy but admitted there was a squabble going on between them and the Yugo-Slavs. The Chief then said he would get in touch with the Yugo-Slavian government to see what they could do in the matter. That clinched the matter. The Italians didn't want their neighbours butting in, and that's how we got things moving."

"But did the Chief send you alone?" asked McLean incredulously.

"That's the funny part. Superintendent Kitson was chosen to represent our people, and to meet his opposite number in Trieste, and as a special concession I was allowed to go with him, but when we were at the airport the Superintendent was suddenly taken ill, and a doctor examined him and said he wasn't fit to make the journey. So I came alone."

"Did you not inform headquarters?" asked McLean.

"No, sir. I thought that time was too precious."

"My goodness!" ejaculated McLean. "You're going to face the music when we get back."

"Who cares?" asked Brook. "It all worked out right, didn't it?"

McLean was compelled to agree, but he still couldn't think why the Marines had been sent instead of the Italian police.

"Matter of prestige," said Brook. "They seem to manage these things differently abroad. If you ask me, the Navy department was dying to put on a little show, and they got their way. Not bad beer this. Almost as good as ours."

They were in sight of the great port when Valerie remembered something which had slipped her mind during that unbelievably pleasant trip.

"Mac, I suppose that as my husband you are now responsible for my debts?"

"What a thing to ask on your wedding day," he protested.

"Yes, or no?"

"Yes."

"Then when we get ashore there's a little matter to be settled with the man whose motor-boat I stole. I shouldn't like to spend my honeymoon in an Italian jail."

"Nice way to start married life," said Donkin. "Anyway, I doubt if you're properly married at all. It was about as phoney as our trial. I'm warning you, Mac."

But McLean needed no such warning, for he had already made certain plans for the future. Within a month he and Valerie enjoyed the luxury of a second marriage, in a delightful little country church, not very far from the cottage which was to be their future home, and on this occasion there was music and confetti.

"No regrets?" asked Valerie, when they were alone again.

"Just one — my failure to solve completely the mystery of that island. But in the absence of a better explanation I take leave to stick to my theory."

"Very nice too," sighed Valerie. "Life would be dull without a few unsolved mysteries."

THE END

A FOOT IN THE GRAVE
Bruce Marshall

About to be imprisoned and tortured in Buenos Aires, John Smith escapes, only to become involved in an aeroplane hijacking.

DEAD TROUBLE
Martin Carroll

Trespassing brought Jennifer Denning more than she bargained for. She was totally unprepared for the violence which was to lie in her path.

HOURS TO KILL
Ursula Curtiss

Margaret went to New Mexico to look after her sick sister's rented house and felt a sharp edge of fear when the absent landlady arrived.

THE DEATH OF ABBE DIDIER
Richard Grayson

Inspector Gautier of the Sûreté investigates three crimes which are strangely connected.

NIGHTMARE TIME
Hugh Pentecost

Have the missing major and his wife met with foul play somewhere in the Beaumont Hotel, or is their disappearance a carefully planned step in an act of treason?

BLOOD WILL OUT
Margaret Carr

Why was the manor house so oddly familiar to Elinor Howard? Who would have guessed that a Sunday School outing could lead to murder?

THE DRACULA MURDERS
Philip Daniels

The Horror Ball was interrupted by a spectral figure who warned the merrymakers they were tampering with the unknown.

THE LADIES
OF LAMBTON GREEN
Liza Shepherd

Why did murdered Robin Colquhoun's picture pose such a threat to the ladies of Lambton Green?

CARNABY
AND THE GAOLBREAKERS
Peter N. Walker

Detective Sergeant James Aloysius Carnaby-King is sent to prison as bait. When he joins in an escape he is thrown headfirst into a vicious murder hunt.

MUD IN HIS EYE
Gerald Hammond

The harbourmaster's body is found mangled beneath Major Smyle's yacht. What is the sinister significance of the illicit oysters?

THE SCAVENGERS
Bill Knox

Among the masses of struggling fish in the *Tecta*'s nets was a larger, darker, ominously motionless form . . . the body of a skin diver.

DEATH IN ARCADY
Stella Phillips

Detective Inspector Matthew Furnival works unofficially with the local police when a brutal murder takes place in a caravan camp.

STORM CENTRE
Douglas Clark

Detective Chief Superintendent Masters, temporarily lecturing in a police staff college, finds there's more to the job than a few weeks relaxation in a rural setting.

THE MANUSCRIPT MURDERS
Roy Harley Lewis

Antiquarian bookseller Matthew Coll, acquires a rare 16th century manuscript. But when the Dutch professor who had discovered the journal is murdered, Coll begins to doubt its authenticity.

SHARENDEL
Margaret Carr

Ruth didn't want all that money. And she didn't want Aunt Cass to die. But at Sharendel things looked different. She began to wonder if she had a split personality.

MURDER TO BURN
Laurie Mantell

Sergeants Steven Arrow and Lance Brendon, of the New Zealand police force, come upon a woman's body in the water. When the dead woman is identified they begin to realise that they are investigating a complex fraud.

YOU CAN HELP ME
Maisie Birmingham

Whilst running the Citizens' Advice Bureau, Kate Weatherley is attacked with no apparent motive. Then the body of one of her clients is found in her room.

DAGGERS DRAWN
Margaret Carr

Stacey Manston was the kind of girl who could take most things in her stride, but three murders were something different . . .

THE MONTMARTRE MURDERS
Richard Grayson

Inspector Gautier of Sûreté investigates the disappearance of artist Théo, the heir to a fortune.

GRIZZLY TRAIL
Gwen Moffat

Miss Pink, alone in the Rockies, helps in a search for missing hikers, solves two cruel murders and has the most terrifying experience of her life when she meets a grizzly bear!

BLINDMAN'S BLUFF
Margaret Carr

Kate Deverill had considered suicide. It was one way out — and preferable to being murdered.